VINTAGE MURDER MYSTERIES

With the sign of a human skull upon its back and a melancholy shriek emitted when disturbed, the Death's Head Hawkmoth has for centuries been a bringer of doom and an omen of death - which is why we chose it as the emblem for our Vintage Murder Mysteries.

Some say that its appearance in King George III's bedchamber pushed him into madness. Others believe that should its wings extinguish a candle by night, those nearby will be cursed with blindness. Indeed its very name, *Acherontia atropos*, delves into the most sinister realms of Greek mythology: Acheron, the River of Pain in the underworld, and Atropos, the Fate charged with severing the thread of life.

The perfect companion, then, for our Vintage Murder Mysteries sleuths, for whom sinister occurrences are never far away and murder is always just around the corner …

GLADYS MITCHELL

The Devil at Saxon Wall

VINTAGE BOOKS
London

Published by Vintage 2014

13

Copyright © The Executors of the Estate of Gladys Mitchell 1935

Gladys Mitchell has asserted her right under the Copyright, Designs and Patents Act 1988 to be identified as the author of this work

This book is sold subject to the condition that it shall not, by way of trade or otherwise, be lent, resold, hired out, or otherwise circulated without the publisher's prior consent in any form of binding or cover other than that in which it is published and without a similar condition, including this condition, being imposed on the subsequent purchaser

First published in Great Britain by Grayson & Grayson in 1935

Vintage
Random House, 20 Vauxhall Bridge Road,
London SW1V 2SA

www.vintage-books.co.uk

Addresses for companies within The Random House Group Limited can be found at: www.randomhouse.co.uk/offices.htm

The Random House Group Limited Reg. No. 954009

A CIP catalogue record for this book
is available from the British Library

ISBN 9780099582236

Penguin Random House is committed to a sustainable future for our business, our readers and our planet. This book is made from Forest Stewardship Council® certified paper.

Typeset in Meridien by Replika Press Pvt Ltd, India
Printed and bound in Great Britain by Clays Ltd, Elcograf S.p.A.

To

HELEN SIMPSON

'Strength and honour are her clothing;
She laugheth at the time to come;
She openeth her mouth with wisdom,
And the law of kindness is on her tongue.
Give her of the fruit of her hands,
And let her own works praise her.'

Proverbs 31.

FIRST MANIFESTATION

DOMESTIC INTERIOR

'I have the Ratsbane ready. I run no Risque; for I can lay her death upon the Ginn, and so many die of that naturally that I shall never be called in question. But say I were to be hang'd—I never could be hang'd for anything that would give me greater Comfort than the poisoning that Slut.'

JOHN GAY,
The Beggar's Opera. Act III, Scene VII.

Chapter One

'Here, for example, is a young woman
with hysterical paralysis of the legs.'

ROBERT S. WOODWORTH
Contemporary Schools of Psychology

IT WAS not until 1920 that Hanley changed.
Constance could date the change; she fixed it from
a certain afternoon in April of that year when he
returned from what he referred to, vaguely, as a
London conference. Constance did not find the
reference vague, because she possessed the type
of mind which automatically invents all that it
does not know. She assumed that her husband
had served during the war, presupposed, since the
only kind of conference she had ever heard of
was a medical one, that Hanley was a doctor and
had been attached to the R.A.M.C., and, since it
was obvious that he was not in practice when
she married him, that he had sufficient private
means to warrant his giving up the profession of
medicine.

Since her marriage Constance had been happy; not riotously, gloriously or even drunkenly happy, but merely royally happy, and having a sense of uneasiness all the time as befitted one who was wearing (truth to tell, unexpectedly) the matrimonial crown.

She could not remember having been happy before, because she could not remember having been all her life anything but a failure. Even as a little girl at her first private school the only prize their consciences would permit them to secure to her (on the guiding principle of the private schools of her day that each pupil must be awarded at least one prize on Speech Day) was a Longfellow's Poems for Ladylike Deportment, and, even then, in ascending the steps of the rostrum to receive the prize from the hands of the kind lady who had graciously consented to present it, Constance tripped, stumbled, shot a bag of spherical sweets out of the leg of her knickers and, in failing to regain her equilibrium, made a conspicuous hole in the knee of her left stocking. She slunk back to her seat (after one philosophical glance at her mother's mortified countenance) not a bit of use as an example of deportment, ladylike or otherwise.

Certainly she had never expected to marry. Even her mother, a most sanguine and optimistic woman, had never expected that. Her mother, in fact, was inclined to shake her head over Constance, and to tell herself, without bitterness but also without the slightest fear of contradiction from any quarter whatsoever, that Constance was not a trier.

Constance's mother liked triers. She herself was one, and whether Constance was designed to counteract the excessive energy of her mother, or whether she began, out of almost inspired cussedness and at an unusually early age, to cease trying, it is idle to attempt to decide, for the result was the same, whatever the contributing causes. She failed at everything, including an attempt to pass the entrance examination of a girls' public day school at the age of thirteen, and an attempt to commit suicide at the age of twenty-three.

Constance's father had made jam during the war, so that there was no particular reason, financially speaking, why she should attempt to earn a living, and at the age of twenty-four she accompanied her parents to Naples because her mother had heard that it was much cheaper to live in Italy than in England. It was impossible to go to Naples without visiting Pompeii, they discovered, and it was at Pompeii that Constance found Hanley Middleton.

Her mother was seated despondently upon a ruined wall; her father, led by an incomprehensible but unyielding guide, had been taken to see the interior decorations of a first century brothel, and Constance was poking about, aimlessly enough, in a house whose floor was a mass of flowering weeds, when she became aware of a man who was gazing down a well. He turned his head and regarded her sombrely. Then he said:

'Are you psychic?'

Constance assured him nervously that she was not.

'Then come and look down here,' he said, 'and tell me whether there's anybody at the bottom.'

Gingerly Constance approached the brink, and peered into the well.

'Nothing there,' she said, with great relief. The young man began to take off his coat and boots. Constance, sickeningly apprehensive lest he was preparing to commit suicide, emitted a faint shriek and ran to fetch her mother. Her mother, delighted at the thought of a little human interest in a place which, as far as she was concerned, was excessively boring and hot, (and whose entrance fee, she informed her husband and daughter angrily, she considered an unnecessarily high one considering the rate of exchange,) charged joyously to the rescue of the professor of hari-kari, and insisted upon retaining a firm grip of his coat sleeve until she got him back to her hotel.

The young man, whose name was Hanley Middleton, proposed to Constance after dinner, and Constance accepted him, but did not tell her mother.

Middleton had a place in Hampshire known as Neot House. Having fled with Constance to England, he married her at a registrar's office in Kensington and then conducted her to her new home.

Constance's mother was delighted with everything she saw there. Her father, whom much jam-making had rendered hard, suspicious and untrusting, and who disliked the thought of the marriage, and said so, made a new will, one clause of which he was at particular pains to make public. It provided that not one penny of his quite respectable fortune was to come to his daughter in the event of his death. Only to one person (and that one was not a member of his family) did Constance's father disclose the reason for this apparently harsh provision. He was willing, he said, for Constance to have a large allowance of money, as long as she lived. Provision had been made for that. But as he suspected her husband not of suicidal but of homicidal tendencies, it might be as well to ensure Constance's safety as far as was humanly possible. He did not say this to his wife, and Constance's mother had no idea of the way her husband's mind was moving. She herself did not care for her son-in-law, but was pleased to think that Constance, the most unlikely candidate for matrimony that she had ever seen, was safely introduced into Hymen's temple. Hanley's somewhat anti-social trick of staring into the darkest corner of any room he was in as though he was watching something materialising out of the shadows, and a way he had of standing aside politely every time a door blew open as though to allow somebody to pass, seemed oddities of behaviour which she felt she ought to allow to pass unchallenged. His habit of making a long low mound of sifted earth at the bottom of the garden, and of planting a stick in it she attempted to dismiss from her mind, but his brooding silences seriously upset her nerves. She was a woman who believed in noise and activity.

Constance however, seemed pleased, and if she felt the slightest twinge of misgiving and alarm when her father and mother left her with her husband in the large, old house surrounded by its garden and its park, she did not show it. Truth to tell, beyond the fact that she found her husband a silent and apparently preoccupied man, enamoured of long lonely walks and whiskey by the half-bottle (for which, incidentally, she noticed that he never appeared the better or the worse) Constance enjoyed married life as much as (with her almost visible limitations of mind and spirit) she would enjoy anything.

Her mother wrote often; her father never more than once in four or five weeks; but while her mother's letters were redundant with 'tell Hanley' this, that or the other, her father contented himself with the curt and, to his daughter, cryptic command to tell Hanley that he had not altered his will.

Hanley appeared equally unimpressed by both parents' efforts to interest him. He was always polite to Constance and never complained about his food. Once a month he attended a conference in London, and once, when Constance told him on his return, after an absence of five days, that she had sent for six London dailies and that not one of them had had sufficient initiative to report the conference, he had looked at her with such darkening suspicion that she had shrunk back in terror. But immediately his expression had altered. He had smiled and had informed her that what scientists in conclave had to say was of no interest to the newspaper-reading public.

The village of Saxon Wall, where they had come

to live, was in a remote part of Hampshire. It was an ugly, straggling place, and Constance disliked and feared the people. They were like no villagers that she had ever seen. She had a poor memory for verse, but every time she encountered any of the inhabitants of Saxon Wall there came into her mind the line 'ugly, squat and full of guile.' They had thick, dirty, fair hair, unkempt and more like frayed rope than anything else she could think of, narrow, shifty eyes under curiously straight brows, low foreheads, big splayed feet, as though they were unaccustomed to the wearing of hard leather boots, and large, coarse hands on the ends of abnormally long arms. Both men and women seemed stupid and ferocious, so that, mixed with her fear of them, was a good deal of disgust. Even the children were ugly, and most of them threw stones at her whenever they saw her.

Hanley laughed when she told him how much she disliked the people. He himself never went into the village by daylight, although rumours reached her from her own kitchen of nocturnal excursions from which he returned too tired even to take his clothes or shoes off. For weeks Constance slept alone and breakfasted alone, and, from motives which she herself would not have been able to explain (since it was too unreasonable to admit even to herself that she was growing to be afraid of her silent husband) she did not question him nor make any reference whatever to his neglect of her.

The vicar, an elderly man named Pullborough, called on her one day and persuaded her to consent to open the church bazaar in the autumn, but when Hanley knew that he had been up to the house and inside it, he flew into such passionate ragings that Constance, in more acute alarm than, so far, she had experienced, promised never again to admit the vicar and on no account to attend Church services. She would have promised anything at such a moment, for Hanley had cast himself on the ground and was knocking his head repeatedly against the side of the fireplace. Constance sat beside him, and, clutching his neck, wrenched his head to her bosom and begged him to desist.

Eighteen months passed, and then the first definite indication to Constance that Hanley had changed came with his return from one of his so-called conferences, not alone but with a woman called Wilmina Barrow. Constance, not knowing in the least how to deal with the situation, welcomed Miss Barrow, and ordered the most interesting meals she could think of because Miss Barrow affected to be an authority upon Spanish cooking, which she declared was immensely superior to the salt-and-water methods of the English.

Looking back upon Miss Barrow's visit, it appeared to Constance to have consisted of a series of excuses from Hanley for being out with Miss Barrow for most of the day—for more than a week he was more tractable, human and conversational than Constance had ever known him—and a series of heart-contracting noises—screams, bumps, stealthy footsteps and the like—after dark. Not once during the time the visit lasted did Hanley sleep in Constance's room.

Miss Barrow left before the end of a fortnight. She had contracted a nasty bruise under the left eye where she had walked into the grandfather clock in the dark, and was limping from a rather severe contusion on the left shin where she had tumbled against the sharp edge of the coal-scuttle when she and Hanley had been playing with the dog. Constance had witnessed neither accident. Hanley had never been talkative, but after Miss Barrow had gone he became positively morose. He had never been sunny-tempered, but now the slightest thwarting of his desires was sufficient to bring on a fit of ill-humour which lasted the whole day and sometimes for nearly a week. He ill-treated his dogs, and once threw the cat out of an upstairs window. When Constance got in his way he pushed, and, later, kicked her out of it. If she remonstrated, be it ever so timidly, he swore at her.

He had given up his mud pies in the garden and seemed to have renounced the drinking of whiskey. It was like living with a savage, treacherous animal, for his fits of brooding moroseness lasted for days on end, only to terminate in a bout of crazy, snarling ill-temper which terrified her into locking herself within her room until he quietened down again. The odd thing was that he could always obtain servants. No sooner had a cook or a housemaid given notice than another would be installed. They were always village women, and, in an indefinable yet obvious way, they indicated their allegiance to Hanley and their detestation of Constance.

Worn out and terrified, she braved Hanley's maniacal rage, and went to appeal to the vicar for advice. He advised her to return to her parents. Constance herself had often debated whether this would not be the wisest course to pursue. She was convinced now that Hanley was mad. 'It's as though he had a devil,' said the tearful Constance.

'Demoniacal possession?' said the vicar. 'Well, the village people have tried for years to convince me that the devil haunts here. They even tell me that occasionally he manifests himself. Fortunately I am fully occupied with my Minoans, and have no time for their nonsense.'

To Constance it appeared that he had no time for hers, either. She remembered that she had let him down over the opening of his bazaar, and that, although he was not annoyed with her, neither was he inclined to take her burdens upon himself. He indicated this, she thought, politely but unmistakably, and Constance, more sensitive than might have been expected of her mother's daughter, went back to the house. To her relief Hanley was in silent mood. He glowered at her, but said nothing. That night she followed him out of the house and into the village to find out where he went, and, if possible, what he did, on his now frequent midnight excursions. She thought, in a muddled but tenacious way, that if she could go to a London doctor with definite evidence of Hanley's peculiarities, he could be removed for treatment and cured. In spite of his usage of her, she was full of goodwill towards him, and explained his condition by supposing that he was suffering from shell-shock.

He walked past the small dower house and out into the park. Here he pursued a zig-zag path among the trees for no reason that Constance could see at first. In a few minutes, however, she realised that he was going from elm to elm, avoiding the other trees, and was gently stroking the trunk of each elm tree as he passed it. At last, when she was tired of the apparently interminable pilgrimage, he turned off to the south and left the park by climbing over the wall. Giving him time to get far enough down the road, Constance followed him. It was easy enough to climb the wall because he had loosened at some time three bricks to make footholds.

To her surprise, Hanley led her to the church which was at the opposite end of the village. Pullborough never locked it. She stood just inside the south doorway, filled with amazement and fear, disliking the notion of following Hanley into the blackness of the interior, although she could hear him stumbling as he ascended the chancel steps. She supposed, in her muddled way, that she ought to make some attempt to rid the church of his sacrilegious presence, but was too much afraid of him to betray the fact that she was at hand. Presently she heard in the stillness the murmur of his voice as though he were praying, and, a short time afterwards, his stumbling footsteps coming towards the door.

She stepped aside, into the folds of the doorway curtain, and out he lurched. Again she followed him. This time he walked about the churchyard as though searching for something among the graves. At last he bent down and she saw a circle of light from his electric torch illumining the ground. She crept nearer. The torch went out. Hanley straightened himself, and, turning, began to walk straight towards her. Constance, crouching behind a yew tree, let him go by, then followed him again.

This time he led her to the only cottage in the village which still had a light burning. She knew little of the village homes, and had no idea who lived in this one. Hanley kicked at the little front gate to open it, walked up the garden path, and kicked at the front door. The door was opened to him, and immediately closed.

Constance realised, suddenly, that she was very tired. She knew, too, that it was useless to attempt to peer in at the window, which was lighted, because of the banked aspidistra and geranium plants which formed an effective screen to all that went on in the room.

She sat down on the dew-wet grass by the side of the gate, and waited for Hanley to re-appear. She supposed that he had gone to spend the night with the woman of the cottage, whoever she might be, and she decided that as soon as she was rested she would return to Neot House and go to bed. She had made no plan for dealing with Hanley. Vague ideas of divorce passed through her mind, but she had singularly little idea of what evidence she would require in order to procure an annulment of the marriage, and, in any case, her upbringing had been such that something akin to instinct rebelled at the thought of the dissolution of her vows, made when she had been optimistic about the future and happy in her husband.

But Hanley did not give her very long to rest. The door soon opened, and out he came, and, after him, hanging on the air like a sinful departing spirit, a voice which wailed:

'Bury un in the name of the Old Man, don't ee forget, master, else nothing won't come of your trouble.'

Constance recognised the voice. Three days previously she had been instructed by Hanley to interview a new maid, a girl named Fluke. This was the mother. She had accompanied her daughter to Neot House, and had done most of the talking— more of it, in fact, than Constance herself. She had a reputation for witchcraft, Constance had heard. Witchcraft, which, in London, had seemed a matter of intellectual interest, fascinating geographically, historically and philosophically, seemed a force to be feared and loathed in Saxon Wall. It was all too likely, Constance had decided, that the old creature really was a witch. Were there not stories of the redness of the moon, and gliding snakes, and crouching hounds of hell?

She heard the old woman chuckle. Then the door was closed. Hanley, bearing a burden, passed close to Constance sheltering in the hedge, and, as he passed, a light touch rested on Constance's shoulder as though a leaf had fallen. She put her hand up and her fingers touched a dry harsh stalk. It was a stalk of corn. Exploring carefully, she could feel the ears, and, with a gentle rubbing, she detached the seeds and automatically ate them.

Then she rose and followed her husband back to Neot House.

When they had first come to Saxon Wall to live, Constance had suggested that the ground-floor room immediately under her bedroom should be a kind of little den where she could read and knit and play with her clay-modelling things, and do embroidery, and get out of Hanley's way when he wished to be alone. Hanley had fallen in with the idea, and the two rooms had become, in later months, a sanctuary to her where she could escape from his moodiness and his fits of violence.

Hanley walked round the house until he came to this part of it. Then he laid his sheaf of corn on the edge of the lawn, and, followed by Constance (who was now more than ever convinced that he was mad) he procured a lantern from the stables, lighted it, and went back to the sheaf. From the shadowed flower bed he took a spade. By the light of the lantern, and in the devil's name, he buried the sheaf just beside the wall of Constance's little den, went into the house, and, presumably, to bed.

Constance waited for about a quatter of an hour.

Then, feverishly, she dug up the sheaf, which was fashioned, with pins in the joints of the stalks, into a shape she would have had some difficulty, even by daylight, in recognising as her own, and, having left the catch up for that very purpose, she opened the window of her den, crammed in the sheaf, and scrambled over the sill.

She possessed a small amount of money and, having set fire to the sheaf in the grate, she counted her store, and, weary as she was, set out on foot for the station, determined to stay in the hag-haunted village no longer, but to return to her parents and ask her father's advice about doctors for Hanley. She reached the station at daybreak, waited two hours for a train, and, arrived at her father's house in Kensington, was discovered to be in a feverish condition and in urgent need of immediate medical attention.

Her father and mother were horrified. She was zealously nursed by the anxious and puzzled parents, and, chiefly because of her babblings during periods of delirium, they discovered the cause of her utter physical collapse, and decided between themselves that she must not return to her husband.

Convalescent, Constance proved unexpectedly obstinate. She *must* return, she said. She had spent long hours in brooding over her own curious conduct in having dug up and set fire to the sheaf, and she really believed she must have imagined the incident. However, a pin-prick she had sustained when she tore the sheaf to pieces had festered rather badly, and seemed disinclined to heal.

During the time of Constance's convalescence her mother had made spasmodic but determined

efforts to find out from the doctor the point at
which, in the eyes of the medical profession, oddity
of behaviour was regarded as certifiable mania.

The doctor, who knew nothing of Hanley, and
who thought that Constance's mother was in a
highly nervous state about her daughter's sanity,
was so bluffly reassuring that the poor woman
conceived an unshakable notion that nothing
short of mass-murder would convince a doctor
of insanity. It was in this despairing belief that
she was compelled to give in to Constance's grim
determination to return to Saxon Wall.

Both parents did their best to dissuade her,
but all their arguments were finally defeated by
Constance's reiteration of the statement that her
husband needed her.

Terrified, her mother let her go.

'He must have put a spell on her,' she said. Her
husband grunted, but his eyes were full of fear.

Chapter Two

'What outcries pluck me from my naked bed,
And chill my throbbing heart with trembling
fear?'

THOMAS KYD
The Spanish Tragedy. Act II, Scene V.

AT THE end of a month, having put off the evil hour
as long as her conscience would let her, Constance
decided to return. It was six o'clock in the evening
when she arrived. A cross-country railway journey,
followed by the long drive from the station to Saxon
Wall, had taken five and a half hours, and she was
tired. She had no idea what to expect when she
reached Neot House. She had written three times
to Hanley, at her mother's instigation, but he had
not replied to her letters.

'You had better stay here with us,' her mother
told her. 'Let your father go to Neot House, and
deal with your precious husband. If only you had
been a little more cautious, dear, about rushing
so hastily into marriage with a man we knew

nothing about—beyond the fact that he thought of committing suicide—how much trouble and anxiety might have been saved to us all! But it's too late to think about that now. The only thing is, that you simply cannot go back to him. I won't be responsible if you do anything so foolish!'

'I am going at the end of the month,' said Constance flatly. 'He's my husband, and I ought to go to him.'

'You're mad,' said her mother decidedly, but she was afraid as well as annoyed.

Her father offered to accompany her, but Constance refused his escort uncompromisingly; she did, however, promise him that she would return home if matters proved too difficult for readjustment.

She heard voices coming from the dining-room, and the sound of Hanley's laughter. She had so seldom heard him laugh that the sound of itself was startling. She hastened up the stairs to her room. The double bed had been slept in, was still unmade, and had not even been stripped for making. The sight of tumbled bedclothes and a pair of crumpled pyjamas did not prepare her, however, for what she found when, at length, having tidied up, she descended to her husband.

Hanley was sprawled in an armchair, the half-clad maidservant Fluke, a white-skinned, black-eyed piece, handsomely sullen, in his arms. About the young woman's neck the pearls which Constance had received from her father on her eighteenth birthday scarcely showed up at all against the creamy skin.

Constance halted at the door, turned slightly giddy, and then, recovering, said:

'I——Hanley, I've come back, dear. What would you like for tea?'

Hanley's face lost its expression of amusement and sensual gratification, and became cunning, and suddenly wary. He showed his teeth, but not in a smile, and said to the girl on his knee:

'Delilah, somebody's come to call. Go and order tea, my dear. Go along.' He pushed her off as though she had been an importuning dog.

Constance advanced and said:

'Hanley, I don't want tea. I can easily wait until dinner time. I expect you've had your tea. It's six o'clock or more.'

'No dinner,' said Hanley, leering. 'Not a servant in the place. All gone. They all went away from here when Constance died. You wouldn't remember Constance. Perfect idiot. Couldn't stand her at any price. Drove me mad. Quite glad she's gone.'

There was not a servant in the place as he had said. A pile of dirty dishes and some cups and glasses were in and about the kitchen sink; the scullery reeked of onions. Blood, where, presumably, a joint had been prepared, was staining the wooden draining board; the copper was full of feathers. Three quart bottles which had contained stout lay on top of the feathers, and a row of cocks' combs and feet were nailed to the woodwork of the scullery window.

Mechanically Constance set to work. Then, when she had reduced the kitchen regions to some sort of order, she made herself a cup of tea out of what had been the cook's private store, and, having drunk it, she stole out of the house and went to the doctor, an old man named Crevister, who lived at the far end of the village near the vicarage. There Constance, seated in a dark red leather-covered armchair out of which the horsehair stuffing peeped in the half-pathetic, half-revolting manner of its sort, stated her fears about her husband's sanity. The doctor shook his head.

'Probably suffering from prolonged nervous strain,' he suggested. 'May end in insanity, Mrs Middleton. Did you know that a child has died in the house since you went away? My opinion is that between the lot of them they murdered it.'

'Murdered it?' said Constance, with a ghastly attempt at a smile. 'You can't mean that!'

'The child died, anyhow. And it was a perfectly healthy baby. I saw it into the world myself, and so I know. Oh, the mother didn't want me to! Neither did that old terror the grandmother, I can tell you! But I insisted. Threatened them with the police, you know. I wouldn't trust that old woman Fluke out of my sight with any baby, let alone an unwanted one belonging to her own daughter. Your husband cleared out, by the way. He's only just come back.'

'But all the same, it died,' said Constance, in a toneless voice. Suddenly, without even the warning of a sigh, she fell forward unconscious.

The doctor, who was a kindly old man, arranged for her to stay the night with friends of his, a married couple in the nearest town, a place called Stowhall, and two days later Constance went back to her parents. A week or two after that, to general amazement, Hanley joined her, with Martha Fluke in tow.

He seemed better tempered than Constance had ever known him. Her parents, astonished and utterly dismayed at the *ménage à trois* which was being forced upon them, were at a loss how best to deal with it, or how to end it. They appealed to Constance to assert herself, and then, finding this useless, they commanded her, with hysterical histrionics, to try for a divorce. Constance was no trier. She also realised that, except on the subject of Martha Fluke, from whom he refused to be parted for even half an hour, Hanley appeared as sane as she did. Saner, in fact, for whereas Constance grew thin, peaked, pale and worried, Hanley appeared to be in better health than he had enjoyed since the first weeks of his marriage.

This curious and unlikely state of affairs continued until November, 1923, when Hanley suddenly discarded Martha Fluke, who was again with child, and demanded that Constance should return at once with him to Neot House.

Constance was affronted, terrified and obstinate. Her parents supported her. Her mother went from sentimental pleading to stern command, and from stern command to hysterical wailing. Then the father died very suddenly, at a masonic banquet, and, after the funeral, the exhausted woman gave in, and consented to return with her husband to Neot House.

Her mother pleaded with Constance and threatened Hanley, but off they went in spite of her.

For about three and a half months her life resembled that of the first weeks of her marriage. Hanley was silent but not ill-tempered, and the servants, under his apparently terrifying eye, were outwardly respectful to Constance.

She herself was little more than an automaton. She rose, ate, made a pretence of ordering meals and keeping house, and never travelled farther afield than the end of the park or the limits of the apple orchard.

Towards the end of the third month she consulted Doctor Crevister and was confirmed in her opinion that she was with child.

Since their return, Hanley had never left the house after dark. He appeared to have forgotten Martha Fluke, and did not go near the witch, her mother. He made no comment when Constance told him her news, and all was sufficiently peaceable to cause Constance to speculate whether the tranquillity she was enjoying was not too good to be true.

Hanley, with a jeering note in his voice which rather disquieted her, had found her a new name. She pretended at first to like it, but finding that this apparently spoilt the joke for him and tended to encourage that same kind of moroseness which had led up to his previous excesses, she showed her true feeling, that of petulant mortification, and this seemed to please him so much that she kept it up even after she had become accustomed to the name.

'Griselda!' he would call, and, at the sight of her expression, he would chuckle delightedly. *'Patient Griselda!'* he would continue, and then, when he had extracted all the pleasure he could out of her distress, he would tell her what he wanted.

Besides this, which was the only form of cruelty he appeared to indulge in at the time, there was something which caused Constance such vast uneasiness that she tried all the while to put it out of her mind. A trier at last, she tried in vain. The horrid thought persisted. He was *gloating* over something. At times she surprised upon his face an expression of insane and devilish glee, and it increased, she was perfectly certain, as the time for the birth of the baby drew nearer. Another sinister fact was his censorship over the whole of her correspondence. He would not allow her to write to her mother to say that the baby was coming, and he would not have her invited to the house. Constance, cut off from her only means of comfort and support, grew frightened and ill, and looked into the future with dread. She did not know what she feared. Horror seemed everywhere present. Persistently in her dreams she saw Hanley's devilish face, and woke from her sleep with a scream.

Chapter Three

'and as to the droppings of wax lights upon
the dress of the corpse when first discovered
in a ditch . . .'

THOMAS DE QUINCEY
On Murder Considered as One of the Fine Arts.

IT WAS on a Wednesday that Mrs Pike was brought
into the house, and on the following Friday
Constance gave birth to a son. It had been a tricky
business, and Doctor Crevister had dealt with it
particularly creditably, he felt. He had never set
eyes on Hanley all the time, but he left permission
with Mrs Pike for Hanley to see his wife and child
if he desired to do so.

He was given the doctor's message, and while he
was in the bedroom Mrs Pike thought she might
as well go down to the kitchen and drink the glass
of stout there provided for her.

On the following Tuesday morning Constance
died of septicæmia following puerperal fever, and
Hanley wept on Martha Fluke's shoulder in the

dining-room where he had interviewed her on the departure of Doctor Crevister from the house. The doctor was exceedingly angry with Constance for dying, after all the trouble he had taken, but he had little time for lamenting her indifference to his professional skill, for, very shortly afterwards, Mrs Pike's husband, a sailor home on leave, complained of violent abdominal pains after partaking of food obtained from the cook at Neot House, and Doctor Crevister was called in to attend him. On the second day he seemed almost completely recovered, but during the night he was sick and in considerably worse pain, and early next morning Mrs Pike went again for Doctor Crevister. She was gone for about forty minutes, because the doctor was in bed and had to dress, and in any case it was a good way from her cottage to his house. When she arrived back again with the doctor Pike had disappeared, and the only proof he had been ill again was the mess on the floor and the stench in the unventilated bedroom.

Every effort appeared to be made by the villagers and the puzzled doctor to find him, but in vain. It seemed as though he had disappeared off the face of the earth, but the thing was only a three days' wonder, for it was reported that Hanley Middleton suddenly had developed alarming symptoms akin to those of Seaman Pike, and, against all his known inclinations, had been compelled to call in Doctor Crevister. Operated on, the unfortunate patient died. According to written request, the coffin was screwed down immediately Martha Fluke, dark

under the eyes and more than usually pallid, had
taken a last look at the dead man. Even Constance's
mother, ill with grief at the loss of her daughter,
was refused a last look at Hanley.

Mrs Pike had not only been chosen as midwife
but was to remain in the capacity of wet nurse to
Constance's baby boy. This was at the particular
request of the mother, who could not bear to think
that a child of hers should be suckled by Martha
Fluke.

Martha's own little boy was then about four
months old, and had not been baptised in spite of
the vicar's frequent reminders. Mrs Pike was held up
as a model to Martha, who giggled and replied that
when her own little baby was as funny and ailing
as that of Mrs Pike she would bring it along of a
Sunday to be christened. Then, suddenly changing
her mind, she promised it should be baptised, and
brought it to the church.

But after Mrs Pike had been caring for the little
Middleton about a week, old Mrs Fluke, the witch,
appeared at the vicarage with the news that 'our
Martha's little baby' was dead of the whooping
cough and looked, 'poor little dear,' like nothing
so much as a three weeks old child, so small and
'back-to-birth-looking' he had become.

There were rumours that the babies had
been mixed and given to the wrong mothers,
but gradually all rumours save one died down.
The persistent rumour was to the effect that
Hanley Middleton had been the younger of twin
brothers, and that somewhere waiting to claim

his inheritance was Carswell Middleton, the elder twin.

Where the notion of twin brothers came from nobody knew. It was believed to have been started, like a hare, by old Mrs Fluke, but it gained ground and had a large number of adherents. This was the more surprising considering that the village had known Hanley Middleton since the death of his highly eccentric uncle, a man equally convinced that he was the Emperor Hadrian and that twelve shillings made a penny. It was the latter foible which had endeared him particularly to the inhabitants of Saxon Wall. It was Hanley's odd behaviour which had caused the village to accept him as a genuine Middleton, and when he died Saxon Wall sat tight and, while continuing to employ itself with its dull and sinful concerns, waited for the uncle of Constance's son to turn up and contest the legitimacy of the child, and carry on the traditional generosity and sinfulness of the Middleton family. Saxon Wall was unaccustomed to the principle that legitimacy was a title to inheritance—for breeding in the village was strictly by the law of natural selection—but old Mrs Fluke, who could back up legal with religious proof—for instance, with the story of Abraham, Hagar and Ishmael—and with involved quotations from the marriage service in the English Prayer Book, enlightened and interested them.

Martha Fluke had conveyed to the altar a half-witted cowman named Passion, and village rumour concluded by fathering Constance's baby on the gardener and Martha Passion's on Hanley Middleton. There was nobody to deny the former rumour, so it soon died a natural death, but the latter was so hotly contested by Martha Passion, old Mrs Fluke, and by Passion himself, an undersized moron who was employed by a farmer called Birdseye, that it persisted for long, kept alive by argument, speculation and lewd jest.

Meanwhile, Mrs Pike, never particularly stable mentally, had been overtaken by idiosyncrasy, and was keeping her baby within doors and out of sight of callers. Her excuse and reason for so doing was that she hid it away lest old Mrs Fluke should afflict it by her possession of the evil eye.

The Middleton baby—for Constance's mother refused to take care of it—was soon committed to the care of Hanley's solicitors, and Neot House was shut up. There was no one to notice whether the ghost of Constance haunted the shuttered rooms or walked the galleries, except on Bank Holidays, when the house was open for inspection at a fee of twopence. For a year or two, interested parties visited the rooms where Hanley and Constance were supposed to have spent their last hours.

The vicar died, and Doctor Crevister retired, and the Long Thin Man, the village public house, passed into the hands of a couple from Essex. The other long thin man, the patron and familiar, it was said, of old Mother Fluke the witch, still slept in his long barrow on the hill called Guthrum Down, and for eight or nine years the village peaceably returned to its dirt and its lies and its ugly clodhopping sins and its Saturday pint and a half, the last no longer paid for out of Hanley Middleton's patrimony, but none the less enjoyed, since, apart from any other consideration, it happened to be better beer, and even the inhabitants of Saxon Wall, dead to all other decent feeling, could distinguish and comment upon the difference.

SECOND MANIFESTATION

CONVERSATION PIECE

'Everything seemed to me to be transformed
and altered into other shapes by the wicked
power of sorcery and enchantment, insomuch
that I thought that the stones which I found were
indurate and turned from men into that figure,
and that the birds which I heard chirping, and
the trees without the walls of the city, and the
running waters, were changed from men into
such kind of likenesses. And further, I thought
that the statues, images and walls could go, and
the oxen and other brute beasts could speak and
tell strange news, and that immediately I should
see and hear some oracle from the heaven, and
from the gleed of the sun.'

The Golden Ass of LUCIUS APULEIUS, in the
translation of William Adlington, edited by
F. J. Harvey Darton.

Chapter One

'I pray thee, friend Bellephoron, sit still,
and according to thy accustomed courtesy,
declare to us the loss of thy nose and
ears.'
The Golden Ass of Lucius Apuleius, in the
translation of William Adlington, edited
by F. J. Harvey Darton.

HANNIBAL JONES had earned a dishonest livelihood
for seventeen years by writing sentimental novels.
It was the less excusable in Jones to get his living
this way in that he knew—none better, since
he had lectured in Abnormal Psychology for a
year or two in an American University before
taking up his rather more nefarious career as
author—that such novels as he wrote tended to
encourage morbid day-dreaming on the part of
their readers, and that cooks and dressmakers,
mothers of families, spinsters in all walks of life—
even his own female relatives—were developing,
because of him and his works, a Cinderella-

complex of the most devitalising time-consuming type.

It was the size of his income which prevented in Jones the acute shame proper to his situation, but, fortunately for the chances of his soul's salvation, the habit of sentimental writing proved to have grave physical risks as well as pecuniary advantages.

One day in the early Spring, his publisher invited him to lunch, and put forward a new proposal. Jones listened carefully. The same notion had been in his own mind time and again, but he had put it from him because of the trouble it would be to put in some serious work after all his years of laziness and easy money-making. Said his publisher:

'Why don't you do some melodramatic stuff? The big scene in your last book was sheer melodrama, and went well. Slums in a riverside district, or in a big port. Plenty of meat, and plenty of sob-stuff, like a film, but solid and fairly long. You know what I mean.'

Jones took the idea very seriously and began to work very hard. But the harder he worked, the more difficult it seemed to write the book. The result of his labours was disastrous. He became nervous and began to suffer from insomnia, but still he persevered. He collected reference books, newspaper cuttings, statistics and even facts, and at the end of six strenuous weeks he tore up the novel which he had hoped and anticipated, was to be startlingly, arrestingly, nudely modern, and, at the same time, an example of English prose at its best.

He worked tremendously hard and sent his wife considerable sums of money on condition that she was willing to extend her holiday on the Riviera until the novel was finished. But it was years since he had settled down to serious work. He grew irritable, morose, and quite unlike himself. In addition, he lost weight, he lost appetite; he began to lose interest in the book. His publisher bullied him, at first over the telephone, and then, when Jones refused to answer it, by telegram. With the business acumen which is often, although not invariably, one of the first-fruits of writing solely for money, Jones had insisted upon a substantial advance before he began work on the book, and the publisher was desirous of being assured that Jones really did intend to write the novel. This, under the circumstances, was natural enough, but it goaded almost to insanity the nerve-ridden and harassed author.

Having at last reassured him by word of mouth in a pithy sentence which, had it appeared in the novel in question, certainly would have been deleted at sight by the Censor, Jones toiled on, despairing but undefeated. Two secretaries gave notice, and the third, a suggestible young man whom Jones' rapidly collapsing nervous system could not fail to affect, hastened the approaching nervous breakdown by appearing five nights in succession at his employer's bedside, sleep-walking, and babbling disconnected lines from the poems of William Blake.

Jones gave him an excellent testimonial and

dismissed him. Then, after spending eight weeks in a nursing home, he consulted a famous psycho-analyst—her reputation was sufficiently established for her to be able to continue the use of an out-of-date term with which to describe her profession—and was given an appointment. She was a small but terrifying woman with the grin of a hungry crocodile and sharp black eyes, and her whole appearance and personality were in direct contrast to those of the nerve-ridden, extraordinarily lanky and cadaverous Jones. She put him through the usual tests, physical and mental, cackled at him, prodded him in the ribs with a yellow forefinger and advised him to take up gardening.

'And mind you return your publisher the advance on account of royalties which he paid you,' she adjured him. Jones, who had not mentioned the advance, was astonished and impressed by her perspicacity, but declined to consider for one moment her advice that he should take up gardening.

'When I was a boy,' he said, 'my father had an allotment. Do you know what that is?'

The little old woman said that she did.

'And on Good Friday mornings,' continued Jones, 'It used to be my detestable duty to walk beside him dropping seed potatoes into the holes he made. Since my fifteenth birthday, when the job passed automatically, according to my father's promise, to my younger brother, I have avoided gardening and never wish to look upon a potato dibber nor a garden fork any more.'

'Well, then,' said she, 'get out your third-best car and travel until you find a sufficiently interesting and secluded village. Make yourself part of it. Study the people, but resolve never to write about them in a novel. Love them. Quarrel with them. Begin a lawsuit. Play village cricket.'

'But look here—this book I'm on!' wailed Jones. 'I'm contracted to finish it at the end of the next two months. I can't let my publisher down. It's essential I should finish the book by September. You don't understand!'

'Very well,' said the psycho-analyst. She gave him back his cheque. 'Go and write. But don't ask *me* to appeal to the Commissioners to release you from a lunatic asylum later on.'

Jones wrote to his publisher, returning the advance, returned her fee to the formidable, reptilian psycho-analyst, closed his flat, got his third-best car from the garage, and started out in quest of his village. It took him nineteen days to discover and annexe the village of Saxon Wall. It was long, straggling and unkempt. It was away from main roads and apparently unacquainted with the progress of what people who put cleanliness before godliness call civilisation. The farmyards of its immediate vicinity smelt sourer, its inhabitants looked more dour and unfriendly, its cottages were uglier in conception, arrangement and colouring and its public house more surprisingly named than any of the others he had passed by or encountered during his tour, so he adopted it at sight, and decided to stay in it a good long time.

'As good a place in which to get over a nervous breakdown as any in England,' thought Jones, drawing up at the entrance to the Long Thin Man and getting out of the car.

Over a tankard of beer—the nuttiest he had drunk for years—he invited opinion upon his chances of finding a suitable cottage for the summer.

'Easy,' said the landlord. 'I'll tell Birdseye to turn out old Mother Fluke for you. She won't have paid the rent three months or more.'

'But what will she do?' asked the humanitarian Jones.

'Her? Oh, that'll be all right. I'll tell Birdseye she can have that little cottage that was built sometime back for the barman when he got married, before he went to the war. I haven't had a barman—haven't needed one, like—since I've been here. It's a little old tumble-down place enough, because I haven't looked to keep it in repair, but old Mother Fluke, most likely, won't live long enough to know much different. I'll tell Birdseye to put a couple of shillings, say, on to your rent, and I shan't charge the old woman nothing for my little cottage, say. Then I can settle up with Birdseye, and nobody won't be the loser as far as I can see.'

Digesting the ethics and the economics of this delicate manipulation of the facts of the case, Jones agreed, and finished his beer. He never came into contact with the accommodating Birdseye, but by the end of the day everything was settled, including which articles of furniture Mrs Fluke was going to leave behind in the cottage for Jones' use, and which were going to accompany her to her new home, a little further down the road. Jones had the felicity of assisting to load her belongings on to two perambulators, the property of Mrs Passion and Mrs Pike, the daughter and next-door neighbour respectively, of the old woman he was dispossessing. Of Mrs Fluke herself he saw nothing, she having preceded the perambulators by a quarter of an hour, so that she could decide where everything was to go when it arrived at the cottage. Jones was considerably lightened in conscience to hear from Mrs Passion that 'mother will be only too glad to be quit of Birdseye for a bit, with his everlasting coming of a Monday morning for the rent just when she'd got the clothes on the boil and the copper fire going nicely!'

The Passions, he learned, were to be his next-door neighbours on the other side. They had seen aeroplanes but not motor-coaches, and both thought that the inventions of wireless telegraphy and vacuum cleaners were in direct contravention of the will of God. Of the divine wishes and intentions, Jones soon discovered, the village had wide and infallible knowledge.

On the second day of his stay he telegraphed to London for a new bed and for various small amenities, and proceeded to make his new quarters habitable. He then began the book for the second time. It was useless. He had dried up completely. He was considerably alarmed. He put his writing materials out of sight; hid his typewriter underneath the bed; went walking every day; explored the countryside and refused to think of work, proposing to court ideas by pretending to ignore them.

The neighbourhood was pleasing without being in any way remarkable. His favourite walk was across the village green and over the rounded hill called Guthrum Down by way of a stretch of heath, bracken-covered, springy underfoot with heather, and pleasantly bracing.

There were slow-worms and adders on the common, and Jones found that these creatures were held in peculiar horror by all the village people except old Mrs Fluke, who had a name for being able to make them dance on their tails by moonlight, and spell the names of the angels of darkness by their contortions at witches' sabbaths.

It was repeated, too, that the devil himself had visited Mrs Fluke at the cottage which Jones was occupying, and there had made his pact with her. Jones was amused and interested, but could find nothing sinister about the cottage itself, which was clean and in good repair, and overlooked arable fields. Mrs Fluke herself, when her daughter spoke of her to him, seemed to be a much-maligned old woman, poor, honest and respectable.

'You wait till they quarrels,' his other next-door neighbour, the simple-minded Mrs Pike, informed him. She was mild-mannered and clean, and possessed the most pronounced squint that Jones had ever seen, but apart from this, and the fact that she had a beautiful fair-haired, delicate-looking son, a boy of nine or ten, who appeared to have sufficient intelligence for the pair of them,

Jones found her unremarkable. She expressed her goodwill by sending the boy along with presents of vegetables out of the garden. Jones, who liked garden peas, returned the compliment by sending in chocolate and bananas from the village shop. He had suggested paying for the peas, but Mrs Pike had burst into tears.

Her devotion to him soon became sycophantic, but not sufficiently obtrusive to be annoying. Her greatest joy was to encounter him in the village street so that he should raise his hat to her, and this usually occurred upon another walk that Jones took through the village, which was a very straggling one, out past a big house standing in a park. He tried to find out the history of the house, for it appeared that no one except a caretaker had lived there for some time, but the villagers were peculiarly, and, to Jones, who had the writer's lust for a story, irritatingly reticent. They told him the name of the mansion, Neot House, and that was all.

Gradually the desire to write his book began to leave him. He no longer took it out twice a day, sighed, and put it away again. He began to go to bed earlier and to sleep better. He had never known such peace of mind and body in his life. He lived sparely, and spent very little money. He received no letters—for nobody, except his wife, who was beginning to tire of Nice, and the people at the shop to which he had sent for the new bed and other necessaries, knew where he was living, and his publisher re-commenced to telephone his London flat in vain. He ceased to be Hannibal Jones, accursed best-seller of novels the proofs of which he could not bear to read and correct, and became Mr Jones of the village of Saxon Wall, again at last a nonentity, but one in a state of grace.

Chapter Two

'Indeed, I must confess that the study of the Anglo-Saxon laws often reduces me to a state of mental chaos. I may know, as a rule, the meaning of individual words; I can construe, though not invariably, the separate sentences. But what it all comes to is often a total mystery.'

CHARLES PLUMMER
The Life and Times of Alfred the Great.

BY THE time he had lived six weeks in the village, Jones' acquaintance with its affairs was wide but not particularly profound. He knew, for instance, that about half a mile from the vicarage there was a ruined castle, but he could not discover by hearsay who had lived there, or when or for what reason it had been abandoned. He knew not [only] that at the other end of the village, on the road which led to the coast, was Neot House, unoccupied save for a caretaker; he knew also that in its grounds stood a dower house which had been let to two maiden ladies, sisters, who were known in the village as Miss Harper and Miss Phoebe. Opinion, so far as he could gather, was divided about them on account of their pet goat. This creature, which, needless to say, and without regard for what Miss Somerville and Miss Ross call 'the accident of sex in the brute creation,' they had named Gerald, was permitted the run of the house, and was taken out for exercise and on shopping expeditions. One section of the *habitués* of the Long Thin Man, where Jones repaired mid-mornings and every evening for a glass of the excellent ale, apparently regarded the goat with affectionate veneration from their having conceived a mistaken idea in respect to the significance of the theory of the scapegoat in Holy Writ; the others, who were in the majority, confined themselves to head-shakings and mutterings, except for the very boldest, who talked loudly of cloven hoofs and observed that they would like to know what sort of things went on inside the Dower House at certain phases of the moon.

Jones made the acquaintance of the two Miss Harpers and their goat outside the post office one afternoon. He had been in to buy tobacco, they to purchase stamps and a ball of string. A mongrel dog, the village scavenger, began to bark at the goat, and nanny, for the animal was female, undeterred by the noise made by the dog, rushed at him, jerking his lead out of Miss Phoebe's hand. Before the Amazonian Miss Harper could interfere, Jones had driven off the dog with a well-directed half-brick, which scared but did not strike it, and had placed the end of the goat's lead again in Miss Phoebe's hand.

His reward for this service was to be invited there and then to tea at the Dower House after a short, audible and trenchant colloquy among the sisters and Mrs Gant, the shopkeeper and postmistress.

'Cheese cakes, sister?'

'Of course, sister. I made them this morning whilst you were going the rounds of the runner-beans.'

'Now what about a pot of your strawberry jam, Mrs Gant?'

'Thank you, ma'am. Eightpence, please, ma'am. Thank you, ma'am.'

'What else, sister? There's the carraway cake.'

'Gentlemen detest seed cake, sister. Isn't there a clutch of eggs in the house?'

'Yes, sister. Birdseye sent them in this morning.'

'Then all is well. Will you come to tea with us this afternoon, Mr Jones?'

Tea over, Jones stayed longer than he had intended, for the ladies gave him the gossip of the village, together with the history of Neot House. He learned that the owner of the house was a boy of nine, a heavy-faced, unresponsive, sullen child—according to the sisters—who was at school in Sussex and spent his holidays in London with one of the trustees of his estate.

'Such a dreadfully sad story, poor child. No wonder he is such a quiet boy,' said Miss Harper. 'His mother, Mrs Middleton, died when he was born, and his father three weeks afterwards—of grief, they say, although personally I am more inclined to think that it was—that he took his own life. Too terrible.'

'You ought not to say such things, sister,' observed Miss Phoebe. 'After all, surely a doctor's word should be believed.'

'Oh? What did the doctor say he died of?' inquired Jones, who found it difficult to conceive that a medical practitioner would countenance the suggestion that Mr Middleton had died of grief.

'Oh, Doctor Crevister thought at first that it was heart failure following a severe bout of indigestion,' said Miss Phoebe, 'but later on they operated for appendicitis, in my opinion most unwisely.'

'Nonsense, sister.'

'But, sister, he was sick. Dreadfully sick. You know what Mrs Passion said.'

'Yes, of course I do. But he might just as easily have poisoned himself.'

'Well, the doctor didn't think so. After all, he couldn't have been as fond of his wife as all that.'

'Why not?' asked Jones.

'Well, you see,' began Miss Harper enjoyably, but she was called to order by her sister.

'Now, Sophie, *please!* Mr Jones does not want to listen to scandal.'

'Of course he does!' retorted Miss Harper. 'Everybody wants to listen to scandal. It's most interesting. Shall I continue, Mr Jones? Just as you wish, of course.' She looked malevolently through gold-rimmed glasses at her sister, and then changed her expression to one of triumph and pleasure, as Jones diffidently confessed to a taste for scandal as long as it was not malicious in intention.

'There you are, you see!' she said. 'I wonder where Sheridan would be if everyone were as pernickety as you!'

'Does it matter, sister?'

'Of course it matters! What else could I produce at Christmas with the Girls' Guild? Even the vicar approves of Sheridan.'

'Really, sister, even if the vicar does approve, I ought to remind you that our dear mother did not. If I can trust my memory, Sophie, she would never allow a copy of his collected works within the four walls of our house.'

'That was Shelley, not Sheridan, sister. Or Shakespeare, possibly.'

'Another subversive writer,' said Miss Phoebe angrily.

Jones gently recalled them to the subject under discussion. 'What was the scandal connected with Mr Middleton, then?' he asked. Miss Harper leaned forward confidentially and, undeterred by Miss Phoebe's headshakings and grimaces, answered readily:

'They say he was unfaithful to his wife!'

'Before marriage, Sophie!'

'It's the same thing, sister.'

'Rubbish, sister. You can't be unfaithful to your wife before marriage! Ask Mr Jones.'

Jones modestly disclaimed any special knowledge of the subject, and the situation was not improved by

Miss Harper's sibilantly relieving herself of the word 'Gaffe! Gaffe!' in her sister's pink and embarrassed ear. It was a most effectual interruption of his protestations, however, and, with a last withering glance at the now utterly defeated Miss Phoebe, Miss Harper continued with great eagerness.

'And they *do* say that the child down in the village—the Widow Pike's little boy—is as like the late Hanley Middleton as a son can be like his father.'

'Really!' said Jones. 'Is that the little boy the villagers say is a changeling. He lives next door to me.'

Miss Harper nodded, and Miss Phoebe, suddenly recovering her poise and, with it, her good-humour, said suddenly and explosively:

'I never would have thought it of the Widow Pike, from what I know of her! A *most* respectable woman, quiet and hardworking.'

'Not very intelligent,' said Miss Harper, pursing her lips. 'Not *very* intelligent, would you say?'

'Mentally defective, in fact,' said Jones, whose training in morbid psychology caused him to take an interest in Mrs Pike's deficiencies.

'Well, I cannot speak as to *that*,' Miss Phoebe admitted candidly, 'but there certainly have been no *lapses* on her part since we came to live in the village, Phoebe, have there?'

'You weren't at the Dower House, then, when Mr Middleton was alive?' said Jones, who had not grasped this fact.

'Oh, no. But we came soon after the funeral. We

have been here just eight years at the end of the present month. We come from Tunbridge Wells. Do you know Tunbridge Wells, Mr Jones?'

Jones had an aunt there, but he was determined not to allow the promising story of Hanley Middleton to be side-tracked in favour of a discussion on English spas, so he shook his head and said:

'But little Pike is supposed to resemble the late Mr Middleton?'

'He's supposed to be the image of him.'

At this point the conversation again showed signs of petering out, and Jones was about to take his leave when Miss Phoebe suddenly inquired:

'And how does Mrs Passion do for you?'

'Oh, admirably,' said Jones. 'She doesn't bother me, and she keeps the cottage as clean as one can expect, and there's always something to eat when I go in to meals.'

'Hm! You want to beware of those Passions, though,' said Miss Harper. 'I am not sure you wouldn't have done better with the Pike.'

'Oh, but she drinks,' said Miss Phoebe. 'They say that just before Mrs Middleton's confinement—Mrs Pike was the midwife, you know. Not certified, of Course——'

'Certificated, sister.'

'It's all the same, sister. As I was saying, Mr Jones, one can't expect everything in Saxon Wall, but there *had* been some talk of getting a nurse from London or Manchester or somewhere——'

'Do you know Manchester, Mr Jones?'

'Sister, *please*! But of course it's something to have a woman like Mrs Pike who will wash her hands. But for all that it was blood-poisoning which caused the poor young woman's death.'

'You've left out the part about Passion being taken ill, sister.'

'Dreadfully ill, Mr Jones——'

'*Poison*, someone hinted.'

'But it proved to be nothing but the drink. His wife said he was always taken with melancholy if ever she had to leave him.'

'It was dreadful, though, while it lasted, I should imagine. Mrs Gant at the post office told us all about it. Really too nauseating. Just like the effects of arsenical poisoning, according to a murder trial that she was following at the time, she said.'

'Most revolting,' said Miss Phoebe, breaking in again upon what she regarded as her story. 'Dreadfully sick, you know, and really not at all himself for some time afterwards.'

'It sounds as though he must have taken a good deal,' said Jones.

'Seventeen pints of stout, sworn to by the landlord of the Long Thin Man,' said Miss Harper impressively. 'Besides, they found the empty bottles at the bottom of the garden.'

'And Passion had the hardihood to declare that he had never touched a drop of it,' said Miss Phoebe. 'And there were the seventeen bottles to confute him.'

'And to do the same thing again just before Mr Middleton died!' exclaimed Miss Harper.

'Good gracious!' said Jones. 'How extra-ordinary!'

'They say he didn't want his wife to go off and nurse Mr Middleton through his illness, and that was why he did it.'

'He believed his wife would stay at home and nurse him instead of going up to Neot House, apparently.'

'But she did no such thing. She saved him from the stomach pump, but that was all.'

'Of course, there *is* a look of her about the boy,' observed Miss Harper, slowly.

'Which boy? Do you mean young Pike?' Jones asked.

'Oh, no. The little Middleton, of course,' explained Miss Harper.

'But, sister, Mrs Middleton was certainly brought to bed.'

'But so was Mrs Passion, four months previously. Only *her* baby died.'

'Not until after Mr Middleton's funeral, sister. On the Saturday after, wasn't it said?'

'Mrs Fluke ill-wished that baby. She never liked Mrs Passion,' said Miss Harper solemnly.

'But they're mother and daughter,' said Jones.

'You don't know this village,' said Miss Phoebe.

'The *things* they talk about——'

'And *think* about——'

'It's really terrible.'

'But what happened to the baby?' Jones inquired.

'It went to heaven,' affirmed Miss Phoebe, nodding her head. 'Fortunately——'

'Most fortunately——'

'——it had been baptised at three months old.'

'I mean the little Middleton,' said Jones.

'If it *was* a Middleton,' said Miss Harper, avoiding her sister's eye. 'My personal, private opinion is that if a man is accused of having been unfaithful to his wife, the boot is often enough on the other foot as well. If the little Middleton was not a Middleton, and the little Pike—well, it's really rather confusing, but still, there's no smoke without fire.'

Jones said he agreed, and, his mind still ringing the changes on Pikes and Middletons and Passions, he rose to go.

'Now do promise us that you will come again, Mr Jones,' said Miss Harper.

'And we'll open a pot of our damson jam and see whether you like it as well as Mrs Gant's home-made strawberry,' said Miss Phoebe.

'You know,' said Jones, 'I don't believe I've got it quite right now. Which was the baby that died?'

'Little Passion,' said Miss Harper promptly.

'And no wonder, with a father addicted to drink,' said Miss Phoebe.

'Stout, too, sister.'

'Yes, poor child, it would have had no teeth worth speaking of.'

'Mrs Passion told me that she herself used to be partial to a glass of stout, but after his disgusting orgies with it, the sight of the froth makes her feel quite ill.'

'No wonder at all, sister.'

'Laced with gin, sister.'

'Disgusting man! And to think we used to employ him in the garden before we knew all this!'

Chapter Three

'There are no specifics for the reconciliation of these interests; nothing can avail save tact on all sides and a recognition of identity of aim.'

VON SEECKT
Thoughts of a Soldier, translated by
Professor Gilbert Waterhouse.

JONES walked slowly back to his cottage, and had been sitting at his parlour window for about two hours when he looked up from his book and noticed the old woman in the red flannel petticoat. She had kilted the skirt and was hoeing, why or what Jones was not countryman enough to know.

He watched her for the best part of an hour. She travelled very slowly up and down the field of crops, chopping with sharp, jabbing movements at the ground. It was fascinating and gruesome, this steady, concentrated hacking of the innocent soil, and (to his later astonishment) Jones found himself watching her with a sick anxiety in which he could imagine that he heard the harsh and gritty sound of the edge of the hoe on stones.

It was dusk before the old creature abandoned her labours, and Jones, on his way to the Long Thin Man for his evening glass of beer, found himself perturbed by the remembrance of her.

Next day, at about four in the afternoon, she came on to the field again and continued work. Jones, absorbed in watching her, did not hear Mrs Passion come in, and, his nerves hair-strung and his mind a field whereon the old woman hoed, gave a pronounced start and made a slight exclamation as the tea-tray was dumped on the table beside him.

According to her usual custom and although she had been told five times that he disliked over-sweetened tea, Mrs Passion dropped two lumps of sugar into his cup and then gazed out of the window.

She was a large, slow-moving woman with black hair, and a heavy, stupid-looking face, pallid and not very clean, but Jones decided that her lovers in her younger days might have thought her handsome.

'A heavy-faced, sullen-looking child,' thought Jones. On impulse he said:

'And how is Master Middleton, I wonder?'

Mrs Passion made no attempt to reply. Jones wondered whether she ignored the question as mere flippancy. Instead she said, still gazing out of the window:

'So old Mother Fluke been tending her tetties,

have she?' She averted her gaze from whom Jones' startled memory informed him was her mother in order to swill the pale blue milk of a dairy-farming countryside into his cup on top of the superfluous lumps of sugar before she poured out the tea, and added carelessly: 'Her's been ill-wishing parson, did you hear, sir? And it's him she's been a-killing and a-burying, I shouldn't wonder.'

'That's rubbish,' said Jones, attempting to ensure that the conversation remained on the high level of playfulness which he had first intended. 'You should make wax images, and stick pins into them.'

'Oh, should you, sir? I'll tell her, then,' said Mrs Passion tonelessly. Jones looked at her in astonishment, but her dough-coloured, inexpressive face was set in its usual mask of sullen heaviness, and she scratched her head, just at the top of the parting, with the nail of her forefinger, as she always did, before absent-mindedly dropping two further lumps of sugar into his tea cup. Tired of arguing the point, Jones contented himself with giving her a reproachful glance, fishing them out with his teaspoon, and dumping them in his saucer where he thought she would certainly see them. She did, but her only reaction to the sight of the tea-stained lumps, beyond a sudden and unnerving giggle, was to pick them up between thumb and forefinger, and suck them noisily.

'I do just love a knob of sugar with tea in, don't you?' she said. 'That's how the chaps makes love to ee in this village.'

Jones made no attempt to sustain this aspect of the conversation, but remarked:

'I feel it my duty to acquaint the vicar with your mother's manifestations of ill-will towards him.'

'Ay. Tell parson to set the hounds of hell on she,' was Mrs Passion's severely serious reply to what Jones had intended for persiflage. He smiled, but Mrs Passion's countenance did not change its expression in the slightest.

Jones had met the vicar during his first week in Saxon Wall. He had been nailing up a wall-bracket upon which he proposed to mount a small plaster cast of the Venus of Milo, the only piece of sculpture, except Epstein's Genesis, to which he could put a name with the certainty of avoiding vulgar error. Suddenly, in the midst of his labour, he became aware of a lounging figure in the sitting-room doorway.

'I know you're busy, and I haven't come to hinder you. But I just wondered whether I could knock a few nails in, or hang curtains or anything,' the vicar said.

Since that afternoon they had not met, and it was less the determination to acquaint the vicar with the nature of Mrs Fluke's sentiments towards him than the desire to indulge in friendly gossip which caused Jones to take his way to the vicarage after tea and to hope that he would discover the vicar at home.

His story of the ill-wishing was not received with the amusement he had anticipated.

'Old Mrs Fluke? Oh, yes. I'm not a bit surprised.

You see, she was ill a short time ago,' the vicar said. 'I used to take her some port and things occasionally. Now she has recovered she doesn't get any more. It goes to old Part, the water diviner. I expected there would be trouble, but I had not anticipated that I should be ill-wished, because, as a matter of fact, she's had her revenge another way.'

'Oh?' said Jones. 'How was that?'

'She informs me she is going over to the Baptists. They have several converts ready, I believe, and are only waiting for the rain. Their pastor is an energetic man, and I admire him. He is no scholar, but is evangelically inclined, and experiences peculiar joy in the contemplation of ninety and nine just persons. But the rain is not doing him justice, and the sinners will disappoint his expectations yet.'

'The rain?' said Jones.

'Yes. The Baptists totally immerse their candidates for baptism, you remember. But the drought is so exceptionally serious this summer that, short of going up to the dewpond on the top of Guthrum Down, I don't know how they will manage, unless it rains.'

'But will the Baptists have Mrs Fluke?' Jones inquired.

'I don't see how the pastor can refuse if she offers herself as a candidate for baptism. Anyway, she informs me that she shall not join the Methodists because her mother was one.'

'That doesn't make sense to me.'

'Nor to me. I am glad of it.' He lowered his voice, and put two fingers nervously between his throat and his clerical collar. 'The only time the conversations in this village ever make sense, they are so unthinkably lewd that one is grateful, as in the present instance, for some obscurity in meaning. And these people's amusements are as shocking as their talk. Do you know the first thing I put a stop to when I came here, nearly four years ago?'

'Drunkenness?' Jones suggested.

'Cock-fighting. Nothing less. And in the south of England, too, you know. It must have been an unbroken survival from the fourteenth century or earlier.'

'Really?'

'Yes. I first preached against it from the pulpit and compared its horrors with those of Spanish bull-fighting, but this method met with no result whatever if you except a most inapposite remark rendered by the man Passion, who is, for all practical purposes except the accidental one of 'having a hand with' calving cows, quite definitely half-witted.'

'Oh, really?'

'Yes. Passion is Birdseye's cowman. He came up to me on the day following that on which I preached my sermon, and he said: 'That do indeed seem grand, that bull-fighting you mention, parson. I should like to see some of that there, so I should. But I suppose they bulls don't be the valuable animals over to Spain as what they do be over here? Stands to reason, we can't be keeping them for our own amusement, *nor* theirs, like what they Spaniards can.'

Jones laughed, and the vicar joined in.

'Well, I could hardly let it go at that,' he continued, 'so I went to the backyard of the Long Thin Man, and challenged every owner of a cock to fight me. I lost every time, of course. Took two or three terrific smashings. Broke my nose, and so on. But at last the innkeeper at the Long Thin Man—he's an old pug, you know, and not a local man—I have great hopes of him— turned in his tracks, strangled his own two cocks and backed me up. The only other thing I've been able to do is to stop the killing of adders by the boys.'

'But aren't the adders rather unpleasant creatures?'

'So are the boys—very unpleasant creatures. But nobody thinks they ought to be slaughtered with cudgels. They used to hunt these unfortunate adders in order to destroy them in the most brutal way. It was wanton. It was cruel. I didn't like it. All the boys here sing in the choir. I turned them out. They didn't get any money. I beat a few. They call me Old Satan now.'

'I should have thought the Salvation Army would have been Mrs Fluke's ideal of a religious body,' Jones remarked, to end a considerable pause. The vicar shook his head.

'The Salvation Army is superstitious where we are concerned. Their Captain told me herself that they don't like making converts from the English Church. I don't know why that is. It may be a local feeling, and confined to this one young woman, for aught that I can tell. Besides, Mrs Fluke informed my housekeeper not long ago—on the same occasion, incidentally, as that on which she told him that she was going to be an Immersed Believer when the Lord sent rain enough—that, in her opinion, there was nothing so terrible as an army with banners, unless it was David kicking his tambourine before the Ark of the Lord in Shiloh.'

'Blasphemous old hag!' said Jones, not attempting to hide his amusement.

'Oh, no,' said the vicar seriously, 'not blasphemous at all, and not intentionally funny. She really visualises that scene, and is as shocked by it as Michal was, and probably for the same reason. Have you never noticed that almost identical prejudices are apt to persist in the untrained female mind for generations ? Oh, and by the way, if you are short of water at any time, please do not hesitate to come up here for some. My well has never failed, so far as living memory and the parish records will admit. I believe it used to be the well of a Saxon monastery which was almost certainly built upon this site. My belief is that the village took its name from the well, which was popularly supposed to possess healing properties, and should be known as Saxon Well, not Saxon Wall.'

'That's interesting.'

'So are the people's beliefs. About six months ago Ames, my colleague in the next parish, tumbled into his well. He now sends over here for all his drinking water. *His* reason is that he had been cleaning out his pigsties and his immersion fouled the well, but his parishioners, whose ideas are not materially

different from those of the heathen Jutes and West
Saxons who settled here, persist in regarding the
well as the receptacle of holy water.'

'Because their priest fell into it?'

'Because their priest fell into it. But, really, it's
quite useless to be shocked by their ideas. It is
simplest to disregard them. "This year the heathen
men ravaged Sheppey." Are you a student of the
Anglo-Saxon Chronicle, Mr Jones?'

Jones laughed.

'I used to be a student of abnormal psychology
in my youth,' he said. 'Interesting, rather.'

'I wish you joy of a study of the abnormal
psychology of some of my communicants,' the vicar
retorted. 'I believe you would find it sufficiently
remarkable. And talking of that, you are just the
man to assist us in amusing the children at their
annual Sunday school treat. We are going to have
it in the grounds of the old castle here this year,
because we haven't very much money. I should be
tremendously happy if you would come and help.
We shall give them tea out of doors if it's fine, or
in this house if it's wet, and then we are going to
arrange races and competitions, a scout display, a
wild flower hunt, a display of country and morris
dancing, and all that kind of thing. We shall send
them off home at about half-past eight or nine
o'clock, so it wouldn't really be a very long day
for you.'

Jones shook his head.

'Not me,' he said. The vicar smiled.

'Oh, come,' he remonstrated. 'I know you detest

the idea, and I suppose you'll be bored all the time, but really you've no idea of the difference it would make to me to have another man on the scene. Of course, the ladies are admirable—absolutely admirable—I don't know what we should do without them, but—I should so much appreciate it if you could be persuaded to take an interest in the thing, and come along and help.'

Jones, inwardly cursing himself for a fool, mumbled that he would come.

'That's splendid,' the vicar said heartily. 'I'll make you a judge in the races, then. I usually do the starting, and one or two of the ladies hold the tape and judge, but it's been unsatisfactory because they've nearly all got children in for the sports, and it's apt to provoke a partisan spirit, with the result that a certain amount of unpleasantness almost invariably follows the distribution of the prizes.'

'Oh, Lord!' groaned Jones. The vicar reassured him.

'Nobody will question *your* decisions,' he said.

'As long as I don't suffer personal violence at the hands of mothers whose sons have been listed as "also ran" I suppose I must be prepared to put up with unpopularity,' said Jones. 'When's the affair?'

The vicar was about to tell him when the housekeeper came in. He was a Japanese whom the vicar had brought with him from a Mission station and whose importance in the eyes of the village was that mothers frightened their children by intimating that the Japanese would eat them if they did not behave themselves in accordance with parental prejudice. This fact the older children invariably rejected upon the evidence of Miss Banks, the school-mistress, who asserted that the Japanese existed exclusively on rice and was forbidden by his religion to partake of the delights of cannibalism. His English was laconic, but unremarkable.

'Mrs Fluke.'

'Show her in, Nao.'

'Very good. Very much upset.'

'What about?'

'Not say.'

Mrs Fluke, whom Jones was meeting face to face for the first time, was indeed upset. She curtsied to the vicar, a sure sign to him that she had come to make what she regarded as a serious complaint, and commenced her story without preamble.

'If you please, Reverend, it be that daughter of mine.'

'Mrs Passion?'

'Martha Passion, as she calls herself!'

'Now really, Mrs Fluke, you must not make these unpleasant insinuations. It isn't right, and it isn't kind. Oh, and by the way, ought you not to go to the Baptist Minister for advice?'

'Nohow,' said Mrs Fluke, emphatically quoting Tweedledum and fixing a rheumy eye on Jones as though daring him to smile. 'I know what I'm doing, and it's not joining no Baptists I am. They're un-Christian.'

'Un-Christian?' said the vicar. 'You really must

not make these—these exceedingly disconcerting statements.'

'I am aware of what statement I'm making, Reverend, although you might not think it,' rejoined Mrs Fluke. She still kept her eyes on Jones as she added: 'Eighty-one next harvest and fully possessed.'

'Quite,' said Jones in what he trusted was a conciliatory tone, although he remained for the rest of his life uncertain whether she was referring to demoniacal possession or the full possession of her faculties.

'Yes, and she and that half-wit she wedded milking my only cow before my eyes and stealing my eggs off me.'

'Nonsense!' said the vicar sharply. 'Nonsense, Mrs Fluke!'

'But that's just what it isn't, then, Reverend!' shrilled Mrs Fluke. 'They've done it twice, and that's twice more than I can abide. And if you don't speak about it from the pulpit I shall not ever sit under your shadow no more. It's a shame and a disgrace that a respectable widow can't get justice from the only gentleman in the parish.'

'You did *not* see Mrs Passion and her husband milking your cow and stealing your eggs, now, did you?' asked the vicar, unmoved by the specific tribute to his birth and breeding. 'You didn't *see* them!'

Mrs Fluke unwillingly abandoned an impregnable position.

'With the human eye, that is the eye of error,

no,' she admitted. 'But with the eye of the spirit, that which I see yesterday as it were in a glass darkly, yea, and all.'

'Now, look here, Mrs Fluke,' said the vicar angrily, 'I've told you before that if you go in for this crystal-gazing and all this awful rubbish, you'll be damned utterly, for ever and ever, and go to hell! Do you understand that?'

'Ay,' mumbled Mrs Fluke. She brooded, pulling out her lower lip between thumb and forefinger. Suddenly she brightened.

'You do speak beautiful, Reverend, when you've a mind to,' she said.

'But it's precious seldom you have a mind to, I must say!' quoted Jones under his breath. Mrs Fluke averted her eyes from him, and crossed herself.

'What on earth are you doing now, woman?' cried the vicar.

'What's he muttering at me for?' she mumbled, pointing at Jones, but without looking at him.

'I was quoting,' Jones answered guiltily.

'From the Good Book, I hope, young man.'

'Well, no.'

'I thought not.' She looked triumphantly at the vicar. 'As for the Baptists, I'll tell you. You call to mind the story of Elijah?'

'I do.'

'How he poured water over the altar?'

'Yes, yes.'

'And yet the fire came and burned everything up?'

'Certainly.'

'Yes, well then, why can't the Baptists get us some rain sent down? Immersed believers!' Jones choked back a spasm of irreverent mirth. 'Water's their god, and he have no use for them! So *I* have no use for them either.'

'Now, really, Mrs Fluke!' said the vicar, very severely, 'I cannot allow you to make these extraordinary remarks in my presence. I am not here to defend any denomination of nonconformist persuasion, but I really will not listen to these disaffected and mischievous suggestions. Are you a heathen, woman? Don't you realise that, in good time, under Providence, rain will come?'

Mrs Fluke shook her head more in sorrow than in anger.

'Now, Reverend, you know better than that,' she said. 'It's so that Mr Turphy can't immerse his believers, that's what it is. And if I can't neither get water nor stop that Martha Passion milking my cow on the sly, I will catch her up in the branches of a tree, like the young man Absalom, and there let a soldier run his sword through her.'

'I'll speak to Mrs Passion, but I'm convinced that it's all a lot of nonsense,' said the vicar hurriedly. Mrs Fluke dropped another curtsy, and seemed inclined to prolong the conversation, but the vicar pressed the bell, so she contented herself partially by saying, as a kind of parting shot:

'Well, thank you kindly, not but what it's your bounden duty to help me carry my burdens, and now I've got what I came for, here's fourpence towards the children's treat, though I hear the behaviour last year was a disgrace to man and beast, and it's a pity Elisha and his bears aren't in this village sometimes.'

The vicar accepted the fourpence without thanks or comment, took a large book, ruled for cash, out of a table drawer, and entered Mrs Fluke's name and the amount of her contribution.

'Queer old party,' said Jones when she had gone. The vicar, who had filled and lighted a pipe, removed it from his mouth, and was about to make a remark when the Japanese again appeared.

'Mrs Passion, master.'

'Show her in, Nao.'

'Very good. Daughter of above Fluke and ditto.'

Mrs Passion was more than ditto, thought Jones, regarding her dead white face and quivering nostrils with interested apprehension. Like her mother, Mrs Passion came straight to the point.

'Firstly, sevenpence towards the outing for they boys,' she said. The vicar took out the cash book and entered the amount. Again, to Jones' surprise, he made no attempt to thank the donor.

'Second,' said Mrs Passion, her voice barely under control, 'the lies that wicked old devil have told against me notwithstanding! But there! Well is it said we wrestle not again flesh and blood, but again all the rulers of the darkness of spiritual wickedness.'

'Come to the point, Mrs Passion. Are you complaining about your mother?'

'No mother of mine, no and all, she isn't. If you ask me she have a mouse in——'

'Enough! Say what you have to say.'

'Her's bewitched I. That's what I have to say.' Her greenish eyes, the colour of stagnant water, gleamed suddenly and evilly at Jones.

'Rubbish, and you know it is! Be sensible!'

'But it isn't rubbish, sir. She *have* bewitched me! Passion too, poor man.'

'What has she done, then?'

'We can't stir out of our house without we hear the crying of little lambs. Piteous it is. But there isn't lambs about now, as *you* know, sir.'

'You're making this story up. And why do you milk your mother's cow and steal her eggs from her?'

The woman looked at him sideways and giggled.

'Mother surely do beat everything for wicked lies,' she said. 'She doesn't have no fowls. Her steals my eggs and I takes them back again. That surely ain't stealing, is it?'

'Be off with you!' said the vicar, suddenly losing his temper. 'Go on, and be quick about it!'

'Yes, and all,' said Mrs Passion mechanically. She seemed to have forgotten her grievance, and, after a moment, suddenly giggled again. 'That Lily Soudall does be on her way to you, about the long thin man it is.'

'And who is the long thin man, Mrs Passion?' asked Jones. She did not answer, but directed her next remark to the vicar again.

'Why do they call it Godrun Down, sir? Do there be any explanation of that, do you know?'

'Guthrum Down, woman, Guthrum Down.'

'Ah, you says so,' said Mrs Passion, unconvinced, 'but there's more things in this village stranger nor they Salvationists speaking with the sounds of brass, or with a tinkling cymbal either, for that matter.'

When she had gone Jones ventured to remark that it was extraordinary how often one found that biblical quotations had become part of the everyday speech of the country people in remote villages. The vicar snorted.

'If only they'd quote correctly it might not be so bad,' he said. 'But when you know, as I do, what a blasphemous lot they are, and what pools of filth their minds, and how bestial their intelligence, it is terrible to listen to them mouthing words to which they attach any significance but what was meant according to the context. I won't attempt to take sides in a quarrel between Mrs Fluke and Mrs Passion. They're as bad as one another. They vilify each other to me, on an average, once in every six weeks. All the accusations are based on some sort of actual reality and then are built up of lies upon lies until it's profitless and maddening to attempt to dig up the truth. The one time that they did join forces the village was flooded with anonymous letters. Nobody ever discovered who wrote them, but I'm prepared to swear that it was those two beauties in collaboration. Mrs Fluke supplied the bulk of the filth, and Mrs Passion wrote it down.

Here, let's have a whiskey, and wash away the taste of them. By the way, I wonder what the long thin man has been doing to Lily Soudall?'

'Who is she?'

'Maid at the doctor's. I should have thought her too sensible a girl to be affected by local legend, but one never knows.'

'Isn't she a village girl?'

'Oh, no. The doctor won't have a village girl. Says they're sluts and hussies, although I don't know what he knows about it. He came just after I did. He's not exactly popular, but he's feared. It's rather extraordinary.'

'And are they sluts and hussies?' Jones inquired.

'Oh, yes. I suppose they are. Lily comes from Surrey. I'm sorry she's turning out to be silly and superstitious.'

'What's the story of the long thin man?'

'He's our elemental spirit. Are you interested in psychic research?'

'Not actively. I've had the usual crop of people tell me the usual crop of "authentic" ghost stories, of course, and certainly have not believed them. But I confess to an unreasoning disinclination to sleep in reputedly haunted rooms and the like, so I suppose I am an unconscious subscriber to the doctrine that "there are more things in heaven and earth, Horatio——"'

Both laughed, and the vicar was putting back the siphon on to the tray when the Japanese entered again.

'Miss Soudall. Business not stated. Has wept.'

Lily Soudall was a pretty girl neatly dressed. She certainly had been weeping, and was not entirely mistress of herself. It appeared to cause her considerable confusion to be confronted by Jones as well as by the vicar.

'Oh, Mr Hallam,' she said. 'Couldn't I speak with you alone, please, sir?'

Jones started for the door.

'Next room,' said the vicar, calling after him: 'Read a book or something. Shan't be long.'

It was not more than five minutes before the vicar recalled him.

'This concerns you, Jones. These back-biting women! What on earth am I to do with them? Tell him, Lily.'

'I couldn't bring myself, sir.'

'Very well. *I'll* tell him. It's that wretched Mrs Passion, Jones. Swears that you've been sleeping with this girl.'

'Glad of the chance,' said Jones, with a bow and a smile. Lily hiccupped and giggled.

'That's better,' said the vicar. 'Dry your eyes, sit down, and let's consider what is best to be done. Is Mrs Passion annoyed with you, Jones, do you know?'

'I haven't any reason to suppose so.'

'No, I thought as much. Then it's Lily she's determined to annoy. Now, Lily, what have you done to make her angry?'

'Nothing at all, I'm sure I haven't, sir.'

'Now, Lily, think again.'

'Nothing, I'm sure, sir, unless——'

'Aha! We're coming to it. I thought we should.'

'But I don't think anybody could possibly think I meant any harm, sir. I'm sure they couldn't. Besides, it was a rare long time ago.'

'Out with it. I expect we're on the track.'

'Well, if you remember, sir, last harvest festival the little gentleman from Middleton's, sir, came into Sunday School and sat among my boys.'

'Lily is quite our most dependable Sunday School teacher, Jones.'

'Well, sir, I happened to say to Mrs Passion on the Monday, me having had a good chance to study the features of the little gentleman, sir, how very like her in the face he was, thinking it a bit of a compliment, in a way, sir, and certainly meaning no harm, seeing he never hardly comes anywhere near the village, sir, and is so rich in his own right and simply no connection whatever with the likes of us.'

'Mrs Passion is a funny woman, Lily. It's apparent that the remark offended her. Look here, I don't think I should take this any further. It will die down all the sooner if we show ourselves superior to it, won't it?'

'Yes, sir.' She paused.

'Go on,' said Jones. 'Young man turned sticky on you because of what has been said about you and me?'

'How did you know, sir?'

'They always do. Take my advice and kick him in the gizzard. That'll learn him.'

'I don't like to quarrel with him, sir.'

'Who is he?'

'Jasper Corbett, at the—at the——'

'At the Long Thin Man. He's the inn-keeper's son, Jones, as a matter of fact,' said the vicar, 'and as nice and steady a young fellow as you could wish for. Good prospects, too.'

'I've met him. I'll have a word with him,' said Jones. 'I expect I can settle his hash and make him see reason.'

The girl looked as though she would like to protest, but with the instinct of her class to feel that the ways of men are higher than the ways of women and therefore suitably beyond their comprehension, she took her leave.

'Queer how she funked the name of the pub,' said Jones.

'Not queer at all,' said the vicar, who seemed to perceive a jest that was withheld from Jones. 'Ever looked at yourself in a full-length mirror, my friend?'

Chapter Four

'The snowflakes settled swiftly on his
hair, his beard, his shoulders. But soon
the traces of the sledge-runners vanished,
and he, covered with snow, began to
resemble a white boulder, his eyes all the
time continuing to search for something
through the clouds of snow'

ANTON TCHEKHOFF
On the Way, translated from the Russian
by R. E. C. Long.

WHEN Jones got back to his cottage, supper was
on the table, and Mrs Passion had taken off her
apron as a sign that she was ready to go home.
Her hat she always wore except when she brought
in Jones' tea.

Jones tackled her.

'Look here, Mrs Passion, what's all this about that
girl Lily Thingummy and myself? Do you want to
give the girl a bad name or something? Understand,
you've got to take it back! I won't have it.'

Mrs Passion's heavy face did not change.

'I don't know what you mean, sir. Asking pardon, but nothing I said again Lily Soudall could have anything to do with you, sir.'

'But, dammit, you've been telling people she slept with me!'

'That, sir, I certainly have not.'

'But she says you did. A girl of that age wouldn't invent such a tale. Come, now!'

'What I did say, and what I admit to, Mr Jones, is that she slept along of the long thin man, which was by way of being my little joke about her being engaged to young Jasper Corbett, whose father keeps it, and that's all sir, and the truth, sir, may I be called Delilah, sir, if not.'

The words of themselves were not passionate, but Mrs Passion herself appeared to be deeply moved. Jones, surprisingly for a man who prided himself upon keeping all his sentiment for his books, was righteously angry, and continued sternly:

'Well, the girl is very much upset, and I'm annoyed. You'd better see that things are made all right, and that all ridiculous rumours are contradicted. Do you see?'

'Very good, sir.' She took the cover from a dish of eggs and bacon, pushed a tureen containing cabbage towards him, and, with dignity, made for the door. Jones grinned.

'Good night, Mrs Passion.'

'Good night, sir.' But she did not turn her head although she shut the door without undue force.

Jones looked at the clock. It was half-past nine.

There was plenty of time to finish his supper and still get to the Long Thin Man before it closed. So far as he could make out, Saxon Wall had never heard of the licensing hours.

The Long Thin Man did not boast a bar-parlour. Jones walked in at the double gates which gave on to the yard, stooped to pat the dog, and entered the taproom. The man he sought was in charge, a fine big boy of twenty-two or so, with a face burnt the colour of red brick and intensely blue eyes.

'Busy, Corbett?'

'No, Mr Jones, not if you want me.'

'Well, I won't get you away under false pretences. I want to curse you.'

'Very good, Mr Jones. Just wait while I call dad to mind the custom. He's nearly finished his supper.'

'It's this,' said Jones, when they were away from the house. He came to the point, with an incisiveness which surprised himself, still glowing with a righteous indignation he had not experienced for nearly twenty years. 'What are you upsetting Lily What's-her-name for?'

'Lily Soudall, sir?'

'Lily Soudall.'

Young Corbett cut at the rank nettles with the switch he was carrying.

'I made a mistake, sir, and no doubt said things I hadn't ought to.'

'And are too pig-headed to take them back, I suppose?'

'It don't do girls any good to own yourself in the wrong, sir. I thought best to let it blow over, like.'

'And what about me? No thought of *my* good name in the village, I suppose?'

Young Corbett grinned.

'Gentlemen like their fun, sir, and never take no harm from it, as I suppose.'

'And where do you get that idea?'

'Miss Phoebe lent me a book by a bloke of your name, Hannibal Jones, where a chap called Kaspar Dillmotway behaved wrong with a young girl, sir. So far as I could see, the man done what he liked, and if he was to be punished it would only be after he died.'

'My sins be upon my own head!' said Jones. 'Let that go, then. But look here, Corbett, you don't believe that tale about Lily?'

'Not now, sir, I don't.' He looked abashed.

'Why not?'

'I thought it over and I see I was hasty and—well, I reckon I had a bit of a guilty conscience, Mr Jones, over going with Vilert Teezy one night, and that made me speak sharp to Lily when I hadn't ought to.'

'Well, it's none of my business what you've been up to with any other girl, but if you'll take my advice, you'll be a sensible chap and stick to Lily. And you go and eat humble pie. It won't do you any harm, and you deserve it.'

'That's right enough, sir. I'll go and say I'm sorry. I *am* sorry too. Rare and sorry. But that isn't right to let Mrs Passion off free. She's a real wicked woman, that one.'

'How do you mean, lad?'

Young Corbett's face was serious.

'What do you think about them little babies, Mr Jones?'

'What little babies?'

'Didn't Miss Harper and Miss Phoebe tell you? They told dad they'd told you. Miss Harper said you was a London gentleman, and could put two and two together, so she reckoned, quicker than most. And Miss Phoebe said it was all of a crying shame—that was her own words—and that if there was anything to be done you'd do it.'

'But in what connection? I don't know what you mean.'

'Them little babies. Middleton baby, Pike baby, and Passion baby, sir. Miss Harper and Miss Phoebe said they told you all they dared.'

Jones shrugged.

'I heard a tale of sorts about some babies from Miss Harper and her sister, but it didn't mean much to me. As a matter of fact, and as man to man, I put it down to old maids' love of scandal.'

'My mother's fine and angry about Mrs Passion and the lies she telled about Lily Soudall and you, sir,' said young Corbett earnestly. 'And she believe there's something in the tale. Would you come back home with me, and talk to my mother a bit? Mother was wondering if someone didn't ought to have the law of her for doing of it.'

'Who? Mrs Passion?'

'Ay.' He cut again at the nettles. They had come to a break in the hedge and ditch, where a stile invited the pedestrian to walk over Guthrum Down. Jones put his foot on the wooden step of the stile, laughed and suddenly clapped Corbett on the shoulder.

'And do *you* want your mother to talk to me?' Corbett's brick-red countenance flushed deeply, and his blue eyes blazed.

'I'd like fine to see that damned old woman in trouble, so I would.'

'You go and make it up with Lily, then, and I'll go and talk to your mother. But, mind, I make it no business of mine to punish Mrs Passion, although she told that silly tale about me. You understand?'

'But if my dad and mother told you all they knew about her, you'd advise them whether to take the law of her, sir, wouldn't you?'

'Probably. But it's more than possible I should not know whether they had a case. I might be able to advise them whether or not it was worth while laying their facts before a solicitor. I doubt whether I could take the responsibility of going further than that.'

Young Corbett nodded. 'Very good, sir. Well, I'll get off to the doctor's. It's Lily's evening out, but I doubt she hasn't gone home to her mother. She's fair and upset, Lily is, and she don't want her mother to know what the folks are saying. She's a hard old woman, is Mrs Soudall, sir. She's a Methodist, and they can't abide anything that's got to do with morals. They're strict, the Methodists are.'

Jones laughed.

'You'll have a good time making-up the quarrel, anyway,' he said. 'I'll see you later, then.'

For some time after Corbett had left him, he remained at the stile, and gazed across a barley field to Guthrum Down. The rounded hill, close-cropped by sheep, still green in spite of the drought, humped itself like a giant creature asleep, its dorsal curve clear-cut against the sky. A chalk-white path climbed round and up and over it, and away towards the west lay the neolithic chieftain in his grave, possibly the uneasy spirit that brooded upon the village, possibly the original of the long thin man himself.

There was menace in the brooding hill and menace in the unnatural heat and dryness of the air. Jones sighed, and longed for rain. The thought of it made him thirsty. With no intention of taking sides in the suit of Corbett versus Passion, he walked slowly down the lane towards the inn.

Mrs Corbett saw him coming. She stood beneath an arch of Paul's Scarlet climber which had been trained over the side entrance to the house, and greeted him as he was about to walk into the tap-room by way of the double gates.

There was nothing for it but to give in gracefully, and listen to what she had to say. She took him into the dark, bow-windowed living-room and shut the door. Then, having leaned far out at the open window and turned her head from right to left

and back again, she shut the casement, smiled
conspiratorially at Jones, set before him cherry
pie and port, and, having congratulated him upon
his changed appearance since the beginning of his
stay at Saxon Wall, made graceful allusion to Miss
Harper and Miss Phoebe.

'I go to their At Home, Mr Jones. We're very
close friends. It's so nice for Jay. They lend him
books, you know, and invite me and Corbett to their
little swarries. Very genteel and nice, they are. Of
course, we don't see much society in Saxon Wall,
there being no lady at the vicarage, so we have to
do what we can between ourselves. There's Miss
Harper and Miss Phoebe, me and Corbett—when
I can get him to come, although you'd think a
hotel proprietor would be more sociable—little Miss
Banks the school teacher, a very refined young lady,
you'd be surprised, and I'm sure the *behaviour's* been
better, of course poor Mrs Woods was getting very
old— over seventy, they said—the pensions forgot
her, living so far from the railway, and in her way
a bit *peculiar*, nothing much, but she would keep
telling us Hamelin town's in Brunswick by famous
Hanover City, and something about a river washing
the walls, quite interesting the first time you heard
it, and I wish we *could* get a little rain, of course,
we do more with the bottled this weather, though
that's not everything, is it, as I tell Corbett, and I
hope I'm a Christian woman, I said.'

Jones, deliberately interrupting her, replied that
he thought there must be rain on the way, and,
talking gravely on past a counter-interruption from

the lady, led her back to her starting point. He guessed that the bulk of her remarks so far had been in the nature of a digression from the main theme, although intended as an introduction to it. Re-started on the subject of the social life of Saxon Wall, Mrs Corbett picked up the scent in faultless fashion from where she had made her detour, and headed for open country with an animation which suggested that she found the acquisition of a fresh auditor for a more than twice-told tale peculiarly stimulating.

'Well, that was four of us, and Corbett you might say five, and Mrs Birdseye six, although farmers' wives in general I don't know whether they make such good company, and the wife of the Baptist minister before she died, poor woman, although, between ourselves, Mr Jones, well, perhaps it's not for me to criticise, belonging to something a bit more toney, which I always think the Church is, somehow, but all that shaking hands at the chapel door on Sunday nights with every member, well, I call it American, myself, but it's not for me to judge, but, to my mind, not altogether in the best of taste, somehow.'

'The Middletons, I suppose, were not often living up at the house?' said Jones.

'Well, of course, it was just a week before we came when it all happened,' continued Mrs Corbett, smoothing her black silk apron over her thigh, and warming to the tale, 'and of course we was all too shocked to start our thoughts about it all straight away, but when both the funerals were over, and the new nurse came and took the Middleton baby away, and then Mrs Pike never bringing hers into the light of day, which, fresh air or not, as you believe in it, it did seem queer she didn't want to show it off to people a bit, and then Mrs Passion's own little baby dying, well, you see, it struck us a bit funny.'

'I see,' said Jones patiently. 'You mean you thought that there was something extraordinary about Mrs Pike's baby? That it was deformed, perhaps?'

Mrs Corbett shook her head. 'Nothing of that sort at all, Mr Jones. But, if you'll believe me, and to crown all, the little Pike to be the very living image of dead and gone Middletons unto the third and fourth generations, as anybody could see who had ever been over the picture gallery up at the house on a Bank Holiday, and if that can't be called proof positive, I'd just like to know what can!'

'Proof positive of what?' asked Jones; but Mrs Corbett could not stop to explain. She merely flicked her head, and continued: 'But just fancy that Mrs Passion daring to do it! And her own baby four months old if a day, and the little Middleton only three weeks, if that! And his father and mother— well you'd really wonder they wouldn't rise out of their graves!'

'You think, then, that Mrs Passion substituted her own four months' old baby for Baby Middleton, and that Mrs Pike is in the plot and is bringing up young Middleton as Henry Pike, her own child having died?' said Jones. 'Quite likely, I should say. Such things have been done before.'

'That's what I think, Mr Jones, I do, really. Can you imagine it! But one thing I don't believe, and that is that poor, simple Mrs Pike knows anything about it. She's nothing but a Natural.'

'But she *must* know whether Henry is her child or not. Even if she's half-witted she'd know that.'

'Ah, that, yes. She'd know whether he was her own child or not, I daresay. Although, really, she's that simple! But I reckon she had young Middleton passed on to her as a Passion. That's what I reckon, Mr Jones.'

'Then why should she have hidden him within doors as you say? If she thought Mrs Passion had parted with Baby Passion . . . anyway, what happened to Baby Pike?'

'Why, as like as not, that wicked woman told her that she'd lose the child if people found out it weren't hers, you see. And what I think is, little Pike, he died. You go and see Mrs Pike when you get the chance, Mr Jones. She'd take in anything. I never, not in *any* village—and we kept a house in the Epping Forest district before we came here and bought the Long Thin Man nine year ago—see anyone so simple. And she fair dotes on the little boy. No doubt of that. It would be cruel to take him away. That's what troubles me, Mr Jones. What to do for the best. It don't seem right that woman should push her own child into the Middleton money and lands if it belongs of right to little Henry Pike, and yet——'

'It's hardly little Passion's fault,' said Jones, 'if things are wrong.'

'Then you wouldn't go to law, sir?'

'Difficult,' said Jones. 'You couldn't prove anything from the ages of the children, and I doubt whether a family likeness would count for much in a court of law. Besides, the present little Pike, né little Middleton, may be the illegitimate off-spring of a Middleton-Passion union. Had you considered that point?'

'But a little Middleton, legitimate, was born, Mr Jones, and has to be accounted for. Besides, the family likeness was the spit and image both ways.'

'Both ways?' said Jones, befogged.

'Yes. Henry Pike for the Middletons, and little Middleton—so-called—for that Passion woman. There isn't any doubt, Mr Jones, about that. I've talked to people, and I know.'

'Well, I don't know. It's difficult,' said Jones, amused by the story and not prepared to commit himself to the extent of offering advice. 'To my mind, the best plan, possibly, might be to wait until the little Pike comes of age, and then persuade him formally to claim the estates. But, at present, where's the money coming from, even if you thought he had a case?'

'I see what you mean, Mr Jones. Yes, better let it rest, it being not of our business whichever way you look at it, except that right is right, and personally we have always kept a most well-ordered house.'

'Of course, you ought to have your facts quite clear about all three of the children, in case anything ever turns up,' said Jones as he rose to go. 'Let's see. Little Passion was four months old, you said, at the time when Mr Middleton died. Then little Middleton would have been three weeks old at the time of his father's death, and little Pike must have been—how old, would you say?'

'Two months, almost to a day, Mr Jones. Oh, I can see well enough what you meant about not proving anything, but it's a crying shame he shouldn't have his rights!'

'Yes, but, you see, as Mrs Pike kept her little chap—or possibly someone else's little chap—so carefully under cover for the first few months of his life, it wouldn't be at all easy to prove that substitution had taken place. The thing seems self-evident, I grant you. She must have made the substitution following, or even just before the death of Mr Middleton. I wonder how long he was ill?'

'Oh, it was all most sudden, Mr Jones. Of course, he grieved after his wife, as was only natural, seeing they hadn't been married so very many years and the baby being their first-fruits, as you might say. But die! Nobody didn't think that of him. A big surprise to everyone it was, and he such a villain to her all the time with his light-of-love behaviour.'

'Was there an inquest, then?'

'Oh, dear me, gracious no! There didn't have to be no inquest, Mr Jones. The doctor wrote out the certificate all right. It was Doctor Crevister then.

Now it's Doctor Mortmain. Quite a nice man he is, but all in favour of these operations. Told me Jay did ought to have had his tonsils out when he was a little boy, but there, as I said to him, all our family have outgrown them quite all right, and there's no doubt Jay will do the same. I don't believe in all these operations. "Sawn asunder, slain with sword," as the hymn book tells us, and quite right too. "I don't believe in interfering with Nature, Doctor Mortmain," I said, "nor in making the crooked straight before its time."'

Chapter Five

'In this same interlude it doth befall
That I, one Snout by name, present a wall.
And such a wall as I would have you think
That had in it a crannied hole or chink,

. . . .

And this the cranny is, right and *sinister . . .*'
WILLIAM SHAKESPEARE
A Midsummer Night's Dream.
Act V, Scene I.

BETWEEN the mysterious Birdseye and the Reverend Merlin Hallam there existed a complete and inviolable understanding, based on the necessity for preserving in the middle of the village green a well-rolled, closely-mown and jealously guarded cricket pitch.

Cricket was not a pastime native to Saxon Wall. Jones, in fact, watching one of the Saturday matches between the vicar's eleven and Birdseye's eleven, came to the conclusion—inevitable in the circumstances—that the object of the fielding side was not to get the batsmen out but to disable them. Even put in the most charitable words—those, incidentally, of the doctor—it appeared that body-line bowling had been practised in Saxon Wall long before its introduction into first-class cricket.

Neither Birdseye nor the vicar played in these matches, which were essentially games for the young and active, but it was the custom for Birdseye to release Passion from his cowman's duties every Friday afternoon so that he might get the pitch into some sort of condition ready for Saturday's game. If Passion, later on, went into the vicarage for a drink of beer, and remained to earn three-pence by weeding the vicar's gravel paths, nothing was said about it on either side.

Jones had made a careful study of the poor little moron, and had come to the conclusion that from him, or from no one, could be learned the truth about the changeling children of Middleton, Pike and Passion. Amused curiosity, alone, and not any desire to assist the righteous Mrs Corbett to establish law, order and justice in the village, impelled him to question Passion upon the subject, but time began to hang on his hands a little, although he was still unwilling to return to his ill-fated novel.

On the Friday afternoon following his talk with Mrs Corbett, Jones tracked Passion to the village green. He left his cottage at half-past three, followed a shady footpath which led from his home in the direction of Guthrum Down, and, keeping the village roofs in sight, branched off and skirted the village green. Then he lay down in the shade of an oak and watched Passion rolling the pitch.

At the end of half an hour he rose, brushed himself down, walked over to the solitary worker and hailed him. Passion, torn between the necessity of finishing the rolling and mowing of the cricket pitch, and the inadvisability of offending his wife's employer, came to an uncertain halt, his hands still on the handles of the cutter, and, wagging his large head mournfully, gave Jones greeting.

'Carry on,' said Jones. 'Nearly finished, haven't you?'

'Ay, nearly finished.' He hesitated, and then went on with his work. Jones studied his hunched shoulders, tortoise-poking head and snail's pace, then, concluding that the task would take some time at Passion's rate of working, stretched himself on the brownish grass again, and tilted his hat over his eyes as a shield against the blinding glare of the sun. Elms at the edge of the green were heavy with summer. Their leaves swam together in the swooning heat of the day, and massed their light and shadow against the sky's unclouded depth. Beneath them the ground was almost bare where cattle had trodden away the grass when seeking shelter, and bracken, at the far side of the common, was brownish at the edges of its fronds.

At the end of a quarter of an hour, Passion trundled the roller to the shed, came back for the mower, and then returned with a birch broom. As he swept the pitch, he bent and ritualistically scattered handfuls of short grass behind each wicket.

Jones had debated carefully within himself the possible means of approach to that nebulous and uncertain entity, Passion's intelligence, and had decided that shock tactics would probably yield the most satisfying results in the shortest time.

'Passion,' he said, coming up with him and speaking very sharply, 'what has your wife been up to?'

The question had an unforeseen result, for Passion stared at him a moment, his mouth working nervously and his little eyes wide open, and then said explosively:

'Ah, if I only knowed! Sick as a dog again I was! Sick as a dog last night! And all on account of Mr Middleton coming into his own again! I telled she I couldn't help it. "No fault of mine," I said. "It was always on the cards," I telled her. But she! Ah, kill me she will if her beant careful, and so I telled her. Sick as a dog! Sicker nor *two* dogs! And in all this heat! It's cruel!'

'Tell me about it,' said Jones. Passion dropped the handful of grass he was holding, then picked up another and wiped his brow with it before he threw it down.

'It's that old devil my mother-in-law,' he said. 'Can't tell ee here, Mr Jones. Come you down to the Long Thin Man after you had your tea, and I'll tell ee, sure enough, if so be you'd want to know.' He leered cunningly at the prospect of free beer.

'No, no,' said Jones, 'you tell me here and now. We're alone. You've finished in rare good time. It isn't five o'clock yet. Let's walk to these elms over yonder and sit and smoke.'

'Not under ellums,' said Passion. 'They'm treacherous, ellums be. Yon oak's the tree for me. There amn't no caterpillars on her yet, be there?'

'Not yet,' said Jones, who had not the slightest idea when the caterpillars might be due to arrive. 'Now you won't let on to mother as I've telled ee aught?'

'Certainly not,' said Jones. Determinedly he collared the conversation. 'Now listen, Passion. What I want to know is this. Did you ever have a son?'

'Ay, sure enough. Mother give un away.'

'What?'

Passion chuckled, pleased at Jones' surprise. 'She did that. She's a clever one, is mother, though her cooking do poison I at times. Ay, she give un away up at the Hall when their little babby died. "Here, take you on mine," her said to Mr Middleton. And sure enough so 'twas.'

'*What* happened to the Middleton baby, did you say?' asked Jones, who found this version of the tale considerably more intriguing than Mrs Corbett's.

'Poor little fellow died. Ay, and was buried, too and all, and mother give 'em our'n, to quieten and comfort 'em, like, so upset and all they was.'

'But did you agree to that?' asked Jones, amazed

at the half-wit's simplicity. Passion gave him a sidelong glance, cunning and full of cupidity, and answered slyly:

'Oh, I agreed all right. Why shouldn't I agree? 'Twas my son as well as mother's and when the little chap grow up to be twenty-one year of age, the notion were that he'd be having mother and me to live with him, and teach him how to mind his money, like.'

'But does he know that you and your wife are his father and mother, Passion?'

'Not until he's twenty-one year of age, he doesn't. Then we shall tell him what mother done. Did ought to be grateful, didn't un?'

'But surely the Middletons knew nothing of all this?' said Jones. He was delighted with the story, found it incredible, and wanted to see how far the man would go.

Passion wagged his ungainly head and leered.

Jones, although he repeated the question, could obtain no answer, so he tried another method of approach.

'What's the matter with little Henry Pike?'

'Ah, him,' said Passion. He hesitated, glanced from left to right, and then at Jones, grimaced at him, turned himself widdershins about, crossed his fingers and then said, softly and hoarsely:

'He'm a changeling, Henry Pike. Grandmother Fluke did that.'

'Really?' said Jones.

'Ah. Widow Pike, she kept him dark so long as her could, but it wasn't no manner of use in the end. Out he had to come, soon as he were breeched. Couldn't keep Master Mischief within cottage doors once he could run about, and then it was "Who'd a' thought it?" when the village see him. Who do you think they say he is, Mr Jones?'

'I know who they say he is,' returned Jones evenly. 'And what's more, Passion, I believe them!'

Passion shook his head.

'Oh, no, you shouldn't say that, Mr Jones,' he said. 'Because you see, sir, mother give 'em ours. No. Henry Pike isn't no Middleton babby, don't you believe it. He's like the Middletons because, you see, he isn't 'uman. He was give to Widow Pike in place of the little Middleton that died. But no odds now at all.'

'How do you mean?' asked Jones. Passion looked slyly at him, drew near, and whispered low:

'Mother said as I wasn't to tell ee.'

Jones produced sixpence, but Passion shook his head. Jones put another beside it on the palm of his hand. At this the cowman grinned, picked up the coins and said:

'That Mr Middleton as died was but the second eldest.'

'Well?' said Jones, who had heard this tale before.

'They say Mr Carswell Middleton as died missing in the war has just come home again.' He hesitated, repeated the sentence to himself, as though to be sure he had it by heart, and then said it aloud again.

'Yes?' said Jones, trying to sound interested and failing. Passion's lip drooped sadly.

'Don't ee want to hear what I got to tell?'

'Of course I do. Go on.'

'Took bad I was when Mr Middleton died. Ah, and no other time till now. That's funny, that is, you know. Ain't that funny, now?'

Jones returned to his cottage, to find Mrs Passion standing beside a kettle which, she informed him, had been on the boil and over for the past twenty-five minutes good.

Jones looked at her, but her heavy pallid face was expressionless, as usual, and her dull eyes gazed unseeingly into his. Jones turned and walked away, and, after a minute or two, Mrs Passion followed him into his sitting-room, bumped down the tea-tray beside him on the table and, leaving him to milk, sugar and pour out the tea—a task she generally insisted on performing for him—she stood with arms akimbo looking out of the small casement window on to the cultivated field beyond.

Jones followed her gaze, half expecting to see old Mrs Fluke at her hoeing, but nothing was in sight save a gigantic raven. Mrs Passion, gazing earnestly upon the bird, said solemnly:

'Ah, there you be, then, be you? You old devil, you! Just like Satan, so you be, going to and fro in the earth and walking up and down in it.'

Scarcely had she apostrophised the bird when Jones was aware of a considerable tumult. It sounded a cross between a Spanish fiesta and an

English cattle sale, and it waxed in volume as he listened.

'They be going along to burn out parson,' said Mrs Passion, still without a change of countenance, but with a note of indulgent approval in her voice which caused Jones to glance at her sharply as he asked:

'What on earth do you mean?'

'Give un a taste of his own fire and brimstone, like,' continued Mrs Passion. 'Happen I'll go along and see the fun, maybe.'

Jones grabbed his hat, and, before the astonished woman could say another word, his long legs were carrying him in great strides down the village street ahead of the advancing noise.

He reached the vicarage to find Nao, armed with a shot gun, being ordered sternly by Hallam to lay it aside.

'What's all this?' demanded Jones, hurdling over the low gate with a grace and style that he thought had long deserted him.

'Do go, my dear fellow,' said the vicar. 'I'm in for trouble, I think. Do go.'

'Not I,' said Jones. He removed his hat and hung it on a bush, passed a hand through his sweat-damp hair, adjusted his flannel trousers, and listened to the approaching sounds.

'What's the matter with them?' he inquired.

'They're getting short of water. I've told them they may come up here and draw water from my well, but that won't satisfy the worst of them. They blame me because it doesn't rain, and that wicked old woman Fluke quoted part of the story of Elijah at me this morning in a screech that would have done credit to Jezebel herself.'

'Did Jezebel screech?' asked Jones, interested. But the promising conversational opening was rendered void by the appearance of a procession round the bend of the road. Prominent among the noisiest of the band, Jones observed the half-wit Passion who had stretched a reeking ox-hide over a small barrel, and was beating upon it tom-tom-wise with muffled drum-sticks. The vicar groaned.

'I wonder who taught that wretched fellow a rhythm as complicated as that?' he said. 'I shouldn't have thought—but there! I am always being surprised in some way by these people.'

'Cheer up,' said Jones. 'I'll address them in my capacity as justice of the peace.'

'But you are not a justice of the peace, my dear fellow.'

'Never mind,' said Jones. He raised his long arms above his head, and, in the glittering hexameters of Homeric heroic verse, he thundered forth the story of Aphrodite's intervention on behalf of Paris.

The villagers, who had ceased their noise, waited until he had finished. Suddenly Nao knelt upon the ground. At this a panic appeared to catch the villagers and suddenly, for no reason that occurred to Jones, they scrambled and pushed past one another to get out of his sight, and in a few moments the street was empty save for an enormous black cat which had appeared from nowhere and which now lay down in the road and commenced to wash itself.

Its nonchalance delighted Jones. He watched it for some time. Then he tackled the vicar.

'You'll have to ask for police protection, Hallam, you know.'

Hallam shook his head.

'They feel that they have a grievance. I pray for rain, and the rain does not come.'

They both looked up at the empty sky. Jones shrugged, and shook his head.

'It's serious. Very serious. Are they capable of causing trouble, do you think?'

'I'm not alarmed, but I am sure they are. Still, I shall go to Neot House, where, I understand, the other Mr Middleton is in residence, and see what he's prepared to do about his well.'

'Who told you he was there?'

'Old Mrs Fluke. Has she told your fortune yet?'

Chapter Six

'Hey diddle diddle, the cat and the fiddle,
The cow jumped over the moon;
The little dog laughed to see such fun,
And the dish ran away with the spoon.'
Nursery Rhyme.

SOME days later Mrs Passion brought to Jones three
news-items, the first with his breakfast, the second
with his mid-day dinner, and the third with the
high tea which she had suddenly and unaccountably
introduced in place of the cooked supper with which
she had been accustomed to regale him.

'Better for you,' she announced with finality,
and her face had been a shade less pallid and her
expression a trifle more alert than usual.

The first piece of news was that Mr Carswell
Middleton had been in the village some days, and
was already installed in two rooms of the Big House,
although no one had set eyes on him except the
Tebbutts, husband, wife and son, who had come
to mind the house for him.

'So the baby business comes unstuck,' said Jones.

'Sir?' said Mrs Passion vacantly. Jones grinned and began upon his eggs and bacon.

The second was that the pump in the back yard had refused its office and was rendering the foulest of slime instead of water. Jones had been expecting this, and merely grunted.

'So you'll have to give over washing your chest, sir,' said Mrs Passion austerely. 'A lick and a promise is all that any of us has any right to expect, the famine being very grievous in the land.'

'Better still, I'll give up drinking tea,' said Jones obligingly. 'Beer is best, as the advertisements would say.'

The third was in the nature of a complaint. She stood over Jones, breathing audibly, whilst he consumed reluctantly a plate of dark, rich, heavy stew—of the type, he surmised sorrowfully, which had upset Passion's digestion and had made him sicker than two dogs—and three thick slices of bread and butter, the last slice topped with the strawberry jam which she had made that same afternoon 'for him alone' as she informed him with a simpering smile. At last he was moved to demand of her what it was she wanted.

'A word of gentlemanly advice, Mr Jones, if you please, sir,' Mrs Passion answered.

'Oh?' said Jones, unaccountably surprised by the modest request. (After all, he reflected, he had several times been asked by servants to give them some advice. If the woman was in doubt, and her moron of a husband could not assist her, it was natural that she should appeal to him.)

'Yes, Mr Jones, if you please, sir. That wicked old mother-in-law of Passion's been and put a spell on me.'

'Oh, yes. I heard about that at the vicarage, didn't I?' said Jones, somewhat amused at her elaborate avoidance of the recognition of consanguinity between herself and Mrs Fluke.

Mrs Passion shook her head, picked a lump of sugar out of the bowl, dipped it, without any apology except a slightly hysterical giggle, into Jones' second cup of tea, and crunched it with enjoyment.

'Not that spell, Mr Jones. Another one,' she said. 'A nasty smell.'

'A what?'

'Yes, Mr Jones, a nasty smell,' repeated Mrs Passion firmly.

'Nonsense, Mrs Passion! It's the drains!'

'There aren't no drains in Saxon Wall, sir,' Mrs Passion reminded him morosely.

'Well, you know what I mean. It's a result of the water shortage. There are smells everywhere. Abominable smells. We shall be lucky to escape an epidemic. You understand? There are no such things as spells.'

'Yes, Mr Jones,' said Mrs Passion. Jones was reminded by her voice and expression of a group of negro students to whom he had lectured in America. The same polite, lip-service acceptance of his statements together with the same obvious, instinctive repudiation of them as facts was to be observed in both cases. He decided to improve the hour with a little rationalistic propaganda.

'There is no such thing as magic, Mrs Passion, you know. All that stuff about charms, spells and curses is simply moonshine.'

'Yes, Mr Jones. Like the Witch of Endor raising up Samuel.' Her voice was still agreeably respectful. Jones looked at her reproachfully. Mrs Passion seized another lump of sugar, dexterously wetted it as before, and crunched it. This time she did not giggle, but looked at Jones with such an unmistakably ogling glance that he coughed aggressively and hurriedly left the table so that she could clear it. But Mrs Passion had not done with him.

'Everywheres I go I smell this smell. Horrible it is. And I wash myself all I know. I used scented soap the last time. Do I seem to you to smell when I come in here of a morning? Or of an afternoon? Or of an evening when I lays the high tea for you?'

'Certainly not,' said Jones.

'Well, then! And yet this old smell follows me whithersoever I go. It do, surely. So what be I to do? They *do* say—' She ogled him again—'that if only you can get a tall gentleman to go up along they ruins over by the vicarage, and say a verse of poetry for ee, like—but where be I to find such a fine, tall man?'

'I couldn't say,' said Jones. He eyed his plate and then added:

'And who's Mr Carswell Middleton, anyway?'

'Didn't Passion tell ee?'

'Why, yes, he said—' Jones, suddenly remembering what he had said, allowed his voice to tail away, and waited for her to finish the sentence.

'He said as Mr Carswell Middleton were own brother to Mr Hanley, that died so sad three weeks after his poor young wife was buried.'

'Very sudden sort of occurrence, wasn't it?' asked Jones, carelessly. Mrs Passion looked at him suspiciously.

'The poor young gentleman was tooken very ill,' she said impressively. 'Very ill he was tooken. Very, very sad, it was.'

'I suppose the whole village was plunged into mourning,' said Jones. Mrs Passion's sombre eyes searched his face, but it did not betray his thoughts.

'That's the worst of educated gentlemen,' she observed. 'Their looks always belie them.' She sounded disgruntled. Had she appeared just slightly less bovine, Jones would have said that she was nervous.

'Come, come,' said he. 'Surely it's usual for a village to be grieved when the local landowner dies suddenly?'

'That's as may be,' replied Mrs Passion. 'All I know is, there were those as were glad to see him gone, and there were those as wished him back again, and there were those as thought their own thoughts and kept their eyes to theirselves and the back door locked after dark.'

'Magnificent,' said Jones. After she had gone he sat there thinking, for an hour or more, while he gave himself time to digest the heavy stew. There was something odd about these Middleton deaths, he told himself. There seemed no reasonable doubt that Mrs Passion had changed over the babies, and that Mrs Pike, innocently or otherwise, was bringing up a child that was not her own.

He rose at last and went over to the vicarage. Hallam had not been in the village when the deaths occurred, but he might have heard rumours. He might be able to shed a little light on occurrences that seemed to Jones murky in the extreme.

'Look here, Hallam,' Jones said as soon as he arrived. 'I suppose the deaths of Mr and Mrs Middleton were all right?'

'All right?' said the vicar, puzzled. 'How do you mean?'

'I don't know how I mean, and I don't care to put into words what I mean, but—well, look here, Hallam, was the doctor satisfied?'

The vicar looked at him oddly.

'I suppose he must have been. I never heard that there had been an inquest. That's what always happens if a doctor isn't satisfied, I think. Was there an inquest on the Middletons?'

'There was no inquest,' replied Jones. 'That's the extraordinary part of it.'

'I don't know much about their deaths, you know,' said Hallam. 'You see, I wasn't here when it all happened. It seems to have been a very sad affair. They were quite young, I think.'

'I know you weren't here. The Corbetts weren't either, and, in any case, they're so frightfully prejudiced that one can't accept what they say as evidence of anything. I've never known people so biased. And the two Miss Harpers weren't living in the village then, either, bless their hearts, so all that they can supply is also the result of hearsay, probably from the Corbetts, which doesn't get me any further.'

'Birdseye wouldn't be any good. His farmhouse is a good three miles from here,' said Hallam slowly. 'I don't know who could give you information, I am sure.'

'How about the chapel people?' asked Jones.

The vicar shook his head.

'The Methodist chap came here last year. They have a circuit scheme, you know. The Baptist minister came here after I did, and the Salvation Army officers are just as much birds of passage as the Methodist preachers. You'll get nothing there, I think. Why don't you go and talk to the present doctor? He wasn't here nine years ago, when the Middletons died, of course, but he may be in his predecessor's confidence. But what's in your mind, man? What are you after?'

'Predecessor dead or retired?' asked Jones, disregarding the vicar's question.

'Retired. Of course he may be dead by now. He went to live in Tunbridge Wells, I think.'

'Cheerful, isn't it?' said Jones.

'But what are you getting at?' asked Hallam, determined this time to be answered.

'I think the Middletons were murdered,' Jones

replied, and before the vicar could repudiate the theory, he added, 'so that Mrs Passion could substitute her baby boy for theirs.'

'But——'

Jones held up his hand.

'What's more, I think the present Mr Middleton was in deadly peril the moment he set foot in Saxon Wall.'

The vicar laughed at this. He seemed relieved. 'Spoken like a man and a novelist,' he said. Jones grinned.

'I know you think I'm talking through my hat. But, look here, this is what I had from Passion only the other afternoon: First, he tells me that he's been sick again, and blames his wife. Second, he connects the fact of his sickness with the restoration of the elder Mr Middleton to his inheritance. Third, he admits that Mrs Passion gave away their baby son. Fourth, he assures me that the Middleton baby died, a thing I believe to be untrue. Fifth, he declares that he and his wife are going to blackmail the boy who is now called Middleton as soon as he is of age. Sixth, most important, and therefore last he declares that he was taken ill in similar fashion just before the deaths of Mr and Mrs Middleton. Now, what do you say to all that? Doesn't it seem to you about the fishiest lot of dirty work, one way and another, that you ever heard in your life? What do you think of it?'

The vicar stroked his jaw.

'Inconclusive,' he said cautiously.

'But, honestly, now,' persisted Jones, 'don't you

think it just a little odd that Mr and Mrs Middleton died so opportunely?'

'Opportunely for whom?' asked Hallam.

'Well, you admit that the evidence is in favour of Mrs Passion's having changed over the babies, don't you?'

'I think there is a possibility she changed them, but as for evidence——'

'Well, she couldn't have changed them if Mr and Mrs Middleton had lived. I'll tell you what I think occurred,' he went on, as the vicar began to speak. 'I think Mrs Middleton died in giving birth to the child, and I think that Mrs Passion, who may have been called in to nurse the baby, saw her opportunity and took it. She poisoned Middleton—arsenic, I expect—and swapped over the kids. To make the thing slightly more complicated, she handed the stolen baby Middleton to Mrs Pike, whose little one had died, and buried the dead baby in her own name, Passion.'

'The baby that died *was* buried in the name of Passion,' Hallam answered. 'There's a wooden cross in the churchyard.'

'Well, there's my case against Mrs Passion, then. She's a murderer, a kind of kidnapper, and a baby farmer as well. The thing is, what can be done about it?'

'Nothing, my dear man,' said the vicar slowly. 'You'd need to have Middleton's body exhumed before you could prove a word of this. And, in any case, it wouldn't bring him back to life, murdered or not, you know.'

'True enough,' said Jones. He left the vicarage, still ruminating, and, on his way home, called upon Doctor Mortmain.

'Crevister? Yes, I have his address if you want it.'

'Thank you,' said Jones, writing it down.

'Don't take your custom out of the village, please,' said Mortmain, smiling at him. Jones grinned. Suddenly he remembered what the vicar had said of Mortmain.

'So the village people fear you,' he said, with no diminution of the grin, which had, however, become slightly sardonic. Mortmain laughed aloud.

'They don't fear me a tenth as much as they fear you,' he retorted. 'What do I hear of your demoniac cursing of a deputation to the vicarage the other day? Is it true that none dared stay to look you in the face?'

'They did slink off in a manner that struck me as being more than a little odd,' returned Jones. 'I thought it was Mrs Fluke who possessed the evil eye?'

'She does; at least, rumour has it so.'

'Well, one evil eye in a village is surely enough.'

'It is surely enough,' Mortmain agreed. 'Incidentally, what's all this about another Middleton coming to live at Neot House?'

'So you've heard it too? Is it true?'

'I should say so. Some people called Tebbutt seem to have taken the place of the original caretaker, who was a relative of Birdseye, and I understand that the new owner has already installed himself. I'd always understood that he was expected to turn up some day and take over the property. The younger of twins, I heard.'

'The elder, I think, isn't it? Well, thank you again, for Crevister's address. I want to ask him if he knows what Hanley Middleton died of.'

'Peritonitis,' said Doctor Mortmain. 'Crevister told me about it. He himself didn't think an operation would do any good, but for some reason it was performed.'

'And the patient died as a direct result of the operation?'

'Don't think the operation made any difference really. Man was in the last state of collapse, according to Crevister. Remember talking it over with him when I first took over the practice. Incidentally—although it's most indecorous of me to say so—he's the most fearful old fathead you're ever likely to meet, and decidedly old-fashioned and prejudiced, especially as regards the dispensing of physic. Don't let him prescribe for you, whatever you do.'

Jones laughed.

Chapter Seven

'"Pen," she said, holding it to her eye to
make sure that the nib was clean. She
stood back to see that the arrangements
were satisfactory; then suddenly clicked
her tongue and threw up her hands.
'"Herr Gott, blotting paper," she cried.'
ANTHONY BERTRAM
The Avenger.

AFTER Winchester, Jones found the way plain sailing,
and he reached the Public Library at a little after
two, having lunched with his aunt and taken his
time over the meal.

The retired Doctor Crevister lived in a small,
neat, rather obviously detached house in a
road which Jones found without much trouble,
and his daughter, a woman of forty-six or so,
who kept house for him and for her brother,
another doctor, recognised Jones' name and
person, the first because she was an admirer
of his books, the second because she had seen

his photograph at the top of some of his earlier reviews.

After desultory conversation, Jones explained his errand. The daughter, fortunately, had a better memory than her father.

'Surely you remember, dear, the Middletons of Saxon Wall. I'll go and get your case-book for the year that Mr J. Hannibal Jones refers to. Let me see. About nine years ago, Mr Jones, you think?'

'Nine or ten,' said Jones. There were advantages, he could see, in being a household word. To no obscure seeker after truth would the same welcome have been extended, or the same willingness to fall in with his whims have been displayed. He sat expectant, and discussed Test Match cricket with the old man until the daughter returned with the book.

'This will be the one, I think,' she said, as she handed it to her father. It took the doctor a long time to find what Jones required, for he was continually lighting upon some forgotten case which caught his interest, and the details of which he seemed compelled to re-absorb as he lived over again those hours which had held birth, death, dread illness and quick recovery in their careless hands, and had disposed the destinies of sufferers as fate decreed.

At last he came to the case of Constance Middleton.

'Septicaemia. Yes, yes, I remember. Most annoying. Really very provoking indeed. A boy baby and, afterwards, some utterly uncalled-for carelessness on the part of the midwife. Certainly the woman seemed very much upset, but so was I! The case should have presented no difficulties, none whatever. Everything going well. Then, through somebody's wretched carelessness, the young mother contracts puerperal fever. Irritating. Irritating.' He clicked his tongue, in anger rather than in sorrow, over Constance Middleton's untimely death.

'Yes, I see,' said Jones. 'And—er—when was the husband taken ill? Could you tell me anything about that? We have to establish identity, you see,' he added, hoping that the vaguely-worded excuse would suffice to account for his persistence.

'The husband, yes. Now *that* was rather odd. I was called in by one of the servants—Pike, I think she called herself—she had nursed Mrs Middleton, you know, and I shouldn't be a bit surprised if she were the extremely careless person who allowed that wretched fever to—well, it's no use to think about that now, I suppose, but still—well, never mind. The thing is that I was called in to attend a man in her cottage who was—who obviously needed to be operated on. Well, I sent to the town—what's it called now?'

'Stowhall,' said Jones.

'Yes, yes, that's right. And a certain Doctor Little came prepared to operate. It was hopeless to think of moving this fellow to a hospital or anywhere, you understand—that's why I was so astounded when—well, never mind that now—but, anyway, I'm not a bit surprised the chap died. Nasty case of strangulated hernia, you know, and acute peritonitis was the result. Well, now, the extraordinary thing was this: When I came to see this chap the second time, he had completely disappeared.'

'Disappeared?' exclaimed Jones.

'Absolutely. We sought him everywhere, and found him—where do you think?'

'I couldn't hope to guess,' said Jones, thoroughly roused and excited.

'Up at Neot House. It hadn't been Pike at all, but Middleton in Pike's cottage. Now, what can you make of that?'

'Had Middleton—of course he had all the usual symptoms?' asked Jones, cursing himself for his abysmal lack of medical and surgical knowledge.

'Symptoms! God bless my soul, yes! *All* the symptoms! All the *possible* symptoms. Shivering, vomiting, severe pain, rapid and shallow breathing, knees drawn up almost to his chin, temperature of 105 degrees Fahrenheit—my dear fellow, if he'd known what the symptoms *were* he couldn't have thought of many more! Doctor Little operated, but the fellow died. I really wasn't surprised.'

'Thank you very much,' said Jones. 'I mustn't trouble you further.'

'Oh, Mr Jones, you'll stay to tea?' begged the daughter almost tearfully. 'We can have it now at once, if you're in a hurry.'

So Jones stayed to tea, and, after tea he signed all of his own works that Miss Crevister possessed, and was about to take his leave when Doctor Crevister suddenly smote the table and said loudly:

'I didn't note it down, although I always meant to. Here's a queer example of mental aberration if you like!'

'Yes?' said Jones, fidgety to get away because of the long drive home, but disguising the fact beneath a mask of almost sycophantic interest. 'What was that, Doctor? Sounds amusing.'

'Well, I don't know about amusing. I had a note from Doctor Little the very next day after the operation to say: "Regret patient died so that operation now unnecessary."'

'Whatever did he mean?' asked Jones. The doctor chuckled.

'I've no idea. I never heard from him again.'

Jones was as anxious now to hear the whole of the story as he had been to get away. He said, trying not to sound too eager:

'Tell me, sir. When the operation was performed—it *was* Middleton who was operated on?—were you in the room with Doctor Little?'

'Oh, yes. I helped administer the anaesthetic.'

'But—look here, Doctor, there's something extraordinary behind all this. Did you know Doctor Little?'

'Oh, no. I telephoned the hospital, that's all.'

'You didn't know him, even by sight, I take it?'

'No, no. Of course I didn't. And, of course, in his surgeon's dress——'

'So any one could have passed himself off to you as Doctor Little? You wouldn't have known the difference?'

'But why on earth should any one ever think of

such a thing? Besides, the operation was perfectly performed. A very good job.'

'Oh, really?'

'Oh, yes. A nice, bold job. I admired it very much. Incidentally, it was Doctor Little who diagnosed the cause of the peritonitis.'

'And you were in there all the time with him?'

'Yes, certainly.'

'Er—in what condition was the patient when—look here, I suppose you're *sure* it was Middleton?—how was he, would you say—er—well—before the anaesthetic was administered?'

'In pain, of course. The pain was exceptionally severe, and there was vomiting. It struck me, as a matter of fact, that the patient was very near collapse. I suggested to Doctor Little that an operation was really beside the point. I believed the patient to be approaching insensibility and death. He disagreed, however, and the anaesthetic was administered. But wasn't that odd of Doctor Little to forget the operations?'

'So odd,' said Jones slowly, 'that I suppose he wasn't right, by any chance, and really had received an intimation that you no longer required him to perform the operation because the patient was already dead?'

'You mean that it was *I* who suffered from mental aberration? But the doctor *came*, I tell you, and the operation *was* actually performed.'

'Yes, I know. I didn't mean that,' said Jones. He felt helpless. 'Well, I do indeed think it extremely odd, Doctor,' he said lamely. Then the obvious psychological explanation came to him, and, with it, a feeling of deflation and disappointment. Doctor Little must have been suffering from that Forget-because-it's-something-that-gives-me-pain-and-annoyance-to-remember form of amnesia noted by Freud and other psychologists. He had been upset because the operation had been unsuccessful, and therefore he had forgotten that he had performed it, and had even invented, unconsciously, the message from Doctor Crevister.

But the point that Pike had disappeared was exceedingly interesting. It opened up distinct possibilities of villainy on the part of Middleton. Jones decided that he would have to question Mrs Pike, to see whether she could give any indication as to the seriousness of her husband's condition when she had gone for Doctor Crevister. If only it could be proved that Pike had been suffering from appendicitis—or arsenical poisoning!

He had reached this point in his musings when he was recalled to a sense of his surroundings by Doctor Crevister, who suddenly exclaimed:

'Young fellow, I believe you're right!'

'In what way, sir?' Jones inquired.

'To ask me whether I'm certain the man was Middleton! You know, I'd not attended either of 'em before—before I was first called in by Mrs Pike, I mean.'

'Neither Pike nor Middleton?'

'Neither of them. And, really, what with their symptoms being identical——'

Jones became more than interested.

'You think it was Pike after all?'

Doctor Crevister shook his head.

'How could it have been? The operation was performed at Neot House. You're hypnotising me, young man!'

Chapter Eight

'She is rotten and unsound from stem
to stern.'
> *From a report made in 1852 on the*
> *battleship 'Warrior'.*

FULL of the problem of Pike's disappearance and the uncanny resemblance of his symptoms to those of Hanley Middleton, Jones returned to the vicarage at about half-past nine that night to enlist the vicar's interest and aid on behalf of the new owner of Neot House.

It proved to be an inauspicious time to attempt to interest him in anything, for the vicar, his face completely muffled in an enormous woollen scarf, to the left side of which the devoted Nao insisted upon holding hot bricks, announced in a voice husky with agony that he was suffering so severely from neuralgia that he doubted his ability to entertain his guest in any manner whatever. He seemed so morose and ill-humoured that Jones, whose sympathy would have been aroused fully by the spectacle of anybody in such sorry plight, felt particularly unhappy to think that it should be Hallam to suffer so. He found himself a little surprised that pain should have had quite the effect on Hallam which he perceived—indeed, the man seemed altered almost beyond recognition—but he reflected that no one is proof against hideous agony.

'What have you come for?' was the vicar's next remark.

Jones described his visit to Doctor Crevister.

'But what do you want to meddle for? It's nothing to do with you,' said the vicar, muffled, peevish and annoyed.

'But what about Mr Carswell Middleton? I can't stand by and watch him being done to death,' protested Jones.

'Of course you can't. But why should he be done to death?' asked the vicar. Jones said impatiently:

'Isn't he the heir to the property? What's to become of young Middleton-Passion now he's turned down in favour of this long-lost uncle? And if the man happens to be married, and has children of his own——'

'He isn't married,' said the vicar. 'Mrs Tebbutt, the housekeeper he brought with him, told Mrs Gant at the post office.'

'That's something, anyway,' said Jones.

'So you need not allow your imagination to run away with you,' said the vicar. Jones' long mouth set obstinately.

'There's no imagination about it, except the kind of imagination that's needed to put two and two together and make it into four, Hallam,' he said. 'There's something terribly wrong about this Middleton business, and I'm going to find out what it is before I leave this village.'

'There's something terribly wrong about the village itself,' said the vicar, beginning to giggle, 'but murder isn't part of it. Nothing as clean as murder. Nothing as definite. You'd be amazed. Really, I know you would.'

'Yes?' said Jones, suddenly watching him closely. The vicar, blinking his eyelids very fast and speaking in a hoarse, broken whisper, launched into a chronicle of Sodomic excess which left Jones speechless. As a novelist Jones was unshockable, but as a psychologist he was appalled by the vicar's obvious pleasure in the details of the recital.

'And that old woman Fluke,' the vicar concluded. 'Cut the head off a Rhode Island cock and strung its tail feathers from side to side of my summer house doorway, so that I can't get in.'

'Can't get in?' said Jones. Instinctively he gripped the mantelpiece, conscious that he did not want to hear what the other was going to say.

'No!' said the vicar, his voice rising dangerously. 'Can't get in! Can't—get—in!' He gave a sudden shriek of laughter and began to beat his breast. Jones flung him down on to the sofa, held him there, and shouted for the housekeeper. In came the Japanese respectfully, and stood with folded hands. The vicar lay quietly.

'Get water, man!' said Jones. 'Your master's ill!'

'No water,' said the Japanese politely. 'All the water very bad. Plague of frogs in the water. Frogs all dead. Very bad water when frogs all die. The water is poisoned master, and the frogs are poisoned. Yes, I think so.'

The remark about the frogs seemed to revive the vicar. He put Jones' hand aside, sat up, and whispered, pressing his hand against his aching jaw:

'The frogs may be poisoned, but the water is not.'

'All right, of course it isn't,' said Jones, endeavouring to sound soothing. The vicar laughed, but this time in a more natural manner, although still in a voice oddly unlike the one that Jones remembered.

'I mean it. My well is too deep, you see, for frogs, so if there are dead frogs in it, they were killed before they entered the well,' he said.

'I see,' said Jones. 'Well, let's go and inspect the well.'

Even in the semi-dusk of the summer evening, the well was not a pretty sight. At least two dozen bloated-looking frogs, with here and there a puffy, spotted toad, blotched, hard and repulsive, lay on its brink with the vicar's fox-terrier looking at them doubtfully, his head on one side. When he saw the vicar, he snarled angrily. Nao swept him up in his arms and bore him off, while Jones inspected the frogs.

'Nasty,' said Jones sympathetically. The vicar went over to the woodshed and brought thence a garden fork and spade. Without a word, without any sign of repulsion, he went to the nearest flower bed, dug over the hard dry ground with the fork, took out loose earth with the spade, and then, shovelling up the frogs and the toads in heaps, he interred them, stopping occasionally to twitch into place the scarf which was still about his head.

'Look here,' said Jones, when they were back again in the house. 'You want a rest. Why don't you see a doctor, or go for a holiday or something?'

The vicar shook his head.

'No, I'm all right. The frogs and things are old Mrs Fluke's reminder that it's time I gave in to the village, and prayed for rain. I don't mind those, but the feathers are a different matter. I've lived in the West Indies, you know, and I've seen some rather odd things.'

'Come home with me tonight,' suggested Jones.

'I'm all right. It's the heat. I'll go easy for a day or two, perhaps. But there's nothing to worry about.' He looked at Jones as though he hated him. Jones smiled patiently and waited at the garden gate until he had given him time to return to his study, which was at the back of the house. Then he ran swiftly and on tip-toe to the summer house. There, visible in the eerie half-light of the midsummer dusk, was the string of dangling feathers stretched across the door. Jones snapped the string, and, twisting it up, crammed the badly-smelling collection into his jacket pocket, and walked quickly but soberly home.

It had not been his custom to lock his cottage door at night, and, in spite of a slight feeling of panic, he did not do so on this occasion.

He undressed in the almost-dark, opened the casement wide—for Mrs Passion always closed and fastened it when she swept the room—gazed out over the fields towards Guthrum Down, and then got into bed.

He was just on the point of falling asleep when he was startled into complete wakefulness by the sound of quiet footfalls on the stairs. He sat up, unconscious that his left hand clutched the counterpane. His voice was loud, and higher-keyed than he intended, when he spoke.

'I say! Who's that?'

A giggle answered him. Jones began to sweat. He sprang out of bed, located a candle and struck a match. The door opened slowly, and round the edge of it appeared a pallid, terribly expressionless face, and a woman entered the room quietly, and gazed at Jones. She wore a black hat of unimpeachable respectability, a pair of farm boots and a man's raincoat.

'Good God!' said Jones, aghast.

She playfully blew out the candle, and the next instant her arms were about Jones' neck, and she was clinging to him with all her countrywoman's strength. Using her considerable weight, and the strategic advantage of having taken him entirely by surprise, she began to force him backwards towards the bed.

Jones braced himself. It was no time for chivalry. He wrested her arms from about his long thin neck, and flung her away from him. Then he re-lighted the candle and stared at her sternly. She had slid down the wall to a sitting position, her legs stretched out in front of her (the absurd boots looking larger than usual with their toes turned ceilingwards), her hands on either side of her upon the floor and her head dropped forward on her breast, whence her eyes looked up at Jones with an expression of hideous coyness. She dropped them, and put her left thumb into her mouth. Jones seized her ankles, hauled her roughly forward, so that there was a space of about a foot between her back and the wall, darted behind her, grasped her under the armpits and with a heave that strained every muscle of his diaphragm, tried to set her upon her feet. She hung with her whole weight on his arms and would not stand. Swearing savagely, Jones hauled her to the door and pushed her on to the landing.

'Go home! Go home!' he said, and slammed the bedroom door on her and locked it. The thought that someone might see her leaving his house at that hour of the night occurred to, but did not trouble him.

He looked at his watch. It was nearly eleven o'clock. For the next twenty minutes, the woman alternately wept and giggled on the landing outside. Then he heard her descending the stairs. He blew out

the candle, went over to the window and watched
her as, like a shadow, she crossed the front garden.
The moment the garden gate had shut itself behind
her by virtue of the spring which Jones had fixed on
it, he descended the stairs and locked and fastened
the ground floor doors and windows.

His last thought before he fell asleep was a
semi-humorous reflection that she had not been
mad but drunk. He wondered how she would
review the incident when she came to herself in
the morning.

He was still asleep when a decorous tap on his
bedroom door announced Mrs Passion's arrival
next day. Jones descended to wash under the
pump, as was his custom, and, upon passing the
kitchen door, glanced in. Mrs Passion bobbed him
her usual greeting. Her hat was still on her head,
but her ordinary walking shoes had been replaced
by coquettish twin horrors of black patent leather,
embellished, garnished and titivated with strips
of putty-coloured suede. Between hat and shoes
stretched the godly, righteous and sober garments
of a village woman out to oblige. Her face was
expressionless, her eyes unfocused and serene.
Jones began to believe that he had dreamed the last
night's incident. Could she have made her way into
the cottage like that in the dead of the night? . . .
He shook his head. The temptation to mention
the invasion of the cottage was overpowering,
though.

'Headache this morning, Mrs Passion?' She turned
her cow-like eyes on him.

'You heerd the news, then, Mr Jones, like?'

'News?' said Jones. She picked up a lump of sugar, adroitly immersed it in his cup of tea and nodded as she sucked.

'What news?' asked Jones. His thoughts went to the vicar, whose nerves were going to pieces. 'Mr Hallam?' he said. Mrs Passion shook her head. The black ostrich plumes and the sequins on her headgear quivered with denial.

'Not the vicar, no, sir. Mr Carswell Middleton.'

'Not——?'

'Dead, Mr Jones. Yes, Mr Jones.' There was an odd little breath of a pause, and then she added: 'Just about eleven o'clock last night, it must have been.'

Chapter Nine

'"Murdratus est," says the sublimer dialect
of Gothic ages.'

DE QUINCEY
On Murder Considered as One of the Fine Arts.

IT WAS at just after half-past six that the police
had been summoned by Mr Carswell Middleton's
housekeeper, and at nine Mortmain dropped in
on Jones.

'A police inspector has just arrived from Stowhall,'
he said. 'Middleton's been murdered. Poker seems
the likeliest weapon. Housekeeper, a London
woman, found his body at six this morning and
'phoned the police. Died between half-past ten
and a quarter-past eleven last night. As it happens,
the woman and her son can fix the time, and
their statement coincides with the police doctor's
opinion. I haven't seen the body myself, but the
Tebbutts, people who have until quite recently been
in the employment of the late Mrs Middleton's
parents, are certain that Middleton went up to

his bedroom at half-past ten. They noticed the time because it was so unusually early, and appear to have commented about it and so fixed it in their minds.

'Then at a quarter to eleven the housekeeper and her husband went up to their room, but the son, a lad of about sixteen, remained in the housekeeper's room downstairs to finish a threepenny blood.

'At just about a quarter past eleven this lad himself went to bed. He had finished his book, and, feeling certain in his own mind that his employer was safely in bed, he confesses that he sneaked along to the dining-room to help himself to a handful of biscuits out of the sideboard cupboard. He was still outside the room when he saw to his very great astonishment that Middleton was not, after all, upstairs. He was lying on his back on the leather-covered settee, the boy says, with one arm dangling to the floor, and his knees drawn up, just as the boy had seen him often enough when he was resting or reading. Oh, and they found a dead cat, a pretty mangled one, on the floor.'

'And the lad hopped it up to bed without saying anything to Middleton, I suppose?' said Jones.

'Exactly. But here's the queer thing. The pool of blood on the floor, where Middleton must have tumbled against the edge of the fender and cut his head when the murderous blow was struck, is at least ten feet, they say, from the settee on which he was found. Of course the head had bled a bit on to the settee as well, but it's easy enough to see where he fell when the blow was struck. It caught the left——'

'Won't mean anything to me,' said Jones apologetically.

'Well, the point is that the murderer must have lifted him up and placed him on the settee in an attitude which would be recognised by anybody who happened to glance into the room. That implies two things.'

'First that the murderer was a person who knew the dead man's habits,' said Jones, nodding.

'Quite. And, secondly, someone with considerable physical strength. Middleton weighed somewhere about twelve or thirteen stone, I should imagine.'

'As much as that? A woman couldn't have done it, then,' said Jones.

'What makes you think of a woman?'

Jones told him what he knew of Mrs Passion.

'Sounds feasible,' the doctor said. Jones shook his head. 'Why not?' persisted the doctor. 'Motive's everything in a case of murder, and she certainly had a motive.'

'Oddly enough, I can give the wretched woman an alibi,' said Jones, 'if the time of the murder was as you suggest. How long, should you think, does it take to get from Middleton's house to this cottage?'

'A quarter of an hour, good,' the doctor answered promptly.

Jones shook his head.

'Twenty minutes, at a good brisk walking pace,'

he said. 'It's quite a bit more than a mile, you know.'

'I suppose it is. But what if one ran the distance?'

'Mrs Passion didn't run.'

'No, I imagine not. But——'

'She walked in here at about ten minutes to eleven last night, fresh as paint and wearing a raincoat a hat and a pair of boots, and I had to chuck her out. I thought at first she was mad, but I conclude now she was tight.'

'Ten to eleven? Sure?'

'Near enough.'

'But——'

'Not on your showing. Couldn't have done it in the time. How could she? Middleton went upstairs at half-past ten. She'd have had to get him downstairs, kill him, put the body on the settee, get rid of her bloodstained clothing and possibly wash her hands, and get to me all in the twenty minutes which was what she had at her disposal.'

'How was she dressed when she broke in on you?'

'Oh, a raincoat, a hat and some boots.'

'Good Lord! Not Mrs Passion?'

'Yes. That's what I keep saying.'

'She'll have to be certified.'

'Oh, I really think she was drunk.'

'You have to be damned drunk to break into someone's cottage at eleven o'clock at night.'

'Of course, if she had just done the murder she may have been trying to give herself an alibi.'

'Yes, but why advertise the fact that she was up and doing at that time of night when the murder was committed?'

'That's true.' Jones fingered his chin. 'I give it up. I say, if you're not busy, I wish you'd go along and have a look at Hallam. He's overdoing it.'

'Oh?'

'Yes. Someone's started a Hoodoo or Voodoo or something in his summer house. Look here.'

He went into his bedroom and took from the side of the window the string of cock's feathers.

'Blood and all,' said the doctor. He shook his head. 'These country parsons ought to be married, Jones. Celibacy plays the deuce with Englishmen.'

'You English?' asked Jones.

The doctor laughed. 'I had an Irish mother.'

'I a Welsh father,' said Jones.

Both laughed; then Jones, remembering the doctor's errand, said:

'Nothing I can do about Middleton, I suppose?'

'Well, there is, if you wouldn't mind. He was expecting the little boy, the nephew, down today, so the housekeeper's husband tells me. The child has been sent away from school because of an epidemic. His guardian naturally had handed him over to Middleton's care since Middleton established his identity, and it appears that at the moment no one is responsible for the little chap. He can't stay up at the school. They're afraid they've got a case of infantile paralysis. So if you'd meet his train and take him on for a day or two until we can get into touch with the former trustees of the estate——'

'Of course I will,' said Jones.

'Incidentally, rumour has it that the vicar was up at Neot House last night. You won't mind, then?'

'No, I shan't mind a bit. In fact, it will liven me up. How old is the boy?'

'I believe he's nine or ten.'

'Oh, yes. Of course. He would be. What time is the train?'

'Look here, I could meet the train and bring him to you in my car. Can you have him to lunch?'

'Oh, yes, if they haven't arrested Mrs Passion by then.'

'Good man. I'll bring him along, then. How's the time? Half-past? Just got time to look in on the vicar first. Good-bye. I'll let the housekeeper know I've parked the boy. Tough luck on them. The police are behaving very suspiciously towards them.'

'Are they?'

'Very suspiciously indeed, although the poor devils obviously have everything to lose and nothing whatever to gain by Middleton's death.'

'I suppose Scotland Yard will come into it if there's a fuss?'

'I don't know about that.'

'Later on,' said Jones, 'when you're not busy, I should like to have a serious talk with you about the death of the other Mr Middleton.'

'The death of this Mr Middleton attracts me a

whole lot more. It interests the Tebbutts, too, I'll bet. The man has already taken to his bed, overcome with shock and horror. He's drugged himself into insensibility, if I'm any judge. The woman looks like death, although she doesn't say much, and the lad is obviously scared nearly silly. Of course the police are all over the house and grounds, and the police doctor from Stowhall agrees with me that Tebbutt can't yet be questioned.'

'Funny, isn't it?'

'Well, it all looks a bit suspicious, certainly. In fact I should say they are behaving very foolishly indeed. Still, it's no concern of mine.'

'But what about this?'

And Jones gave the doctor a summary of the information he had obtained from Doctor Crevister.

'I've heard the whole story from Mrs Corbett, of the Long Thin Man,' said Mortmain.

'And do you believe that Middleton died of peritonitis?'

'It sounded like it, from what Mrs Corbett told me.'

'Oh, well, from what Mrs Corbett told *me* it sounded like arsenic,' said Jones. 'And, in view of what's just happened to the new Mr Middleton—'

'Lot of difference between administering arsenic and coshing a man over the head with a poker,' said the doctor.

'Academically speaking, yes,' Jones agreed.

'Psychologically speaking, yes a lot more,' said

the doctor warmly. 'There's the whole difference between a man and a woman in the difference between murder by poison and murder by violence.'

'The resemblance of the sexes one to another is more fundamental than their differences,' said Jones. The doctor smote him between the shoulder blades.

'You lap-dog novelist!' he said. Jones grinned. He liked the doctor; watched him affectionately as he walked down the path of the cottage garden to his car; had inquired once, in all innocence, what the man was doing in a place like Saxon Wall.

They were drinking bottled beer in Jones' small sitting-room, and the doctor, gazing thoughtfully into his glass, which was three-quarters full, had answered:

'Illegal operation. Syphilitic lover. I was let off for lack of evidence.'

'Yes, and talking of all that kind of thing,' said Jones. 'What's your opinion on eugenics and so on? Interesting subject in its way. Used it in a novel once, but not particularly satisfactorily, I thought. Not enough sentimentality about it for my kind of stuff.'

The doctor raised his glass and, shutting his left eye, gazed with his right at the beautiful amber liquid with its crest of froth. Then he wagged his head, and misquoted solemnly:

'"For malt does more than *Malthus* can
   To justify God's ways to man."'

Chapter Ten

'"Won't she answer the helm at all?" I
said irritably . . .
"Yes, sir. She's coming-to slowly."
"Let her head come up to south."
"Aye, aye, sir."
I paced the poop. There was not a sound
but that of my footsteps until the man
spoke again.
"She is at south now, sir."'

JOSEPH CONRAD
The Shadow Line.

MRS PASSION did no house-cleaning of any kind for
Jones except on Wednesdays and Saturdays, so that,
having given him his breakfast, she had left him
talking to the doctor while she returned to her own
cottage for an hour or so. Having performed such
domestic duties there as, presumably, suggested
themselves to her, it was her custom to return to
Jones at about half-past eleven in order to prepare
and cook his midday meal.

Between her going and her return on the day Mr
Middleton had been found dead, no fewer than four
persons called upon Jones to give him the news.
Miss Harper and her sister were the first, and they
had scarcely gone before Mrs Corbett appeared.
She was followed by Lily Soudall. In addition to
the news, (which, being a girl of some intelligence,
she assumed that Jones had heard) she brought a
message from the doctor.

'He says he don't like the sound of the Reverend,
and thinks he ought to see a specialist. He wrote
out what was the matter with him. Here it is.
'Suffering from'—I been trying to make out the next
word coming along to tell it you, if you couldn't
read his writing. All doctors write bad, don't
they?'

She was a very different creature from the grief-
stricken girl Jones had seen at the vicarage on
the occasion of her quarrel with Corbett. Jones
smiled.

'That's so that unauthorised persons shan't be
able to read what they've put,' he said. The gentle
rebuke was lost upon Lily.

'What is the word, anyway, sir? My mother's
sure to ask me, time I get home.'

'Hallucinations,' replied Jones gravely. She looked
at him for enlightenment, but Jones, grinning
wickedly, gave her sixpence for bringing the note,
and went indoors.

Lily and the returning Mrs Passion encountered
one another at the garden gate. Lily spat into the
middle of the garden path. Mrs Passion curtsied

ironically at the insult, and held the gate open for the girl to pass out.

'You don't seem popular with Lily Soudall,' said Jones, a little later. Mrs Passion lifted her lacklustre eyes to his and answered without apparent ill-feeling:

'She's been brought up nice, Lily has. A very respectable young woman.'

'Any more news about Mr Middleton's death?' asked Jones, watching her closely. Mrs Passion shook her head.

'I been up there this hour or more. The police from Stowhall are there. Both of them. They've been very sharp with Mrs Tebbutt and her lad.'

'How do you know that?' asked Jones.

She answered: 'Oh, news travels about, sir, doesn't it?'

'Sit down, Mrs Passion, a minute, and shut the door, I want to speak to you,' he said, acting upon a sudden impulse, which, as suddenly, he regretted.

She sat on the edge of a chair, and rolled her hands in her apron. Jones found it difficult to begin.

'You remember last night, Mrs Passion?'

'I can't say I do. Not specially, Mr Jones, sir.'

'Good heavens, woman, of course you do!' said Jones. 'Your—your coming here, I mean.'

'Oh, that,' said Mrs Passion. 'Well, what of it? We settled it to our satisfaction, didn't we?'

Completely nonplussed, Jones nodded feebly. Mrs Passion eyed him. Then she added:

'I could see you were a gentleman the first time I set eyes on you. So let bygones be bygones, say I.'

'Yes, but hang it, that's all very well,' said Jones. She waited patiently, but all he could add, in the way of protest, were the words: 'I shall have to discharge you, you know, if you drink to excess. I really can't—I mean—well, it doesn't do, does it?'

'I wasn't drunk,' said Mrs Passion sullenly. They left it at that. After a moment she rose and walked out of the room, pausing at the door to ask respectfully what he would have for lunch.

'Well, what you've got, I suppose,' said Jones. 'There's a little boy coming. Can you make it enough for two?'

'For twenty-two of the kind you mean, Mr Jones,' she answered. 'It's the little nephew, I suppose?'

'It's the little nephew,' Jones replied, and looked at her to see how she would take it. But her face remained impassive. Jones got his hat and, thrusting the doctor's message into his pocket, walked to the village post office to send a telegram. The postmistress, greatly interested, took it and read aloud to her daughter Miriam.

'Bradley Stone House Wandles Parva Bucks badly needed Saxon Wall Hants Hannibal Jones with love.'

A second telegraph form bore an identical message, but was addressed to Mrs Bradley's London house.

'It's over a shilling for each of them, anyway,' said the postmistress angrily to Jones. Jones grinned and nodded.

'Exactly how much over?' he inquired. The postmistress counted each message twice, sucked a pencil, made calculations on a blotting pad, and finally charged him, as she put it, two and sevenpence the pair.

She brooded long over the messages when she had transmitted them, but they remained mysterious as pain, and just about as irritating.

Jones got back to his cottage twenty-five minutes before the doctor arrived with the little boy. The lad's resemblance to Mrs Passion was certainly extraordinary. Jones studied him while they lunched. The boy had thick black hair, a pale, expressionless face, and looked as strong as a little bull. He ate hungrily, but not greedily, and his table manners were above criticism. His behaviour was easy and natural, and he accepted Jones in the oddly attractive way in which young boys do accept men who reciprocate their unsentimental liking.

Jones took him out for a walk in the afternoon, but, before they went, Mrs Pike insisted upon their sampling her home-brewed ginger beer. Henry Pike served them. Jones looked from boy to boy; and, acting on impulse, said:

'Get your hat and come out for a walk with us, Henry.'

They walked in silence towards Guthrum Down, but before they reached the cart-tracks which led on to the common, Henry stopped short and said:

'My mother said I was to ask you if so be you'd seen the gentleman's corp, Mr Jones.'

'The what, old man?'

'The dead gentleman that's supposed to be this little boy's uncle, sir. The gentleman——'

'I'm not a little boy,' said Richard. 'But I should like to see the body, if we may.'

'Well, you may not,' said Jones shortly. There was a short pause, and then Richard asked politely:

'He was knocked on the head in the dining-room, wasn't he?'

'Now how on earth,' said the exasperated Jones, 'do you know that?'

'Your servant told me while you were trying to pump up some water so that we could wash.'

'Oh, did she? What else did she say?'

'That I bore a marked resemblance to my mother.'

'My mother said she didn't believe the corp *was* Mr Middieton,' ventured Henry. 'She said that seeing was believing.'

'No doubt,' said Jones. 'And, no doubt, also, the police know what they're doing, old chap.'

Richard was observing the landscape.

'What's that hill?' he inquired.

'Godrun Down,' said Henry. 'Her's bewitched, that hill is. The long thin man live up top of she.'

'That's the kind of tale to tell kids and suckers,' said Richard, haughtily. Henry looked at him, puzzled by this complete indifference to one of the articles of the village children's creed.

'That's right enough,' he protested. 'The long thin man.' He looked at Jones. 'My mother thought Mr Jones was he till parson told her different. And so did she think the doctor was Old Satan, only that's what they call parson too and all.'

Both boys stared at Jones, taking in his height and his drooping slenderness.

'The long thin man,' said Richard, meditating. 'Hm! Not bad. Your mother must be rather observant,' he added politely to Henry.

'Mrs Fluke always says it's the simple ones that see the most in the end,' said Henry, nodding, 'because folks don't hide up things in front of simple folks like they would in front of you or me.'

'What, for instance, would they hide from you and me?' asked Jones. But Henry shook his head. The remark itself had impressed him, but its application had escaped his memory. At this point Richard noticed a Clifton Blue butterfly, and both boys went in chase of it.

'Well, what did you think of Henry Pike?' Jones asked his guest when they were back at the cottage, and Henry, inarticulate because of a shilling which Jones had given him, had taken his leave of them. Richard, eyeing with great interest the tea which Mrs Passion was placing upon the table, said politely that Henry seemed all right. Perceiving that it was not reasonable to expect his whole-hearted attention until some, at least, of Mrs Passion's efforts to please the guest and tempt his appetite had received just consideration, Jones seated himself at the table.

'Good gracious, Mrs Passion,' he said. '*Four* kinds of cake? And *three* kinds of jam?'

'And a nice egg, Mr Jones,' said Mrs Passion, dumping the egg-cups down. 'We must keep the young gentleman's strength up whilst he's with us.'

'Not half,' murmured the young gentleman, helping himself to bread and butter and watching Mrs Passion as she served him with tea the colour of a black boot, and sweetened it lavishly.

'What a kind woman she is,' observed Richard, when she had gone. 'She seems to like my being here.'

'Yes, it makes a change for her,' Jones agreed. 'Would you have liked it if Henry had stayed to tea?'

Richard, chewing thoughtfully, considered the question.

'Probably have embarrassed him, don't you think?' he suggested tentatively.

'Why so?' Jones inquired.

'Well, he seemed a nice chap, and he's sure to be caddish at the table, I should imagine, and probably knows it, don't you think?'

Jones was amused and impressed. He gazed at the child, comparing him with Passion and his wife. Physically, of course, it looked more than possible. Mentally, he decided, it seemed the reverse. Besides, this boy was attractive. The lack of expression in his face was more than compensated for by the aptness of his remarks, and his candid, intelligent views. They conversed no more until the meal was ended. Then Jones said:

'What time do you think of going to bed and so on?' Richard considered this, too.

'Eightish,' he said. 'I'm in training. Mustn't overdo things, you know.'

'In training?' said Jones. 'That's fine. What for?'

'Boxing. I've brought a set of gloves down with me. I shall have to find someone to spar with.'

He cast an experienced eye round the sitting-room.

'The light's not too good in here, I should imagine, but I dare say it will do to spar in. How big is it?'

Jones replied humbly that he did not know, but that they could measure it in the morning. He inquired what competition the other was entering.

'Oh, only at school,' replied Richard magnificently. 'I want a Public Schools Championship later on. That's one advantage of not having a mater, by the way. Don't you think so?'

Jones replied that the point had never received from him the consideration which he now perceived to be its due. Richard shook his head soberly.

'A number of our men, even our bigger men, find their maters a fearful disadvantage,' he said. 'They do fuss so, the majority of them. Of course, they have to be educated up to a sport like boxing. But it's very bad luck on the fellows who have to educate them. And, of course, a mater will simply ruin your training, if she gets the chance. Takes you out, and stuffs you with sweets and so on.'

Jones, smoking his pipe, nodded gloomily in sympathy, and said that he supposed it was so.

'I'll do my exercises now, if you don't mind. I think I have digested my tea,' Richard observed, two hours later, after a most companionable silence during which he had drawn elaborately and with great mechanical exactitude, every type of motorcycle on the market.

'Carry on,' said Jones. 'Oh, by the way, I'm afraid I can't offer you a bath. We're rather ridiculously short of water.'

'Oh, right,' replied Richard. 'I've got my training towel with me. I'll just have a good rub down, then, after my exercises.'

He disappeared upstairs. Jones could hear him stamping around in the front bedroom overhead. In about three minutes he reappeared, dressed in vest and running drawers. His exercises were complicated, exhausting, and obviously his own invention, and he performed them as one carrying out a religious rite.

'Feel that,' he said to Jones proudly at the end, flexing the muscles of his arms. Jones felt them. At that moment Mrs Passion came in.

'How does the young gentleman like his bath water, please?' she said.

'Bath water?' ejaculated Jones. 'But how on earth have you coaxed bath water out of this thirsty land?'

Mrs Passion looked out of the window.

'Thirsty land, rivers of water,' she murmured. Then turning her eyes on Jones, she added:

'Isn't there a dewpond on the top of Godrun Down?'

'You haven't been up to the top of Guthrum Down for water?'

'Young gentlemen must have their bath,' said Mrs Passion impassively. 'I hanna been brought up in good service without knowing that. We took the yoked milk-pails up there, Passion and mother and me, so there's a drop over as you can wash yourself in, Mr Jones, if you've a mind. Will he take his bath in here or in the kitchen?'

'But I thought you'd quarrelled with your mother,' Jones observed. Mrs Passion looked at a spot on the wall just above his head.

'Mother have her own good reasons for wanting to go up Godrun Down in the heat of the summer, Mr Jones.'

There appeared to be something significant behind the words, but their meaning was lost to Jones. There was a pause whilst he wrestled with an idea which eluded him. At last he gave it up and shook his head.

'No doubt,' he said. 'And how goes the nasty smell?'

'It went from me with Mr Middleton's death.'

'Oh, really? How was that?' Mrs Passion looked from Jones to the black-browed Richard who was waiting to be told where to have his bath. Then she replied:

'"Night unto night showeth knowledge." And

what's more, Mr Jones, someone has ill-wished the vicar all over again.'

'Why, how do you mean?' asked Jones. Mrs Passion put a pudgy hand on her brow and murmured in ominous tones:

'The rose-window in the church have been took away, and the vicar have gashed himself dreadful on the forrid with the glass.'

'Morbid symbolism,' said Jones automatically.

'Very likely. I bean't up in they new diseases. But it's ill-wishing the poor young innocent man that's done it, all the same.'

Jones nodded. Richard said politely: 'Would the kitchen be the best place, do you think? Perhaps it wouldn't matter if I splashed a bit in there.'

'Very good,' said Mrs Passion. Jones could hear them talking as Mrs Passion poured out the heated water for the child. Then she returned to the sitting-room.

'I'll be going now, then, Mr Jones. Could I use the front door, being that the young gentleman is having the use of the kitchen?'

'Surely,' said Jones. He heard the front door close behind her, and twisted his long thin body in the chair to watch her walking down the garden path between the over-heavy roses and the foxgloves and the brilliant poppy-heads. Thetis, thought Jones, must certainly have been the most fearful and most desperate of women. He wondered what, in Richard, symbolised Achilles' heel.

A little later, Mortmain came to see him. He

shook his head when Jones inquired how the vicar was.

'Between you and me,' he said, 'he's insane. But I want another opinion.'

'I've sent for Mrs Lestrange Bradley,' said Jones.

'Good. Yes. He wouldn't allow Nao to admit me, and when I looked in at him through the window he came and positively gibbered at me through the glass. He had a great bandage round his head and completely over one eye, and informed me that he was the Prophet Mohammed, or something else Biblical.'

'*Biblical*, you heathen Chinee?' said Jones, who had been brought up in the bosom, flinty but well-informed, of the Welsh Methodist Church. 'You mean Moses, not Mohammed. He's got water on the brain, Hallam has. Besides, Moses was not a prophet, he was a patriarch.'

'I knew it began with M,' said the doctor meekly.

'So does mutton-head,' said Jones, with the rudeness permitted to friends.

Chapter Eleven

'Poor Brother Tom had an Accident this
time Twelvemonth, and so clever a made
fellow he was, that I could not save him
from those fleaing Rascals the Surgeons;
and now, poor Man, he is among the
Otamys at Surgeons Hall.'

JOHN GAY
The Beggar's Opera. Act II, Scene I.

MRS PASSION had not been gone for more than half
an hour when a restlessness, due, possibly, to the
warmth of the summer evening, took possession of
Jones and compelled him to the first of that series
of actions which had, later, such extraordinary
results.

He sat and listened for a time, to Richard,
splashing and reciting in his bath, and as his ear
became accustomed to the rhythm of the iambic
pentameters, Jones found himself listening keenly
to as excellent a rendering of Mark Antony's oration
as he had ever heard.

He went to the door that separated sitting-room from kitchen and passed through. Richard was standing up in the bath-tub, a loofah of terrifying dimensions in his right hand, his chin raised slightly, his eyes half-closed, his expressionless face woodenly Japanese. His child's voice, heavy and flat with the tragedy of the lines, was saying slowly:

'For Brutus, as you know, was Cæsar's angel:'

'Go to bed,' said Jones. 'What do you think you're doing?'

'Saying my part.'

'Well, say it in bed. Washed yourself yet?'

'Oh, yes.'

'Well, out you get, then. All right. I'll see about emptying that water. I want it for my garden. Give me the towel. Here, you have this small one. Got your pyjamas handy? All right, I'll go and get them. Dry your hair a bit.'

Richard safely in bed and fortified with biscuits and a drink of milk and soda, Jones returned to the sitting-room to read. But suddenly he put down the book, went to the table drawer and took out notepaper and envelopes. He wrote two letters, one to his wife, the other to his lawyer.

The first read:

'I've found a boy of ten I want to adopt. What do you say?'

The second ran:

'How does one proceed to adopt an orphan boy ten years of age? He is supposed to be the nephew of the murdered Middleton, but I believe him to be the son of a couple in the village here.'

He decided to post the letters immediately instead of waiting until the morning. He stamped the envelopes and then went upstairs on tip-toe. Richard was not asleep.

'I want to go as far as the post office,' said Jones.

'All right.'

'You don't mind being left?'

Richard grinned. Jones grinned too.

'Sorry,' he said. 'I knew you didn't, really.'

He decided, all the same, to be as quick as he could. But on the way back from the post office he encountered old Mrs Fluke. She was bent nearly double and had an empty sack flung over her ancient shoulders. A black cat trailed behind her like her shadow.

Jones accosted her.

'And what are you doing out at this time in the evening?' His voice was loud and good-humoured. The old woman cackled and wagged her head. The cat walked round Jones' legs and purred, and rubbed itself against him.

'It be parson,' said old Mrs Fluke, in a voice of surprising shrillness. 'He be suffering from they plagues of frogs again.'

'What plagues of frogs?' said Jones, remembering

the bloated-looking corpses which the vicar had interred, and beginning to feel slightly sick.

'You should read your Bible, young man, and then so be you'd know,' retorted Mrs Fluke. 'I was going up there with Malkie and my little sack to take his frogs away, but now I ain't a-going to.'

'Very well. I'll go myself,' said Jones. 'Give me the sack.'

She handed it over, chuckling. The black cat, evidently in two minds as to whether its allegiance lay to the sack or to the old woman, walked in a circle, communing audibly with its sense of duty, and then elected to follow the sack. A slight but unmistakable odour of stale fish which clung about the receptacle explained to Jones the reason of its choice.

He thought of the little boy alone in the cottage, but reflected that he had taken the precaution of fastening the downstair windows before leaving him. He also had bolted the back door and locked the front one. There was small chance of the cottage catching fire in his absence, and if Mrs Passion happened to be taken by a wandering fit she could not get near enough to the boy to frighten him. All the same, Jones stopped at the doctor's house and told him where he was going, and mentioned that the child was alone.

'I'm glad you're going to see the vicar,' the doctor said. 'He's baddish. Ought to get right away from here for a bit, but I can't persuade him of anything if he really won't see me.'

'Odd,' said Jones, 'how suddenly the thing came on.'

'What thing?—Look here, I'll send my couple of maids over to your place if you'd care to leave me your key. Nervous about the boy, now, aren't you?'

'As any old woman,' admitted Jones.

'The girls won't mind,' the doctor said. 'It's still broad daylight. If they go over now, you need not hurry away from the vicar if he wants to talk to you. Will Mrs Bradley be coming, do you know?'

'I hope so. Haven't heard yet. Thanks for the loan of the girls.' The girls, summoned and instructed, smiled and announced themselves pleased to go and mind the little boy. Jones rewarded them, and prepared to take his departure.

'You haven't told me what thing,' said the doctor, holding him by the sleeve. Jones had a sudden extraordinary conviction that he could have held him equally well by the power of his eyes.

'Oh, you know. These nervous symptoms. And is it true he broke the rose-window of the church and is cutting himself with the glass?'

'Good Lord! I hadn't heard that! No wonder his head and eye were bandaged. I don't like the sound of that! Poor old fellow! That's bad, if it's true.' But the doctor sounded ghoulishly delighted.

'Yes, very bad,' said Jones. 'Morbid symbolism! Nasty! Mrs Passion told me all about it.'

'How do these people get to know things? It can't have been broadcast over the village, you know, or one of the maids would have told me.'

They found the vicar in bed. His head was indeed heavily bandaged. He hid his head under the bedclothes when the two men came in, and refused to let the doctor take the bandages off, or, in fact, to come within two yards of him. The Japanese butler, impassive as an idol, stood in the doorway. The doctor did not stay for more than ten minutes. He said nothing to the butler until they were at the front door.

The vicar peeped out at Jones. His eyes were bright, as though he were fevered.

'He won't get much out of Nao,' he said, and laughed; then winced, and put a hand to his bandaged head. 'I don't like Mortmain. He makes me out to be worse than I am, you know.'

'Why on earth did you not let Mortmain see your head?' asked Jones, a trifle impatiently. The vicar grimaced; then laughed again, and winced.

'I feel such a fool about it. You know what happened?'

'No.'

'Oh, I thought the village would certainly know.'

'Mrs Passion told me one of her funny yarns.'

'What did she say?'

'Oh, something about the rose-window getting smashed, and your cutting yourself on the glass.'

'Carefully censored version of what she really did say, isn't it, Jones? Why don't you tell me the truth?' His voice was still petulant and was inclined to be hysterical. Jones could not recognise in him the Hallam he had known at first.

'Well, you know what the villagers are. Tell me what really happened,' he said, speaking calmly and pleasantly.

'Oh, some of the boys stoned the window, you know, and one of the stones caught me on the side of the head when I went out to stop them. That's all.'

Jones' training in psychology caused him to suspect that the vicar was lying. It was not easy to say this, so he changed the subject.

'What does old Mrs Fluke mean when she says you have a plague of frogs?'

'She's thinking of those you saw me bury in the garden, I suppose.'

'Oh, perhaps she is,' said Jones, utterly unconvinced. 'No more frogs in the well, then?'

'No. None at all. Not one. Don't forget what I said about coming up here for water, if you're getting short. And I know you must be. Everybody is. Everybody is!' He grimaced with unholy glee, and hid his face again beneath the bedclothes.

'Thanks. I'll remember,' said Jones. He told of how Mrs Passion had pressed Passion and Mrs Fluke into Richard's service to procure for him the water for a bath. They both laughed over that. The vicar seemed particularly amused. He screamed with hoarse laughter. Jones had to quieten him. 'I'm convinced that Richard is her son,' said Jones, 'and I'm certain she murdered Middleton.'

'But why should she murder Middleton?' the vicar demanded, as though the subject had never been mentioned before.

'To secure the inheritance for the boy, of course.'

'I don't believe it,' said the vicar flatly.

'Why not? I'm convinced,' said Jones, 'the woman's capable of anything.'

'Not murder.'

'Why not? I believe she murdered the other Middleton to get her son accepted as the heir.'

'You've said all this before,' said Hallam petulantly, and I don't and can't believe it. The village isn't as wicked as all that. It can't be as wicked as all that. It's my village, and they're my people, and I won't have it said that there's wickedness.'

Jones was puzzled. It was from the vicar that he had heard the most passionate, the most definite, and infinitely the most pessimistic declarations of the wickedness of the village.

'If only it won't rain yet,' the vicar added. 'The continuance of the drought will solve all my problems. Rain would just make all my troubles begin again. Oh, if only it will not rain!'

It was about nine-thirty when Jones left him. Secure in the knowledge that Richard was not alone in the cottage, he walked out into the kitchen to talk with Nao. The Japanese was eating his supper—sardines, bread and butter and a handful of freshly gathered raspberries. The candle-light which illumined his head and hand and plate—for the kitchen was always gloomy, and needed to be lighted earlier than the rest of the house—made him look like a sleek-headed gnome. He rose politely

when Jones entered, and stood waiting for him
to speak.

'Look here,' said Jones abruptly, 'you must tell
me what's the matter with your master.'

'The murder up at Neot House is the matter,'
said the Japanese.

'But he was ill—his nerves were bad—before Mr
Middleton's death. Now don't hedge. Your duty
towards Mr Hallam compels you to tell me the
truth. I want to help Mr Hallam, who is very ill.'

The Japanese smiled.

'My duty to Mr Hallam is to keep his secrets, I
think. I think Mr Hallam is not ill.'

'Well, you think wrongly and foolishly. Don't you
understand that Mr Hallam is not himself at all?'

'I understand. Let us not talk of that. I have
something to put in your charge. Please to
come.'

He picked up the candle and led the way to
the back door. Shading the candle with his hand,
although the night was still, he crossed the yard
to the scullery where the pump was housed, and
stood the candle on a shelf. Then he went to the
great old copper and raised the lid.

'Perhaps the candle,' he said. Jones picked up
the candlestick and brought it to the open copper
hole. He peered inside. The candle-light showed
him a winking gleam of blue at the bottom of
the big cauldron. Nao put in his slim yellow hand
and brought out one by one some pieces of glass,
colours that burned and glowed, rich blue and
comely crimson, clear green and glowing gold.

'Not the rose-window?' said Jones.

'The quatrefoil, yes, Mr Jones. He climbed all alone and took out the beautiful glass. Every little bit he took out with a diamond, Mr Jones, and put it into a basket slung on his arm, and brought it all down and laid it in the bottom of the copper, and charged me on my soul to give it you if anything should happen.'

He placed the glass carefully in a basket, and smiled at the mystified Jones.

'But how do you know that's what happened?'

'I watched him,' said the Japanese serenely. 'And I hoped he would not fall. This vicar then climbed the church tower, but that was late at night.'

'Did he use a ladder?'

'No, no. He climbed. This vicar climbed very high.'

'What?'

'Yes, Mr Jones. Very dangerous. And saying to himself how very few churches have a rose-window with the thirteenth-century glass still there, intact. Oh, yes.'

Jones took the basket to the doorway, and the Japanese closed the copper, and took up the candle. Before they went back to the kitchen Jones asked:

'Did Mr Hallam know that you saw him, Nao?'

'He knew.'

'Oh, *did* he?' said Jones. 'Did he say anything?'

'When he had laid glass carefully in copper he washed his hands under the pump, I drawing up the water, and he said: "What time is it, Nao?" I answered that it was more than half-past eight. Then he said: "It has taken me more than an hour."'

'Now what about this plague of frogs?'

The Japanese showed the first sign of emotion that Jones had witnessed in him.

'That bestial old wicked woman!' he said. 'It was while the vicar was climbing the church tower. She emptied a great sackful of those beastly frogs into the well, yes, certainly she did! I saw her.'

'Great heavens! At what time was that?'

'That was at five minutes past eleven. I told her some wicked words.'

'How long was she here?'

'By the time she had heard me and replied to me, it must have been twenty past. That was in the churchyard, too. That is a dreadfully wrong place to argue with witless old hag-women about sacks full of frogs. Then I made her gather them all up again and be off with her.'

'So at what time did she actually go away?'

'Not until just before the vicar came down from the top of the tower.'

'Very odd,' muttered Jones. 'And what was she doing here this evening?' he inquired aloud. The Japanese shook his head.

'She had better let me catch her here this evening or other evenings,' he said mildly, but with a curious intonation that sent a shudder down Jones' back. He was an imaginative man, and centuries of cruelty had gone to make that curious little hit in Nao's voice. He was thinking so deeply that he missed his turning on his homeward way, went on past the Long Thin Man, and, by the time he came to himself, was only about five minutes' walk from the Middleton house. He found himself wondering whether Middleton's body had been moved, and a sudden onset of curiosity caused him to continue his walk, push open the garden gate and walk up the drive to the building.

He was prepared to find the whole house barricaded and impossible to enter. He was prepared to find other sightseers, as morbidly curious as himself, staring in at the ground floor windows of the house. He was even prepared to find policemen on duty, with orders to admit no one. What he was not prepared for was the painful, shrewd and sudden blow which knocked him out just as he was negotiating an angle of the house on his preliminary tour of reconnaissance.

There was a sharp pain which seemed to flash like a shining sword before his eyes; then a sensation of blackness and of falling.

The next thing he knew was that he was in bed in his own cottage, the victim of a most devitalising headache, with the doctor in half-reproachful, half-humorous attendance on him, and Mrs Bradley, grinning like an alligator and dressed like a macaw, sitting in his best armchair.

Chapter Twelve

'When Socrates heard me rail against Meroe thus, he held up his finger to me, and, half abashed, said, "Peace, peace, I pray you, and" (looking about lest any person should hear) "I pray you" (quoth he) "take heed what you say against so venerable a woman as she is, lest by your intemperate tongue you catch some harm."

'Then (as if in wonder), "what" (quoth I), "is she so excellent a person as you name her to be! I pray you tell me."'

The Golden Ass of LUCIUS APULEIUS in the translation of William Adlington, edited by F. J. Harvey Darton.

'THE village is lousy with superstition of every kind this side actual idolatry,' said Jones. Mrs Bradley forbore (out of deference to what she guessed of Jones' headache) to cackle at this sweeping statement, but the expression on her face as she received the information would have graced the countenance of any of the gargoyles on Notre-Dame. 'They have decided already that you are Meroe in person, I have no doubt.'

'I believe the vicar thinks so, anyhow, dear child.'

'Oh, Hallam, yes. What did you make of him?'

'He has homicidal tendencies,' said Mrs Bradley. Her low voice, rich and full, took from the words their startling implication, but Jones, propping himself on his elbow and flushing with excitement, said:

'You don't mean *he* killed Middleton?'

'How should I know who killed Middleton?' asked Mrs Bradley, grinning. 'The verdict at the inquest was murder by persons unknown. Tell me about the Tebbutts, child.'

'I don't know anything about them. You tell me about Hallam. What's the matter with him? Overwork?'

Mrs Bradley pursed her lips until they formed a little beak, and shook her head.

'Oh, confessional secrets?' said Jones. 'I may not betray any confidence poured into my unwilling but nevertheless receptive ears by my unfortunate and only partially-responsible patient. Is that it?'

'Possibly,' said Mrs Bradley. 'Go to sleep, child. I am going to take Richard for a walk.'

Richard was silent until they reached the Long Thin Man. Then he asked politely:

'Are we going up to my house just now, Mrs Bradley?'

'Why, yes,' replied Mrs Bradley. 'At least, *I'm* going there, but I don't want you to come.'

'Oh, mayn't I, please?'

'I'd rather you didn't. I want you to go and play in Mrs Corbett's garden, Richard, and, while you're there, you might acquire some specimens of soil. I want to analyse them in connection with the crime.'

'How jolly good,' said Richard, quite reconciled by this means to the alteration in his plans. 'And do you want match-sticks or finger-prints?'

Mrs Bradley gave him a couple of glossy correspondence cards.

'All the finger-prints you can possibly manage to collect on these, and initial them, please,' she said briskly. 'Match-sticks, no. Cigarette ends, no.' She frowned thoughtfully. 'Size of footprints, yes.' She produced a folding ruler. At the sight of it Richard's expressionless face did not alter, but his black eyes shone. 'Notebook for recording data obtained,' concluded Mrs Bradley, giving it to him, 'and——'

'I've got a pencil of my own,' interpolated the child. 'I say, you know, isn't this absolutely topping!'

Mrs Bradley laid a yellow forefinger against her pursed-up lips. Her sharp eyes glanced about her. The boy, laughing with excitement, nodded. From the next bend in the road, Mrs Bradley, looking back over her shoulder, had the felicity of seeing his sturdy little body in its suit of light grey flannel squeezed closely up into an angle of the dark-red house. She had left him in safety and with the maximum of employment for at least two hours, she knew.

The Tebbutts were still nominally in charge of the house. The wife looked ill and anxious, and the sixteen-year-old son unkempt, wild-haired and rebellious. Mrs Bradley said:

'Good morning. I'm not a sight-seer. May I sit down somewhere? I'm very hot.'

The woman produced a chair and placed it in the shade of a laburnum.

'Will you have a drink, madam?' she inquired.

'No, I'll have a talk with you,' said Mrs Bradley.

'Not about Mr Middleton, madam, please.'

'Don't you want to know who killed him?'

'No one will ever know that,' said the sixteen-year-old son.

'Oh, Tom, you mustn't say that,' his mother protested.

'Well, what will they find out bullying you and me?'

'They're doing their best, son. The police can't mince their words, and father will have his character to commend him.'

She was a pale, composed, neatly-dressed woman, heavily built, and fleshy with the onset of middle age. Mrs Bradley studied the woman with her sharp black eyes, and then said suddenly:

'Go away, Tom, please. I want to talk to your mother.'

The boy shrugged at that, glanced at his mother, received a nod, and went.

'And keep right out of the way,' Mrs Bradley called after him. Then she settled herself more comfortably in her chair and looked out over the garden.

'I expect you are very busy, Mrs Tebbutt,' she said. 'I won't keep you longer than I can help.'

Mrs Tebbutt shook her head. She was not looking at Mrs Bradley but at a beautiful bush of syringa laden with blossom along its swaying stems.

'I haven't got the heart to be busy, and that's a fact, madam,' she said. 'We're in trouble, sad trouble, over Mr Middleton's death. And really, although I shouldn't like father and Tom to hear me, because of hurting their feelings, the fact is, madam, it's a relief for me to be able to speak with another woman, if you'll excuse me referring to you like that. These policemen, and the inspector, I don't really believe they think in their hearts poor father had a hand in it, but, after all, what *can* they think, on the evidence? Made poor father quite ill, the shock and that. That's his room, facing west.'

'And what is the evidence?' asked Mrs Bradley gently, her black eyes fixed not on Mr Tebbutt's window, but on a huge bush of fuchsia which was hung with a thousand dark red and purple buds. Mrs Tebbutt shook her head despondently.

'There isn't any, madam. That's the trouble. I can't believe that father and I could have been asleep when it was done, and the inspector, I should say he doesn't believe it either. You couldn't expect him to. And as for Tom—why, he was downstairs all the time. It doesn't seem possible that none of us should have heard so much as a sound.'

'Extraordinary,' said Mrs Bradley absently. 'Tell me about Mr Middleton.'

'Well, he was the elder brother. Both of them went to the war. We were in service, dad and I, with the parents of the second Mr Middleton's wife—Palliner, the name is. Perhaps you know it, madam? Well, *our* Mr Middleton, as we always call him among ourselves, *he* came home safe, not even so much as wounded, but eight or nine months before the end of the war—in the February, I think it would have been—we heard that the *elder* brother, Mr Carswell Middleton, this one that's just been murdered, was missing, believed to be killed.

'Well, that meant our Mr Middleton inherited the London house together with this big house here with its land, and a whole lot of money—the Middletons used to be tea merchants and had their own fleet of clipper-ships, so I've heard tell—so it meant he was very well off, though, of course, he had always been comfortable.

'But, later on—in fact, only a few months ago—Mr Carswell Middleton turned up in a London hospital, suffering from injuries through being knocked down by a car, and it seems the shock brought back his memory that he'd lost, and he remembered who he was and everything. Well, it wasn't hard for him to prove he was speaking the truth. For one thing, Mr and Mrs Palliner both recognised him, and so did father and I. He'd got some papers, too.

I don't know all that part of the tale, I never heard quite all of it, but, anyhow, the little boy's lawyers and trustees fought it, but they hadn't got any case against Mr Middleton's proofs, and he did promise them faithful, so I heard, that he never intended to marry, so the boy wouldn't be disappointed any way about inheriting, it simply put his chances off a year or two, it didn't do away with them. He was to have the little boy to live with him, to be brought up like his son, too and all, and all the arrangements were made, his bedroom got ready and everything, only this dreadful thing had to go and happen to him just as the whole thing was arranged so pleasant for everybody.'

'And did people really believe that Mr Carswell Middleton would remain a bachelor?' Mrs Bradley inquired. Mrs Tebbutt looked cautiously round to make certain that her son was not within earshot, and then said quietly:

'If they did, it was more than anybody could have believed of Mr Hanley Middleton. It's ill work to speak against the dead, madam, but I know it nearly broke Mrs Palliner's heart to know that her only daughter was married to a rake.'

'A rake?' said Mrs Bradley.

'A promiscuous rake,' said Mrs Tebbutt, sinking her voice still further in order to gild the lily with the greater effect. 'They couldn't keep a servant till they got our Martha—Martha Fluke—to come in for them. And then she soon had to get married to that half-witted husband, poor thing, to cover herself against what might be coming to her.'

'Are you speaking of Mrs Passion by any chance?'
asked Mrs Bradley, interested.

'That's right. I always call her Fluke because she
was Fluke when I first heard of her.'

'Have you lived in the village before, then?' Mrs
Bradley inquired.

'In Saxon Wall? Thank God I have not,' replied
Mrs Tebbutt earnestly. 'But everyone that knew
Mr Hanley knew Martha Fluke as well. He used
to bring her up to London regular, in pretence of
having her to wait on poor Miss Constance. Oh,
it was a scandalous thing! I can't think why Mrs
Palliner ever had Martha in the house, unless it
was to get a sight of her daughter sometimes, for
Mr Hanley wouldn't come without the girl, and
wouldn't let his wife go and stay with her parents
without him. It was a nice how-d'ye do, I can tell
you.'

'It all sounds very sad,' said Mrs Bradley. Mrs
Tebbutt dropped her voice again.

'If poor Miss Constance hadn't been first to go, I
wouldn't like to have said who killed Mr Hanley,'
she said bluntly. Mrs Bradley nodded.

'I wish you'd tell me exactly what happened on
the evening of the murder,' she said, and, as she
spoke, she produced from a pocket in her skirt a
notebook and a small gold pencil. As Mrs Tebbutt
talked, Mrs Bradley wrote. The tiny hieroglyphics
were meaningless except to the woman who wrote
them down.

'We spent the evening as usual,' Mrs Tebbutt
began. 'That is to say, madam, we had our tea at

five, Mr Middleton having had his at half-past four, and then, while father went round the flower beds with his little hoe, loosening the soil, which it had been too hot for him to do earlier in the day, Tom cut the lawn in the front, and I got Mr Middleton's dinner ready, and cooked it for seven-thirty, that being the time that he preferred to dine.

'Well, I gave them a nice drink of milk and soda, there being no water nice enough for lemonade, it giving it a funny, musty taste since the dry weather, and cups of tea, even, being anything but what they were; and then father went in and laid the table, and Tom cut a few flowers for me to put in a vase, and then father went to Mr Middleton to see what wine he wanted opened.'

'Where was Mr Middleton between tea and dinner?' Mrs Bradley inquired, without looking up from her notebook.

'Oh, here and there, madam, just the same as usual. He went to the greenhouse, I believe, and he spent half an hour or so in the library where he was making a list of some books, I think, and he went up to his bedroom to dress at about six-thirty, just as usual, and Tom went up to hand him his studs and put the links into his shirt.

'After his dinner he stayed in the dining-room drinking a glass of port, and then he lay on the settee, with his knees drawn up——'

She looked at Mrs Bradley, who nodded, comprehending that the woman was remembering the attitude in which Middleton's dead body had been found.

'He was reading a book,' Mrs Tebbutt continued. 'He always read for a bit after dinner. Then at about nine o'clock he went for a walk in the grounds, and called, I believe, on the vicar, though that wasn't usual. But he couldn't have stayed there long, for he was inside the house again by twenty to ten and ringing for father to bring him his brandy and soda, that he never went to bed without.'

'Tell me,' said Mrs Bradley, looking up from the notebook and dangling the little gold pencil between two yellow fingers, 'was Mr Middleton ever affected by his experiences in France?'

'He never had the nightmare, or anything of that, so far as we ever heard,' said Mrs Tebbutt.

'Did he ever appear to suffer from temporary loss of memory?'

'No. He had a very keen memory, especially in little things. Quite trying it was at times. And always on the fidget till his orders were carried out. Once his memory came back, it came back for good, you might say.'

'He went to bed early that night, I think?' said Mrs Bradley.

'Very early for him it was, madam. At half-past ten he went upstairs, and we never heard another sound of him.'

'Now this is the critical point of the story, it seems to me,' said Mrs Bradley briskly. 'I suppose the police are perfectly satisfied that when your son went into the dining-room at a quarter-past eleven and saw him lying on the settee, that Mr Middleton was dead?'

'They're sure, and the two doctors, the doctor from Stowhall and Doctor Mortmain here in Saxon Wall, are sure of it too. There doesn't seem any doubt about it, more's the pity.'

'Now, why do you say that?' asked Mrs Bradley, eyeing the woman keenly. 'Come along, Mrs Tebbutt. There's something you haven't told me.'

The woman's face suddenly puckered and crumpled. Her voice sounded strangled as she flung herself on her knees at Mrs Bradley's side, clutched Mrs Bradley's hideous jumper and cried heartrendingly:

'Oh, madam, it's my boy! It's Tom! Oh, what shall I do if he's hanged! What shall I do if he's hanged!'

Mrs Bradley soothed her. Then she said:

'Now, tell me what you mean. Don't keep back anything. And then I'll talk to Tom.'

'Oh, madam, I wish you would! I dare not say to him what's in my heart to say. Madam, he's always been such a nervous boy. You wouldn't think it to look at him, so big and strapping a lad he looks since he was turned fourteen, but when he was a little chap we had no end of trouble. I remember once at school. Oh, dear! I was so upset! He thought the master was going to give him the cane, and he turned on him like a little tiger, and bit the poor man in the thumb, and was screaming out and that—I can't think where he gets it from. I'm sure we've never done anything to aggravate it. His father's never thrashed him, never in all his life. The headmaster sent for me.

He said he shouldn't punish him, as he was certain sure that he was too upset to have known what he was doing, but he thought I should be told. We had to give Tom hyoscin to quiet him. And the next time was when he left school and went to his very first job. He threw a hammer at the foreman, and might easily have killed him. That was because the man was going to fetch him a clip of the ear for something he done which was wrong. It isn't temper—not as you and I know temper, madam—it's just his dreadful nerves. And *where* he gets them from I do not know. Even valerian doesn't seem to soothe him.'

'And you think, in a moment of panic——' said Mrs Bradley thoughtfully.

'Who else was there that could have done it? That's what I ask myself,' said the woman despairingly. 'And knowing these turns he gets. It's when he's taken off his guard, you see. Now, boxing, that's different. Used to knock one another about like anything at that. He was a scout, you see, before we came down here. But Tom could stand all that, when he was prepared to be knocked about. It isn't the pain he's frightened of, you see. I've known him as brave as brave when he hurt himself accidental, or at football or anything of that. But it's only nerves. I'm sure he wouldn't mean any harm if only he stopped to think.'

Mrs Bradley looked thoughtful. It was all too hideously possible, she could see. The boy entering the dining-room intent only on the thought of the biscuits he was going to purloin—she had that part of the story from Hannibal Jones—and being suddenly aware of his employer . . . the poker, a smashing blow, a dead man, a boy strong enough to lift the dead man and deposit him on the sofa in such an attitude that anyone coming casually into the room would think him not dead, but resting or reading . . . Mrs Bradley suddenly frowned and shook her head.

Apparently alert for any hopeful sign, the other woman caught at her sleeve and said:

'Don't you believe he did it? Don't you? Oh, if I could see any hope!'

Mrs Bradley pursed her lips into a little beak and shook her head again.

'I certainly don't believe he did,' she said. 'I have had boys under my care who were afflicted with the same kind of nervous trouble as your son. It's curable, you know. I'll cure him of it, if he'll let me. And although a boy like that might strike the blow, I don't believe for an instant that he would have moved the body. Tell me. On the occasion when he bit his teacher's hand, what was the first you knew about it?'

'Why, from Tom himself. He came home dinnertime in the most dreadful state and said he'd bitten his teacher, and did I think the police would put him in prison.'

'And when he threw the hammer at the foreman?'

'Oh, he came home, and cried, and said he'd got the sack, and a fat lot of use he'd be to me if anything happened to father. He's morbid like that, madam. Always thinking father is going to die.'

'The wish is father to the thought,' said Mrs Bradley absently.

'I beg pardon, madam?'

'I think I ought to speak to Tom. Will you trust me alone with him? I won't, of course, suggest anything to him of what you've told me.'

'And you really don't think he did it?'

'From the bottom of my heart, I do not.'

'God bless you,' said Mrs Tebbutt. Then she sat down and cried.

'Now you must bear up, and be very brave about all this,' said Mrs Bradley. 'I want your help. And, look here, Mrs Tebbutt, it won't help me a bit if you remember things that didn't happen! You understand me, don't you?'

'I'm not accustomed to tell lies, madam.'

'I'm sure you're not, or you wouldn't have been in a position of trust and confidence all these years. I'm going to ask you something which may sound a little bit odd. Don't answer it unless you really want to do so. I'm not prying, mind.'

'You're going to ask me whether Tom is Mr Tebbutt's son.'

Mrs Bradley smiled in a mirthless and terrifying way. 'You've answered me,' she said. Mrs Tebbutt shook her head.

'I don't think I have, madam. Tom *is* Mr Tebbutt's son, madam, but he isn't mine. Mr Tebbutt and me have only been married a matter of thirteen years, and Tom was sixteen last May.' She paused.

'Of course, Tom's not legitimate,' she said, 'but I would never hold him up against father for that. Men have their temptations which we're lucky to be without, I often think.'

Mrs Bradley nodded. Tom was explained. So was Mrs Tebbutt. Deep as her distress appeared to be at the idea that the boy might have committed the murder, she had confessed her fear of his guilt. A mother, Mrs Bradley thought, might have been more reticent.

'His mother was a most respectable girl,' Mrs Tebbutt continued. 'Really, so quiet and nice. I can't think how her nature come to overcome her, but she died of Tom, and father brought him up and told me the whole story, quite free, when he wanted me to get married. We never had any of our own except a little girl that died, so it's a mercy we have Tom, and his father's ever so proud of him—quite as proud as I am—that I *do* know.'

Mrs Bradley nodded again.

'Now, Mrs Tebbutt,' she said, much more briskly, 'you say that Mr Middleton went to bed at half-past ten that night. How do you know that that was when he went?'

'He called to father out of the dining-room, I believe, to say he was going. Or it might be Tom that said so. I couldn't be certain now.'

'Did you see him?'

'Father did, I think. Or, wait a minute! Yes, I remember. Yes, of course I saw him going up the stairs.'

'This is what I want to know, Mrs Tebbutt. Are you certain that it *was* Mr Middleton who said that he was going to bed then?'

Mrs Tebbutt looked extremely disconcerted.

'You don't mean it might have been his *murderer* speaking to us, madam?'

'Well, frankly, I don't,' said Mrs Bradley, with her hideous cackle of laughter, 'but it might help the police tremendously if it could be shown that Mr Middleton was dead at half-past ten, instead of, perhaps, say, half an hour later.'

'How could that be, madam?'

'Well, you see, it would mean that various people who can account for themselves satisfactorily after half-past ten, may not be able to do so if the murder took place a little earlier. In this village, for example, people can walk half a mile, we'll say, in ten minutes.'

'What the papers call an alibi, madam.'

'Precisely,' said Mrs Bradley. Her grin was that of a half-fed crocodile as she went in search of Tom. Suddenly she turned about, and came back to Mrs Tebbutt.

'Did you say Doctor Mortmain *and* the doctor from Stowhall had seen the body?' she inquired. Mrs Tebbutt licked her lips.

'I understood so, madam.'

'Ah,' said Mrs Bradley, pleasantly.

Chapter Thirteen

'For heaven's sake, gentlemen, do not mistake me; it was not I that did it.'

THOMAS DE QUINCEY
On Murder Considered as One of the Fine Arts.

'You needn't worry about watching your step,' said young Tom, sourly and rudely. 'I know mother thinks I killed Mr Middleton, but I didn't, and that inspector can ask me what he likes.'

'And so can I, I take it,' said Mrs Bradley crisply. 'Well, look here, child, this is the crux of the matter. Why did Mr Middleton come downstairs again?'

'I wish I knew,' replied the boy. 'He had been out all day, and most of the day before and all the night before, and he went to bed too early, I reckon, and decided he had, and put on his dressing-gown and came down again. I reckon it was all just as simple as that.'

'Yes, but what a bit of luck for the murderer,' said Mrs Bradley pleasantly.

'How do you mean?'

'Well, let us imagine, for a moment, that the murderer was someone who did not know where Mr Middleton slept.'

'Well, there wouldn't be anyone who did know that, except dad and mother and me.'

'Tell me all the people who've been to the house since Mr Middleton arrived. Before his death, of course.'

Tom, his face losing a little of its sullen, rebellious expression, began to consider the point.

'Of course, he'd only been here a day or two, officially,' he said.

'How do you mean, officially, dear child?'

Tom grinned.

'I don't suppose it matters now,' he said, 'but dad and mother and me all had to promise faithfully that we wouldn't let on he had been here a fortnight or more. We were supposed to be getting the house in order, and Mr Middleton, he used to bunk upstairs if ever anyone came. Of course, there wasn't many. It was the postman mostly, and Passion to do the pumping, lent us by Mr Birdseye who farms up Little Horsa, and sometimes an old girl selling taters and peas. Her name was Fluke, I think. But none of them ever set eyes on Mr Middleton, and none of us ever mentioned he was there.'

'But what was Mr Middleton's object in disguising the fact that he was living at the house?'

'He said he knew a fellow who was leaving England, and who he didn't want to let know that he had come into money, so he said, but me, I don't believe it.'

'What do you believe then, child?'

'I believe he wanted to have a think about who done his brother in. That's what I believe.'

'Whatever gave you that idea?'

'It's all over the village. Nobody except the old fool of a doctor who used to be here seemed to think fair play caused Mr Hanley Middleton to die. Mrs Corbett, at the Long Thin Man, she says she knows that someone done him in, and both the Miss Harpers, I believe they think so too.'

'Oh, yes. The people at the Dower House. But they knew, surely, child, that Mr Middleton had been living up here for a fortnight before his death?'

Tom shook his head.

'I don't believe they did. They're proper nosey old parkers, both of them, but never a word did they let out to want to know anything about him. You see, he came in our old car, me driving him from Stowhall railway station, and as I always brought the groceries that way, and the meat and such, mother not liking the way they do the killing hereabouts, though I tell her it's all the same, they wouldn't notice nothing so long as Mr Middleton kept hidden; and that he surely did, for I found him under the seat with the rug hanging down in front of him, when I opened the door to let him out of the car. Half spiflicated, I should say he was, and he poked his head out, nervous as a cat, and said to me: 'Tom,' he said, 'is anybody about?'

'"Only dad and my mother, sir," I said. So with

that he crawled out and hopped it inside quicker than I can tell you, and then he made us promise solemn not to let on he was there till he gave us the word.

'"Where's the room my brother died in, I wonder?" he said, kind of under his breath. "I'll sleep in it. By gum, I'll sleep in it till what's wrong has justice done to it," he said. Then he pokes about in all the rooms till he finds the one he reckoned his brother died in, and made that his bedroom, and that's all I know.'

'Oh, no, it isn't, Tom. Not by a very long way,' said Mrs Bradley gently.

'It's all I'm going to tell,' said Tom. Mrs Bradley poked him in the ribs with a forefinger like an iron bolt. Tom yelped, and moved out of reach.

'Now don't be foolish, child,' she said indulgently. 'Of course you're going to tell me, unless you want your mother and father hanged.'

'What do you want to know, anyway? I've told the police all I can. I don't see why it's any concern of yours.'

'Did you always steal biscuits from the dining-room and take them upstairs with you?' asked Mrs Bradley.

'No, of course I didn't.'

'Why not?'

'Because I didn't. That's why not.'

'Don't become hysterical, Tom,' said Mrs Bradley, gently. Tom's high flush subsided. His face grew set and obstinate. 'I'll tell you why you didn't, if you like,' she continued. 'You couldn't.'

'Oh, couldn't I?' His tone had become brutally offensive, but Mrs Bradley bore with it patiently.

'No, you couldn't,' she said. 'You usually went to bed before Mr Middleton retired.'

'You seem to know a lot,' sneered Tom.

'Yes,' said Mrs Bradley complacently. 'The dining-room door wouldn't open on the night Mr Middleton was killed.'

The sullen expression vanished from Tom's face. He went white. Mrs Bradley continued cheerfully: 'So you went to the window and hoped you could climb in there. Unfortunately Mr Middleton was in the room. You saw him through the window, didn't you? It was dark—as dark as it gets at this time of the year—and it was his white face against the cushion that you saw.'

Tom was sweating. His eyes were large with fear. He bellowed hoarsely:

'I never did it! I helped 'em chase the parson and I see him fall off his bike, but I never done no murder!'

His face was distorted with terror. Mrs Bradley reached out suddenly and clawed his wrist. Pushing back the shirt-cuff, she laid her yellow fingers on his pulse and looked at her watch.

His attention distracted, Tom watched her nervously. She could feel that he was trembling, but he was in command of himself. He was sweating like an overdriven horse. Mrs Bradley released him. Then she said:

'Listen, Tom. Apart from any question of whether you yourself killed Mr Middleton, you realise that it will go very hard with your parents if the murderer is not discovered, don't you?'

'Yes,' muttered Tom, but he volunteered no further information.

There were other questions which Mrs Bradley would have liked to put to him, but she realised that it would be wiser to defer them. She walked away briskly, in spite of the fierce afternoon heat. When she was almost opposite the Long Thin Man, she seated herself on a gate, took out notebook and pencil and wrote swiftly and at considerable length.

Then she sighed, replaced the writing materials, lowered herself very carefully from the gate, and entered the yard of the inn.

Richard had nine measurements of footprints, five kinds of soil, and a collection of seventeen finger-prints, all duly initialled and ready for her inspection.

'The women don't seem to like me to measure their feet,' he complained. Mrs Bradley bought him ginger beer.

Chapter Fourteen

'Have you ever considered how well,
how intimately, you must know a man
to murder him'

> J. C. MASTERMAN
> *An Oxford Tragedy.*

. . . 'the best person to murder was a
friend; and, in default of a friend, which
is an article one cannot always command,
an acquaintance; because in either case,
on first approaching his subject, suspicion
would be disarmed. . . .'

> THOMAS DE QUINCEY
> *On Murder Considered as One of the Fine Arts.*

AMONG Richard's many admirable qualities those
which ranked highest in Jones' estimation were
his willingness to go to bed at the appointed hour,
and his infinite capacity for amusing himself. At
about eight o'clock each evening he announced
his intention of doing his exercises, and, those

performed to his satisfaction, he would go into the kitchen for his bath, the water for which was provided with amusing regularity by Mrs Passion and her pressed men, and then, having eaten his supper and brushed his teeth, he would put himself to bed.

Mrs Bradley had further endeared herself to him by teaching him how to throw a knife. A fine, heavy weapon having been discovered, among other treasures, at the Long Thin Man, Richard spent endless time in the garden, with a target made by Passion, patiently practising.

'He'll kill himself,' said Jones apprehensively, the first time. He picked up the keen-edged heavy weapon and balanced it upon his palm. Mrs Bradley shook her head and cackled.

'Not he,' she said. Then she took the knife away from Jones and, with what looked like a negligent flick of the wrist, sent it flying through the air. It stuck, quivering, in the centre of Richard's target. She drew Jones into the cottage, whilst Richard went to draw out the knife from its mark.

'I can't get it out,' he cried. Mrs Passion ran to help him.

'Mrs Passion is strong,' said Mrs Bradley, watching. Jones nodded.

'Strong as a good many men,' he said. 'Are you thinking about the murder?'

'I am,' replied Mrs Bradley. 'It was an interesting murder in its way, you know.'

'You haven't seen Hallam again, I take it?' Jones inquired.

Mrs Bradley shook her head, led the way into the sitting-room and seated herself on the settee. Jones was using it at nights, since her arrival, as his bed. She had protested at first, and had suggested that she should book a room at the Long Thin Man.

'Mr Hallam's is a curious and interesting case,' she said. 'He will find in the end that it does not pay to be at loggerheads with the village, I think.'

'He always has been, though,' said Jones. 'Stops all their amusements, and so on.'

'He may have annoyed the people before, but not, I think, to this extent, dear child,' said Mrs Bradley. She smoothed the sleeve of her jumper, and shook her head.

'What's happened now to make things worse?' asked Jones.

'If you went to church, you would know,' said Mrs Bradley. 'The vicar, in spite of everything that can be said to him on the subject, refuses to pray for rain.'

'Oh, does he? Odd in a parson, isn't it?'

'Well, he finds the going rather heavy, I'm afraid. He is accused, definitely, by the villagers, of being in league with the devil, as I suppose you know,' said Mrs Bradley, carefully avoiding a direct answer to the question.

'I know they call him Old Satan, for he told me that himself,' said Jones. He laughed, remembering the adder-hunters. 'But what's the connection in this instance?'

'The lack of rain forces them into the belief that evil is triumphant in the village.

"God comes down in the rain,
And the crops grow tall"—

you remember.'

Jones nodded. 'I see. He absolutely refuses to pray for rain, therefore he doesn't want the rain. Therefore he is on the side of evil. Primitive, but, from their point of view, reasonable, I suppose. But I can't understand it. Definitely, I thought, he *did* pray for rain. All the parsons do. Besides——'

Mrs Bradley, gazing at the picture of a blushing girl with a riding-crop in her hand—the jacket of Jones' last novel—sighed and said: 'It's difficult for him. He wants the shortage to become so acute that the people have to go to him for water.'

'Oh, I see,' said Jones. 'Then the faithful will get it—those who repent, and so forth—and the unregenerate will go without until such time as they are brought to a state of grace. Is that his idea? By Jove, you know, I respect Hallam. He's got some pluck. It's certainly a scheme, if he can only guard his well, but I am under the impression—I believe I had the idea—— Oh, well!' He paused, and then said suddenly: 'Good heavens! Then *that's* what old Mrs Fluke was after! Fouling his well with frogs!'

'Yes. He told me about the window, by the way,' said Mrs Bradley. Jones did not attach significance to the fact that she had not concurred in his theories as to Hallam's behaviour if the villagers had to go to him for water. He murmured the words 'Rose-window' under his breath. Mrs Bradley lifted her head.

'I wonder why you call it that?' she said. 'It isn't a rose-window at all. It's a late thirteenth-century quatrefoil. He removed the glass because it happens to be extremely valuable. There isn't so much thirteenth-century glass still in England that he wanted to risk having the quatrefoil panes smashed by youths from the village.'

'But what I can't understand,' said Jones very earnestly, 'is how on earth he could have managed without a ladder.'

'Who said he managed without a ladder? Of course he had a ladder, and of course he had a light. Your old Mrs Fluke even reports that he had horns and a tail as well, according to Mrs Passion.'

'Well, why did his servant Nao tell me lies about the ladder then? Nao said distinctly that the vicar climbed up the wall. I thought it rather odd, but couldn't contradict him. I wonder what idea was in his head? Or do you think he wasn't there at all?'

'Nao is possibly a student of Sigmund Freud,' said Mrs Bradley, with her saurian smile.

'But so are you,' said Jones. 'So, even, once, was I.'

Mrs Bradley cackled and waved a claw-like hand. 'I know, I know, child. But ladders, in the Freudian sense, have no significance for you and me, except when our patients dream about them.'

'You mean——Oh! well, it doesn't matter. But—a Japanese?' said Jones.

Mrs Bradley wagged her head.

'Son of a progressive, and, some say, an enlightened nation,' she observed in her dove-like accents.

Jones, at a loss, harked back to the subject of old Mrs Fluke.

'Did she really tell Mrs Passion that the vicar had horns and a tail?'

'Nothing so depravedly Dickensian,' replied the little old woman. 'What she did say was in the form of a striking, beautiful, and, so far as I am aware, original metaphor. She said, according to Mrs Passion, who has, when she pleases, the supreme gift of accurate verbal reporting:

'"Parson be humbled and parson be exalted by the shadow of the long thin man."'

Jones thought it over, but it conveyed nothing to him. Changing the subject again, he said:

'You talked about the murder being interesting. To me it's about as interesting as that dream one gets of being in a tangled forest with no possible way out.'

'I have never experienced that dream,' said Mrs Bradley with her devilish cackle. 'In any case, the dream and the murder are not analogous.'

'Consider the facts,' said Jones. 'Oh, and the latest—have you seen our village constable?—he's full of it—which, I suppose, strictly and police-forcedly speaking, he ought not to be!——'

'You mean about the poker?'

'The poker. Yes.'

'Too light?'

'Quite a bit, according to their calculations.'

'No finger-prints?'

'Plenty of finger-prints. Mrs Tebbutt's. It's one of the things about the murder which acts for her or against her, you know. There hasn't been a fire in the house since the end of April, therefore the prints are where she has picked up the poker to clean it. Therefore, the prints may not mean anything. Contrariwise, they may. On the other hand, wouldn't she have wiped them off, if they were made when she dealt the blow?'

'That poker should not incriminate Mrs Tebbutt,' said Mrs Bradley placidly. 'It would need a much stronger person than Mrs Tebbutt to kill a man with a light poker by smashing his head in. It must have been a madman's blow.'

'On the other hand,' argued Jones, 'no one could have used that poker, wiped his own finger-prints off it and then imposed those of Mrs Tebbutt. Hers were not superimposed, you see. They are the only prints on the poker at all.'

'Come, come,' said Mrs Bradley. 'If you are going to argue that way, surely you can think of at least two people who would have had both time and opportunity to persuade Mrs Tebbutt to pick up the poker after they had wiped their own prints from it.'

'Oh, you mean Tebbutt and the son?'

'Exactly.'

'Oh, yes, there is that. I wonder whether you ought to tell the inspector?'

'He has probably thought of it for himself. The police aren't half as idiotic as they have to appear in stories, child, you know.'

Jones laughed.

'But there is another possibility,' said Mrs Bradley.

'How do you mean?'

'Imagine it for yourself. You go into the dining-room prepared to murder a fairly active man.'

'Yes, but Middleton was not in the dining-room. He went upstairs.'

'We have only the Tebbutts' word for that, and Mrs Tebbutt did not tell me about the hue and cry that night.'

'Then the Tebbutts *are* implicated!' cried Jones.

'If they are not, then they were most conveniently blind and deaf, from the murderer's point of view. Consider, child. If the Tebbutts are speaking the truth, and the man had gone to bed, he came downstairs again, either at the murderer's instigation, or, if by accident, at the very time when he could most conveniently be put to death.'

'How—conveniently?'

'If the Tebbutts are innocent, the murderer had to get away before the house was locked up for the night. That is to say, on that particular evening he had to leave between half-past ten and a quarter to eleven.'

'Only a quarter of an hour. Yes, I see what you mean,' said Jones. 'The murder had to be premeditated, and he had to know exactly when Middleton was going upstairs to bed.'

'And how to get him down again. The man was certainly in the dining-room when he was murdered. The question is: *was* he Middleton?'

'Now, now! The body was identified, remember. Perhaps the murderer was somebody whom Middleton wouldn't receive in his bedroom, so he had to go downstairs to him——'

'But that implies that the murderer came as a visitor, and the Tebbutts swear there were no visitors. No one ever came to the house. It was Middleton's express command. Middleton was afraid of somebody. From what Tom Tebbutt told me, there can be no doubt of that. He had been in the village a fortnight, and nobody knew it. He was in hiding at the house.'

'From whom?'

'The Tebbutts suggested that he wanted to find out who had murdered his brother.'

'But that was only a theory of my own, that Hanley Middleton had been murdered.'

'It is a theory very widely held in the village, child.'

'Then why on earth wasn't something done about it when it happened?'

'I suppose it was nobody's business, and the doctor gave the certificate without any bother.'

'That's another thing I can't understand,' said Jones. 'Surely, even an old man getting past his job wouldn't have thought it was peritonitis if it was really arsenic or something.'

'What makes you think of arsenic, child?'

'Well, I take it Middleton was poisoned.'

Mrs Bradley chuckled.

'I have an odd feeling that it was not the wrong diagnosis but the wrong man, you know, child,' she said. 'What about the symptoms of Seaman Pike?'

'Yes,' said Jones, frowning, 'I know. But, seriously, about that poker.'

'Yes, what more about the poker, child?'

'Well, (according to the village policeman,) the inspector, his sergeant, the police doctor, Mortmain and the Chief Constable present a united front on the subject of that poker. They don't believe that anybody but the most exceptionally powerful man could have smashed in Middleton's head the way it *was* smashed in by using that particular poker.'

Mrs Bradley nodded.

'I see. That would fit in nicely.'

'What would?'

'The idea that there were two pokers, one with which the murder was accomplished, and another which was merely dabbled about in the blood and brains and left for the police to find.'

'Well, but——'

'What, child?'

'Mrs Tebbutt's prints were on the poker,' said Jones.

'They were.'

'Yes, well, then.'

'How do you mean?' Her black eyes were bright as a bird's.

'She killed him with a heavy poker——Oh, no!
I see. Husband and son stuff again.'

Mrs Bradley sighed.

'It was not ever thus with you,' she said.
'You used to have imagination. Now, I suppose,
through writing those dreadful novels of yours,
you've become earth-bound, a mere elemental, a
curse to yourself and a menace to contemporary
fiction.'

'I am a reformed character, if you only knew,'
said Jones. 'The next thing I'm going to write is
a nice story about murder. Murder's wholesome,
murder is.'

'Did you ever read *Goblin Market?*' asked Mrs
Bradley.

'Yes, I suppose so. Christina Rossetti, and the
heroine's name was Lizzie.'

'True. Is that all you remember about it?'

'By no means. It is a poem, all about fruit.'

'You read it again,' said Mrs Bradley earnestly.
'Never mind the fruit.'

'But I do. It makes my mouth water.'

At this juncture Mrs Passion came in with the
tea. Richard followed her, carrying a plate of cake
and a trifle.

'There's no sherry in this,' he announced. 'It's
soaked in pure fruit juice, and Mr Birdseye gave
Mrs Passion the cream, and I whipped it. I've been
whipping it most of the afternoon.'

'And very nice it looks,' said Jones. 'What do
you think, Mrs Passion?'

Her expressionless face flushed slightly.

'I couldn't have done it better myself. Passion's gathered you some water-creases. It's a bit hot.'

'Passion took me paddling to gather them,' said Richard. 'I cut my foot a bit. Mrs Passion bound it up. Passion's been in bed. He's better now.'

'I let Passion know what for,' said Mrs Passion. 'He means well, Passion do, but he's that simple!'

Mrs Bradley had undertaken the task of pouring out the tea. As usual, Mrs Passion walked to the window and stared out. Turning, she picked up a lump of sugar, gazed wildly for Jones' cup, perceived that it was still empty, and went out with the lump of sugar in her hand.

'She's got about five lumps now,' said Richard, 'and she takes them out and looks at them and mutters: "Seven children by the long thin man." I know because I've heard her. And once she turned to me and said: "Not you for one, little king, not you for one." I think she's an amazingly interesting woman, you know, Uncle John.'

Jones nodded. Mrs Bradley turned to him when tea was over and Richard was gone, and said:

'Has nothing else occurred to you about the murder? Don't you see the strongest reason the police have for suspecting one of the Tebbutts?'

'You still mean to emphasise the point that none of them appear to have seen or heard anything? But then, the murderer was someone so well known to the dead man that the latter does not seem to have suspected anything. There were no signs of a struggle, apparently. Of course, there was that cat. And, by the way, do you think that Mrs Tebbutt

could have been lying when she said that Middleton
had gone to bed at half-past ten?'

'Oh, yes. I'm sure she was,' said Mrs Bradley
briskly. 'As I indicated, she is certainly a most
accomplished liar, and more than a bit of an actress.'
She looked at Jones and chuckled. Then she added
carelessly: 'And certainly Mrs Tebbutt locked the
dining-room door on the murdered man.'

'You bluffed Tom into admitting it, I know. But
that may have been the murderer, not Mrs Tebbutt
at all.'

'But Mrs Tebbutt must have known that it was
locked, because it was she who "discovered" the
body at about six o'clock next morning. If it was not
she who locked it, why didn't she inform the police?
It must have been an unusual circumstance.'

'But it may have been locked quite
innocently.'

'How?'

'Well, I've known people to lock inside doors as
an extra precaution against burglars.'

'Well, but if she was in the habit of locking it,
young Tom would have known that it was of no
use to go to the dining-room for the biscuits.'

'But the key would have been on the outside
of the door.'

'If the door was locked by an innocent person,
yes. But in that case Tom would have turned the
key, gone in for the biscuits, come out again, and
locked the door behind him.'

'Which we know, on his own confession, obtained
by you, that he did not do.'

'Quite,' said Mrs Bradley, beaming.

'What I'd like you to tell me,' said Jones, 'is how on earth you *knew* that Tom hadn't been into the dining-room that night.'

'It was about a quarter-past eleven,' said Mrs Bradley. Jones nodded. 'Therefore it was about as dark as it could be at this time of the year.' Jones nodded again. 'There was no moon. To get anything out of the sideboard where the biscuits were kept, Tom would have had to switch on the electric-light. If he had done so he could not have helped remarking the blood on the floor. He did not notice it, apparently, therefore he did not turn on the light, therefore he could not have entered the room.'

'Simple when once explained,' said Jones. 'Thank you.'

'But,' continued Mrs Bradley, stroking her purple sleeve, 'Mrs Tebbutt could get into the dining-room next morning, therefore she must have had the key, therefore she must have been privy to the fact that some time between half-past ten and a quarter-past eleven the murder had been committed and the corpse was in the dining-room.'

'Good Lord!' said Jones. 'She's guilty, then!'

'Well, the police will think so, I'm afraid,' said Mrs Bradley cautiously. 'If the police found someone in the village who had known this dead man well enough to murder him, they might not be so anxious to arrest one of the Tebbutts. If the man had been Hanley, now——'

'Good Lord! They haven't got to the point of arresting them?' cried Jones.

'One of them. I think so. The question is—which one?'

'I see. You plump for Mrs'

'Not necessarily. By the way, I have discovered that Carswell Middleton does not appear to have been mentioned in the village until after his brother's funeral. Mrs Pike and Thomas Part the water-diviner, independently of one another, are my informants. Does that seem a little odd to you? It does to me. There was an eccentric uncle and a moody nephew—Hanley. Carswell, the elder twin, who would appear to be a possible heir, had never been heard of until after his brother's funeral. Isn't that rather interesting? Even then, no one had actually *seen* him, you know. The fact of his existence was bruited abroad and formed a perennial subject of pot-house argument.'

'I don't know what you are getting at,' said Jones, 'but, yes, it is odd.'

He hesitated and then said suddenly: 'In fact it's more than odd. It's absolutely incredible that there should be an elder brother.'

Mrs Bradley grinned mirthlessly.

'It's more than incredible. It's absolutely false,' she said. 'I don't see how there could *possibly* be such a person as Carswell Middleton. He's a Fluke-Passion myth, invented for some obscure but deeply fascinating reason, all those years ago, possibly in view of just such an eventuality as this murder.'

'You mean this murdered man is an impostor?'

'No, I don't.'

'But he called himself Carswell Middleton.'

'And he wasn't Carswell Middleton, because there never was a Carswell Middleton.'

'Well, then——'

Mrs Bradley leaned forward.

'Did it never strike you that Hanley Middleton might have thought Saxon Wall too hot to hold him?'

'You mean the story Mrs Tebbutt told you?'

'No. I mean the story *you* told me. The unwanted virtuous wife, Constance. The careless nursing. The sudden death from puerperal sepsis. From what I can gather of Hanley Middleton's reputation by talking to the villagers I should say he was a melancholiac of pronouncedly licentious habits with a strong bias towards actual mania. I believe that he became alarmed when his young wife died. He knew what the village knew of him, you see.'

'But why didn't anybody make a fuss and ask for an inquiry into the circumstances of her death?'

'Again, it was nobody's business. If only Hanley had been content to let well alone, what a perfect murder it would have been! Really, I regret the death of Seaman Pike. It was an artistic blunder and should never have been perpetrated. Poor Pike! But still, Hanley provided him, and therefore——'

'*Provided* him?' Jones was horrified. Mrs Bradley's cackle was fiendish. 'But the man must have been a devil! Anyway, I *knew* arsenic came into it somewhere. I felt it in my bones. But how on earth did Crevister come to overlook it? I mean arsenic's obvious, isn't it?'

'Do you remember, child, Doctor Crevister's admission to you that Doctor Little—in other words, our little friend Hanley Middleton, who had telegraphed the Stowhall surgeon not to come—diagnosed that the patient's condition was due to "a nasty case of strangulated hernia?"'

'Good heavens!' said Jones. 'And was it?'

'Hanley Middleton certainly passed Pike's corpse off as his own,' said Mrs Bradley. 'Then I think he fled, and came back a fortnight ago in the guise of his non-existent brother——'

'And murdered this man who's supposed to be Carswell Middleton,' said Jones. 'I know that's what you think, but you can't deduce it from the facts at our disposal. The dead man was identified at the inquest——'

'By Mrs Tebbutt, who tells lies and suppresses truths.'

'Oh!—you mean—I see.' There was a pause. Then Mrs Bradley added:

'There are obvious indications that the dead man cannot be a Middleton.'

'What indications?' Jones inquired. Mrs Bradley waved a skinny claw.

'Ask Doctor Mortmain, child. He attends there every day. Besides, it is quite obvious to everyone but you, that Middleton is still resident in the village.'

'But the dead man *must* be Middleton,' said Jones. 'Consider the question of motive once again. Mrs Passion certainly spent some part of her life as Hanley Middleton's mistress, if we can believe what Mrs Tebbutt told you.'

Mrs Bradley nodded. 'And if we can believe what I have gathered from various other sources,' she said.

'And she is almost certainly little Richard's mother, don't you think?' continued Jones.

'I wish we could prove that,' Mrs Bradley said. 'I think it is very likely, but I should like to be quite sure.'

If she is, that surely gives her the best motive of anyone for the murder. She would not want a Middleton taking little Richard's place.'

'True. But what about it, child? Remember, that only holds good if the dead man is Middleton.'

'Well, she and that old mother of hers (and Hallam and his Japanese, of course) happen to have the most obvious alibis of anyone in the village. It's extraordinary the way they seem to have timed the murder and arranged to be elsewhere. It couldn't happen by accident once in a thousand times that Mrs Passion should happen to come here drunk just twenty minutes after a murder had been committed a mile away. She couldn't possibly have done the thing and come from there to me in the time, as I said before. Yet the more I think of it, the more it puzzles me.'

'What did you say she wore?'

'A hat and a pair of boots and her husband's raincoat. Nothing else.'

'Hm! And you think she was intoxicated, don't you? She sat on the floor, you say?'

'Until by main force I bunged her out and locked the door on her.'

'She sat with her chin on her breast?'

'Looking up at me with a kind of ghastly coyness.'

'You were embarrassed?'

'Naturally. I hated to see a woman—any woman— making an exhibition of herself like that. It made me most uncomfortable.'

'Undoubtedly. I take it that you looked at her as little as possible, and that, in any case, the light was bad.'

'But what's all this about?' demanded Jones.

'Time will show,' was Mrs Bradley's slightly exasperating reply.

'Yes, but how do you explain the conduct of the vicar?' Jones persisted.

Mrs Bradley shrugged.

'I don't think he removed the quatrefoil glass that night, that's all.'

'But that is his alibi.'

'No. That is someone else's alibi, dear child.'

Jones refused to become exasperated.

'Whose alibi was it, then?'

'Well, Mrs Fluke knew the glass had *been* removed, and she declared it was taken out on the night of the murder to give *herself* an alibi in case she needed one.'

'I see,' said Jones. 'So her alibi is dependent on the vicar's, and his on her.'

Mrs Bradley cackled.

'You and your vicar!' she said.

Chapter Fifteen

'Well, I'll let her alone, and go home, and
get another pitcher, and, for all this, get
me to the well for water.'

GEORGE PEELE
The Old Wives' Tale.

'THE next thing to do,' said Mrs Bradley cheerfully,
'is to ask the Chief Constable to dinner. Will you
do it, or shall I?'

'Let's see, who is he?'

'Major Odysseus Featley.'

'Don't know him.'

'Well, I do, therefore I will invite him. I used to
go hand in hand with his mother to a small private
school some—' she calculated on her yellow, claw-
like hands—'sixty odd years ago.'

Jones laughed. Mrs Bradley looked at him
reproachfully.

'And what are you going to say to him?' he
asked.

'I shall tell him he is to dig up the bodies of

Middleton, Middleton and Passion, and re-name
them,' she said.

'Middleton, Middleton and Passion?'

'Yes, child. Carswell Middleton, Hanley Middleton,
and Baby Passion.'

'He won't do it.'

'We shall see. Perhaps he may be able to suggest
some means whereby Mrs Passion's memory may
be stimulated. If she could remember whether they
buried Baby Passion or Baby Pike, it might be very
useful.'

'But she confessed that Richard was her son.'

'Not in writing, nicely signed and duly witnessed,
child.'

'You mean she'd go back on what she told
us?'

'Undoubtedly, to the police.'

'Damn!'

'Not at all.'

'Hanley Middleton will turn out to be Pike, of
course.'

'I hope so.'

'And Carswell is certainly Hanley, you think.'

'Which leaves us with this mysterious corpse,'
said Mrs Bradley cheerfully. Jones, who had tackled
Mortmain, but without any satisfactory result, said
suddenly and loudly:

'Yes, now look here. This unknown man. Who
can he be? It seems we ought to be able to deduce
him, somehow, although I don't know how. He must
have been some sort of acquaintance of Middleton,
I take it? Or, of course, he might have been just a

tramp. He must have been someone who wasn't missed much when he died. I mean, no inquiries seem to have come to hand about him.'

'True, child.' There was a pause, and then, with seeming irrelevance, she asked: 'Have you ever handled a dog which was accustomed to unkind treatment?'

'Are you thinking about that cat?'

'No,' said Mrs Bradley. 'Are you taking Richard to London this afternoon?'

'Yes. I heard from Frances. A telegram.' He handed it to her. Mrs Bradley read:

'Have returned bring boy Frances.'

'I am surprised, rather,' said Jones. 'But I'm taking him. To hell with his heredity.'

'Bless you, my child,' said Mrs Bradley absently. While you are gone I shall go and see Miss Harper. Both Misses Harper, in fact.'

'About the night of the murder?'

'Yes, child. They ought to be getting over the excitement of it by now, ought they not?'

'I should think so. Wonder whether Mortmain would like a run up to town?'

'Unless you are anxious to have his company, I would rather you left him here. I have the vicar to dispose of, and the presence of another doctor is essential to the preliminaries, you know.'

'Oh, Lord, yes. Hallam, of course. But hadn't you better put it off a day, until I get back. If he's violent, you know, it might be awkward.'

'I shall manage beautifully with the assistance of Doctor Mortmain, child. Shall you be back tonight?'

'Oh, rather, yes. At about eleven o'clock, I should think. I shall have to dine with Frances and make a few arrangements about the boy, but——Oh, yes, I shall certainly be back.'

'I am not in the least nervous,' Mrs Bradley assured him. Jones laughed.

'I know, but I don't want to miss a moment in Saxon Wall until this business is all cleared up. What do you expect to get out of the Misses Harper?'

'Goodness knows, child. What ought I to allow them to get out of me?'

Jones laughed.

It was Miss Phoebe who welcomed Mrs Bradley that afternoon. Miss Harper, she explained, was at the vicarage assisting with the last-minute arrangements for the treat.

'And we do so hope dear Mr Jones is not leaving the village for good. We had so hoped to have his valuable assistance with the *Boys*,' said Miss Phoebe, emphasising the last word until it sounded as though the boys had about the same reputation in the village as Alva's soldiers in the Netherlands. 'A *Man* is so exceedingly useful on these occasions. Just a *Word* from him is sufficient. The Boys are dear creatures, no doubt, to those who understand them, but, speaking for myself, I can't *Cope*. I don't really think any Unmarried Woman ought to be expected to Cope with Boys, do you?'

'Well, Miss Banks seems to manage,' said Mrs Bradley, mildly.

'Oh, Miss Banks, yes. Well, they're Trained at College, dear Mrs Bradley, and it Makes a Difference. Training is Everything, I always think.'

Mrs Bradley, delighted to have the chance of interviewing Miss Phoebe separately from her sister, introduced the aim of her visit.

'Training, yes. How true that is,' she said. 'Even in work like that of a housekeeper——'

'You mean the Tebbutts,' said Miss Phoebe eagerly. 'Yes, now. Take the Tebbutts, for example. Most *worthy* people, and, of course, we see a good deal of them, one way and another. Not quite so much *now*, of course, since——'

'I was wondering about that,' said Mrs Bradley.

'The police—most Annoying and Official. "I really can't imagine," I said to the inspector, "what You imagine *We* could know about it. We are Very Secluded here," I informed him. "We are certainly not on the Lookout for Murderers," I said, "and if a Murder should Occur in the Vicinity," I said, "we should keep ourselves To ourselves," I said, "Inspector," I said, "and not Peek and Pry. I am not so much interested in Pools of Blood," I said, "that I need to be looking out for them at Eleven o'clock at Night," I said. Do you blame me, Mrs Bradley?'

'By no means,' Mrs Bradley assured her. 'It would be strange indeed if you did know anything about such a disorderly occurrence.'

'Mind you,' said Miss Phoebe, sinking her voice, 'I don't say I didn't know *anything*. I don't say that at all. But there's such a thing as the Liberty of the Subject, and, in my opinion, it should be respected. As a matter of fact, I have my Own Ideas about that murder.'

'Really?' said Mrs Bradley.

'Yes. On the Night in Question I was very late to bed. We have two bedrooms facing Neot House, you know, because of the Early Morning Sun, and, although I went upstairs at the Usual Time, I did not Immediately Retire.'

'No?' said Mrs Bradley.

'No. I—in short—well, I should not like my dear sister to know, but I am reading the Plays of Ibsen, and I was finishing *Hedda Gabler.*'

Mrs Bradley nodded comprehendingly.

'And, of course, Ibsen being What he Is, and the light in my room being Quite Invisible from my sister's room, and our having agreed From the First to consider candles a Separate Item so that neither of us need make the burning of them an Affair of Conscience as, of course, we should be obliged to do if they came out of the housekeeping, I read on until past ten o'clock.'

'Oh?' said Mrs Bradley. 'How much past ten o'clock, do you suppose?'

'Well, it really is a little difficult to say. At ten o'clock——'

'Yes?'

'Well, at ten o'clock I lighted a Second Candle, and placed it on the mantelpiece. That's how I knew it was ten o'clock, because I always keep my bedroom clock twelve minutes fast in memory of the twelve apostles, and it showed twelve minutes past ten. But how much longer it was before the Affairs at Neot House engaged my attention it is impossible for me to say.'

'Ah!' said Mrs Bradley.

'Yes. I can see the house from my bedroom window, and I was about to draw down the blind while I Prepared for Bed when I became aware that a Disturbance was going on, and scarcely had this dawned on me when the vicar, going very fast— much too fast for safety, I should have thought— shot past my window on his bicycle. There was what I can only describe as a Hue and Cry behind him, and the Man Tebbutt, carrying a hayfork, the Woman Passion, carrying an instrument exactly like the poker with which Mr Middleton is supposed to have been Battered to Death, the Youth Tebbutt, waving the branch of a tree, and the fellow Part, of whom, personally, I should have thought Better Things, came bounding from the front door of the house as though they were all demented.

'It was disgraceful. I blew out my two candles, the better to see what was going on, and pressed my face close against the glass. It seems, mercifully, that the vicar Escaped their Vengeance, but I don't wonder the poor man is in the throes of a Nervous Breakdown. I do not suppose, for one Instant, that he will Occupy the Pulpit on Sunday.'

'Why do you suppose they were chasing him like that?' Mrs Bradley inquired.

'Oh, because of the water.'

'You don't suppose what you saw had any connection, then, with the murder at Neot House?'

'Oh, as to that,' said Miss Phoebe nervously, 'I could not possibly take it upon myself to say. Marks just like Gerald's footprints were found all over the Neot House lawn on the following morning, and Gerald, I know, was shut right away for the night.'

'What *can* you mean?' asked Mrs Bradley, amused and intrigued. Miss Phoebe dropped her voice.

'Where all those human feet had run, and pressed on top of the marks left by the vicar's bicycle where he had turned across the lawn to cut off the big bend in the gravel drive, were hoofprints like those of a goat. What do you make of that, if not something Horribly Supernatural?'

Mrs Bradley wagged her head.

'You are not superstitious, surely, Miss Harper?' she inquired.

'Superstitious?' Miss Phoebe considered the point. 'Well, no, perhaps not. But I do believe in the Supernatural, Mrs Bradley, and if dear Gerald was Locked Away, well Locked Away he was, and *Something* had performed a Satanic Dance upon the lawn of Neot House.'

'And you have not told the police about the chase after the vicar?' Mrs Bradley inquired.

'No, indeed. *Whoever* committed the murder on the Night under Discussion, it was not the dear vicar, and wild horses would not coax me into betraying to the police the fact that he was Anywhere on the Premises at the time.'

'I see. But if the police find out, you may find yourself in court, you know,' Mrs Bradley pointed out.

'And not for the first time,' said Miss Phoebe, proudly. 'Not that I believe in being on Bad Terms with the Neighbours, but a back garden fence is a back garden fence, and nobody is going to nail trellis on to mine.'

'You complained to the police?' inquired Mrs Bradley, interested.

'No, no. Mind you, it was Sophie who actually Threw the Water, but I was with her, Body and Soul, and that is just what I feel about the vicar. How could I feel otherwise, when my duty to the Girls' Guildry compels me to admonish them to Fight the Good Fight and to Put on the Whole Armour? You don't put on armour to go and make daisy chains, Mrs Bradley, you know, and I hope and trust that I shall always find a Little Unpleasantness as stimulating as I do now.'

'But the murder?' Mrs Bradley said, plaintively.

'What is to be, will be,' returned Miss Phoebe. 'And what I have said to Sophie I will repeat to you: It would not surprise me in the very least to discover that the Woman Passion knows a great deal more about the murder than she has Yet Told.'

'I think you may be right there,' Mrs Bradley agreed, and they were about to discuss the point when Miss Harper came in.

'And that wretched Tebbutt never anywhere to be had when he's wanted,' she grumbled. 'Why did he say he would help me in the garden if he never intended to turn up? Taken ill with grief at the loss of his employer! I don't believe a word of it!'

'But the poor man couldn't help being taken ill, sister,' said Miss Phoebe. 'The police questioning and all the suspicion seem to have upset him. So his wife thinks, anyhow.'

'Well, he'd no reason to be upset. They haven't arrested him yet. Besides, he was taken ill before the police questioning began!'

'Callous, sister.'

'Why so, sister?'

'Wait until *you* are in Imminent Danger of Arrest, and see how you feel.'

'I have experienced the feeling, sister.'

'Yes, but Murder, sister, is a Very Different Matter.'

Mrs Bradley, deciding that she had added little to her knowledge by hearing Miss Phoebe's story, stayed another half hour but, finding nothing to be gained by remaining any longer with the sisters, she walked up to Neot House, and inquired of Mrs Tebbutt, who opened the front door, whether Tom would like to earn a little money by coming to Jones' cottage to do some gardening.

'Tom?' said Mrs Tebbutt, eyeing Mrs Bradley with anything but favour. 'Tom's been left the village these three days and nights. Got a job over by

Southampton, Tom have, and very pleased to get out of here, too and all.'

'Whom can I ask, then?' inquired Mrs Bradley, mildly.

'The devil might be able to tell ee. I can't. Tebbutt, he's still a-bed, quite moidered with the police trouble and that, and how I'm to manage without him is what I'd have a rare fine job to tell anybody. What's more, I be very busy.'

She shut the door in Mrs Bradley's face, and Mrs Bradley could hear her footsteps retreating down the passage.

'Hm!' she said to herself, as she turned away. 'There goes a badly frightened woman. This is very different from her previous reception of me. I wonder what has happened?'

Something sang through the air. Mrs Bradley jerked her body to the left. A large hammer swung past her, and cut a chunk of turf out of the lawn when it fell. Mrs Bradley retrieved it, swung it thrice round her head as the arm clothed in white samite once had waved the sword Excalibur, and then darted in amongst the rhododendron bushes that bordered the drive. Keeping well under cover she reached the gate. She glanced swiftly up and down the empty road and then hurried to the Long Thin Man as fast as ever she could go.

When she left the inn to return to Jones' cottage she was escorted by young Jasper Corbett and two labourers from the farm of the ever-present, never visible Birdseye.

Jones was back by ten, and the lads went home.

'What cheer?' he said. Mrs Bradley told him. Jones whistled.

'That's you *and* me,' he said. 'Who is it, do you suppose?'

'I fear it must be one of the Tebbutts, child,' replied Mrs Bradley.

'You'll report it to the police, of course?'

'Did you?'

'Well, no. But then, I was snooping round by night, you see, and they could always declare they thought I was someone up to no good.'

'And I,' said Mrs Bradley, 'was snooping around in broad daylight, child, and they could always deny that they threw the hammer at me. No one was there to see.'

'I bet the Misses Harper saw, all right.'

'Yes, I expect so, child.' She told him Miss Phoebe's story.

'So Hallam *was* up at Neot House on the night of the murder,' said Jones.

'Yes. Too early, though. Besides, we knew he was.'

'But you say Miss Phoebe Harper cannot fix the time.'

'No, but I *know* it was too early for the murder, child.'

'But how do you know that?'

'Because Tebbutt was among the hunters.'

'What's that got to do with it?'

'Everything,' declared Mrs Bradley roundly.

'Come! come!' protested Jones earnestly.

Mrs Bradley cackled.

'Well, what about Hallam?' asked Jones, perceiving that he was not going to obtain a satisfactory reply. 'Did you get into consultation with Mortmain?'

'Oh, yes.' Mrs Bradley smoothed the sleeve of her jumper.

'What does Mortmain think about him?'

'Doctor Mortmain is forced to the conclusion that the vicar ought to be kept under observation for a little while.'

'Where?'

'I suggested my London clinic.'

'Oh?'

'Doctor Mortmain thought it a good place.'

'Not interested in Hallam personally, then?'

'Oh, I wouldn't say that, child. But he is of opinion that the vicar would benefit by leaving Saxon Wall for a time. Mr Hallam is suffering from shock.'

'I'd say he was, too,' said Jones. 'I suppose all arrangements are made, then?'

'All arrangements are made, child.'

'Hallam quite agreeable?'

'To the arrangements?'

'Yes. I mean, does he consent to leave Saxon Wall?'

'He was not asked to consent, child. I suggested to Doctor Mortmain that it would be better to practise a little innocent deception, and not to acquaint the vicar with our proposal that he should leave the village. Ostensibly I was to take Mr Hallam for a drive in your car, and——'

'That doesn't sound too good to me,' said Jones, knitting his brows. 'After all, he could be told. He isn't insane or anything. Not permanently, I mean.'

'No,' said Mrs Bradley thoughtfully. 'But one can't really say that the Long Thin Man is in London.'

'What are you getting at?' said Jones. Mrs Bradley laughed.

'Doctor Mortmain doesn't know it, but I have my own reasons for wanting Mr Hallam to remain in Saxon Wall a little longer.'

'What for?'

Mrs Bradley smiled.

'Because there is a madman after him; and after you, and after me. But particularly after Mr Hallam.'

'Middleton?'

'Middleton.'

'Then you're *certain* the dead man wasn't Middleton?'

'Quite certain, child.'

'You know,' said Jones, 'I can't see any sense at all in this murder, if the body wasn't that of Middleton.'

'There is that disadvantage, child.'

'I mean, what becomes of the case against Mrs Passion?'

'Exactly.'

'Or Mrs Fluke?'

'Yes.'

'Or even Hallam?—Oh, no. There's still a case against Hallam.'

'Oh, no, there isn't,' said Mrs Bradley firmly. 'Mr Hallam left the house too early to have been the murderer.'

'That's what you said before, but you admit that you don't know the time at which he left the house.'

'Tell me, child. As a matter of interest, is there anyone in the village who gives you the creeps, so to speak?'

'Only Passion and Mrs Pike. That's because they are sub-normal. How do they affect you?' asked Jones.

'They don't give me the creeps, child.'

'Another thing,' said Jones. 'If the dead man is not Middleton, once again, *who is he*?'

Mrs Bradley made no attempt to answer the question.

'By the way, I must get hold of Tom Tebbutt,' she said. 'His mother has Made Away with him, as Miss Phoebe would say.'

'Made away with him?'

'As far as Southampton, child. Tom has been removed from our vicinity so that we cannot get at him and question him.'

'Bit suspicious, that, surely?'

'Quite. Never mind. It won't affect our findings. Oh, another point! What do you think of Nao?'

'I never know what to think about the Japanese. East is east, and all that, you know.'

'Sometimes,' said Mrs Bradley, ruminatively, 'I think the murderer did *not* under-rate your intelligence, child.'

Chapter Sixteen

'The "learning curves" showed a gradual
though irregular improvement, with no
indications of sudden transition from not
knowing the answer to knowing it.'

ROBERT S. WOODWORTH
Contemporary Schools of Psychology.

'Now what?' said Jones, passing his teacup for
the second time. With the return into his life of
sugarless, Passion-less tea he felt that a new era
had dawned, and regularly drank three cupfuls at
every tea-time.

Mrs Bradley sighed and leaned back in her
chair.

'I don't believe you've been so well and so happy
for years,' she said.

'Why hasn't he?' asked Richard. Mrs Bradley
diverted his attention by cutting him a large slice
of cake. This effective reply silenced him for the
next five minutes, and she continued, addressing
Jones:

'I wish we could find some irrefutable proof of the parentage. To know the mothers would be interesting; to know the fathers would be stimulating. Don't you think so?'

Jones laughed.

'What would you call irrefutable proof?' he inquired. Mrs Bradley's black eyes twinkled.

'I can think of various tests which would be satisfactory,' she said.

'Blood tests, you mean?'

'Perhaps.'

'You must get the consent of the parties concerned, though, mustn't you?'

'Yes. And a blood test is not more than a negative proof, you know.'

'Yes, I know what you mean. You could prove who wasn't the father or mother, so to speak, but not necessarily who was. Isn't that the catch?'

'I know a man who lets the hospitals have his blood for people who are dying,' Richard observed, eyeing the crumbs which were all that was left of the slice of cake which Mrs Bradley had given him.

'Noble, noble,' she said absently. 'Some more cake?'

'No, thank you. May I have some gooseberries?'

'Certainly. Take a cupful outside if you want to go and talk to Mrs Passion.'

'Oh, thank you. I'm teaching Henry Pike to box.'

'Don't kill one another,' said Jones.

'Of course not,' said Richard, wounded. 'Not sparring. You never go all out when you're teaching anybody.'

'Sorry,' said Jones. Richard's smile forgave him.

'What were we saying?' asked Jones, when the child had left them.

'That Hanley Middleton must have been a surgeon,' replied Mrs Bradley.

'That would account for his being able to perform the operation, of course. Look here, what do *you* think was the meaning of all that business?'

'Just what we said before, dear child. Pike was the victim, of course. Middleton operated on and killed him, and Doctor Crevister, supposing Middleton, whom he barely knew by sight, to be the surgeon from Stowhall hospital, signed the death certificate.'

'It *was* Middleton, then, who telephoned Doctor Little not to come?' suggested Jones. 'Look here, I propose that we interview Mrs Pike and Mrs Passion. One, if not both of them, must know something of what occurred, I should say. Let's tackle Mrs Pike first, shall we? I want to find out how ill she thinks her husband was at the time of his disappearance.'

'I think that would be a good plan,' said Mrs Bradley. 'Let us go now. I wonder at what time Henry goes to bed?'

'No need to bother about Henry. He can come over here for an hour and raise hell in company with

Richard. You know, it's very odd about Richard. I can't help feeling that he can't be Passion's son.'

'Defective mentality is a Mendelian recessive, child, you know.'

'You think he *might* be Passion's son?'

'Well, no, I do not.'

'Hurrah!'

'Get your hat, child. Leave Richard sixpence to spend. Let us be going.'

'Richard has his pocket-money. I don't think we ought to spoil him.'

'Yes, I know. But, morally speaking, ought we to compel him to entertain Henry out of his own pocket-money when Henry is coming here for our convenience?' asked Mrs Bradley.

'Quite,' said Jones, going off and giving Richard one-and-sixpence.

Mrs Pike was reading the Bible. She was tracing the print word by word, and was making very slow progress. She mumbled each word as she came to it, but it seemed as though she must have forgotten the beginning of each sentence before she reached the end of it, she read so very slowly. She curtsied to Mrs Bradley and then to Jones, and feverishly dusted chairs. Mrs Bradley reached out a skinny claw for the testament, Mrs Pike watching her the while, a slightly idiotic grin on her pale long face.

'It be that there story of Jonah and the whale,' she said. 'Parson told us about it once, and I made him show me the place it was writ in the book, and marked it with a pansy off of Pike's grave.'

She looked at them with her timid, deprecating

smile. 'It do be a nice tale, that one, don't it, now?' she said.

Mrs Bradley turned back a couple of pages and began to read it aloud to her.

'Thank you so kindly,' said Mrs Pike, when at last Mrs Bradley put down the book. 'And he really got out again safe? It do seem wonderful, don't it? Out again safe! It do seem wonderful, don't it? Is it true, mam, do you suppose?'

'Oh, yes,' said Mrs Bradley readily. 'Of course it's true. Jonah was a good man. He was a brave man, too. He turned his back on his duty at first, you know, but he was ready to give his life to save the poor sailors, wasn't he?'

'Ay, sure enough,' said Mrs Pike. Her watery eyes clouded over. 'I don't want to go in no whale's belly,' she said, 'and never get out no more.' Her lower lip trembled.

'No, no. And of course you won't,' Mrs Bradley reassured her. 'All the whales are made with small throats now, so that nobody can ever be swallowed any more.'

'Just like the rainbow?' said Mrs Pike, entirely restored to cheerfulness.

'Yes. And a pity it is that we don't get some rain,' said Mrs Bradley. 'I suppose we can hardly remember a drier summer than this.'

'Time I was a gal,' said Mrs Pike, suddenly garrulous, 'we had a mort of dry summers. Ah, and time I come to be married, too.'

'Let's see,' said Mrs Bradley, adroitly, 'you were married in Mr Middleton's time, I think?'

'That's it. Time little Henry was born. It was parson brought my poor Pike up to it. He didn't want to marry me; he said as how I was a Natural, he did. And I beant no Natural. I be an honest woman, because parson did cause him to make me one in front of all the village, and me in a white starched dress and my orange blossom, which Martha Passion never had, no, not in all her life she never did. And then at first if I didn't think it were all no good at all, when my little Henry died.'

'Died?' exclaimed Jones, glancing at Mrs Bradley.

'Died,' repeated Mrs Pike, nodding her long head. Her lugubrious expression brightened, however, to a self-congratulatory smile, as she added triumphantly:

'But I went over to Mr Middleton by moonshine, and he told me to go right along to old Mother Fluke's cottage with my little dead baby in my arms. And I laid him on her kitchen table, pushing away they feathers where her had been plucking two fowls, and I did bid her bring un to life again, like witch did to that there Samuel in the Book. So her promised I her would do it. Her never wanted to do it, but Mr Middleton, he did command her so.

'"Baby may have a bit of a different look about him," her says, "and he'll not favour that husband of yours too much," her says, "that's off to foreign parts out of Southampton Water and tells me he ain't coming back no more to you," her says, "but for all that, you shall have baby again," her says.

"Come you back herealong in three days' time," her
says, "and you shall have the little dear crying in
your arms again," her says. And, sure enough, so
it was! But I was to keep him from harm and not
to let him be overlooked by anybody, for fear he
should die again. So I kept him as close as I knew,
for fear she might overlook him herself, like, her
wicked old tricks being what they are.'

'Then your husband was a sailor, Mrs Pike?'
said Jones.

'Aye.'

'And he went away to sea, and you have never
set eyes on him since then?'

Mrs Bradley leaned forward.

'What I can't quite understand,' she said, 'is how
your husband managed to rejoin his ship when he
was so very ill.'

Mrs Pike looked frightened.

'He be dead. I know he be dead,' she asserted.
'I be a respectable widow woman, I don't trouble
what they say.'

'But he *was* very ill, wasn't he?' Mrs Bradley
persisted.

'Oh, he groaned terrible,' said Mrs Pike. Her
face brightened again. 'He groaned more terrible
than what I ever heard anybody groan in my life.
And he *screamed* terrible, too, towards the finish.
Oh, how he did scream, to be sure! You'd have
thought it was a pig-killing going on.'

'Very interesting,' said Mrs Bradley. 'And at last
you thought he ought to have the doctor?'

'Well, old Mother Fluke, her done the best by

him, but he were too strong for her, were that old devil and all.'

'What old devil?' asked Jones, tremendously excited by what he took to be a reference to the murderer Middleton.

'Why, that old devil inside that tear him and make him scream and moan,' said Mrs Pike, surprised. 'I got old Mrs Fluke to him first, but she couldn't do nothing for him. She told I to call in doctor, else I never would have troubled. And doctor, he seemed to think I did ought to have called him in before.'

'He really was pretty bad, then?' Jones asked sympathetically. Mrs Pike wagged her head.

'Bad as bad can be. But when doctor came the second time, never a sight or sound of him left.'

'But how on earth could that be?' Jones inquired.

''Twasn't on earth, you see, sir. 'Twere in hell,' Mrs Pike informed him with a terrifyingly triumphant smile. 'Oh, he were rare and wicked, were Pike. When sailors be bad they be the worst of any, sailors be. And the old devil, I reckon he were one too many for him at the last. Went clean away from me he did, and the doctor chumbling and mumbling at me as though I wouldn't have kept him if I could. But there! It was just who'd a' thought it, and when Mr Hanley come to die of his operation so sudden afterwards, there weren't a mort of people worriting themselves about Pike, you may be sure. Operation and everything he had, but nothing couldn't save him, and him and Pike dancing hand in hand round Satan's maypole at this very day, because old Mrs Fluke she looked in the dark glass and see 'em, too and all she did, and nowt to be seen in the village but a lumbering old cartload of turmuts and that, so you wouldn't hardly have knowed Old Satan from an honest waggoner.'

Back in Jones' cottage, he and Mrs Bradley looked at one another.

'Pretty clear case here,' said Jones.

'What do you make of it?' asked Mrs Bradley.

'Oh, it's obvious, I should say. Mrs Middleton died, Middleton went crazy and murdered this chap Pike, and the Fluke-Passion partnership found out about it. They began to blackmail Middleton, so he went off, and as everybody was under the impression that he had been dead some time as a result of the operation, that finished things. Then Mrs Passion worked her kid into the Middleton inheritance, palmed off the little Middleton on to Mrs Pike, and now Hanley's come home again.'

'Hm!' said Mrs Bradley. She seemed about to add to this observation when Mrs Passion entered, so she contented herself with murmuring in her beautiful voice:

'"Was this the face that launched a thousand ships, And burnt the topless towers of Ilium?"'

'The thing is,' said Jones, when Mrs Passion had cleared the table, 'how did he manage to get Pike up to the house to *be* murdered?'

'We must discover that. Mrs Fluke would know, but I doubt whether she will tell us. Mrs Pike did tell us, I think, but too much after the manner of the Delphic oracle to be of much assistance.'

'She *must* tell us. Besides, if we knew all about the murders of Mrs Middleton and Pike, it might give us a clue to the identity of this unknown chap,' said Jones. 'I ought to have known that there had only ever been one Middleton, and not two,' he added thoughtfully. He was remembering his conversation with Passion on the village green that time when he had heard from the Harpers and Mrs Corbett about the exchanging of the babies. 'Passion recited his little piece about Carswell Middleton as though it were something which he'd had to learn on pain of death. I knew at the time that there was something fishy going on. Now we know what that was.'

'There are fishier things to come,' said Mrs Bradley, with a hoot of unfeeling laughter. 'By the way, I am off to Kensington tomorrow to interview the late Mrs Middleton's mother. I want to find out whether she ever suspected that Hanley might not have died when he was supposed to have done so. And I want to refute Mrs Tebbutt's incredible statement that she was once in service there.'

Mrs Passion entered at this point of the conversation, and observed that as the dewpond on Guthrum Down was failing rapidly, she thought that Richard would be compelled to forgo his daily bath.

'Once a week, if not more, we'll go up and fetch it down to him,' she said. 'Say that Dick Landlaw what he will.'

'Who is Dick Landlaw?' Mrs Bradley inquired.

'He calls himself a shepherd,' returned Mrs Passion, eyeing with stolid hatred the little old woman whose presence in the house she openly resented. 'But the only thing he'll ever nourish in his bosom is a viper, not a lamb.' She turned to Jones and added: 'And that mother-in-law of Passion's to be ill-wishing the blessed fairy water up above the way she is! By Woden and Thodon I curse her, her and all that she has! May her bones stand out through the skin and her eyes turn black on her like the blackest midnight, and all the ants in the parish eat her alive on Saint Swithin's day if it rains!'

'That's a remarkably picturesque curse,' said Mrs Bradley, writing it out in her neat, illegible script. 'Do they still swear by Thor and Odin hereabouts?'

But Mrs Passion's face was expressionless as ever, although she snorted when she reached the door. Mrs Bradley allowed her to get her hand actually on the doorknob, and then inquired:

'By the way, was it dark or daylight when Pike was taken up to Neot House beneath the turnips?'

Mrs Passion turned and surveyed her doubtfully. Then she answered:

'It was early in the morning. Very bad all night he must have been, and frit that poor daft wife of his with his moanings and carryings-on, so she went for the doctor early—so she told that wicked old mother-in-law of Passion's—and the doctor found him gone.'

'He really *was* ill, I suppose?'

'Ah! And that wicked old woman, she tooken the devil out of him and put him in Mr Hanley that died in Saxon Wall.'

'Extraordinarily interesting,' said Mrs Bradley, making rapid hieroglyphics. 'And do you believe that story, Mrs Passion?'

'As much as I believe any of her wicked old lies, I do,' said Mrs Passion briefly. She looked at Jones, who nodded at her to go.

But Mrs Bradley said quickly:

'One moment, Mrs Passion. Who was it tried the arsenic on your husband every time? You remember how extremely ill he was?'

Mrs Passion fixed her lack-lustre gaze on the wall above Mrs Bradley's head and replied, in her dead voice:

'Madam, that Passion eats the berries off the hedge like all the other childer. That simple he is, don't know what fills belly and what pi'sons blood.'

'I see,' said Mrs Bradley. 'By the way, has Mrs Tebbutt ever been an attendant in a mental hospital, do you know?'

'Our Eliza work at an asylum? Nay, indeed she never did. That's that there husband of hers that you be thinking about.'

'"Even valerian,"' quoted Mrs Bradley, to Jones' mystification and interest, '"*even valerian* doesn't seem to soothe him." And that's how the Tebbutts met Hanley Middleton, child,' she added, when Mrs Passion had gone.

'*In a lunatic asylum?*' said Jones.

Mrs Bradley nodded.

'And have blackmailed him ever since they helped him to escape; I can't prove it yet, but it must be a fact, you know. Think it out, and see, and then find the motive and the corpse, dear child.'

Chapter Seventeen

'And only Dr Pritchard and I knew that
Laura's little son was as brown as a coffee
berry.'

HUBERT S. BANNER
The Gamellan.

'WELL, let's see what we've got,' said Jones upon
Mrs Bradley's return from Kensington. 'What do
you take to be our starting point?'

'That Hanley, according to the late Mrs Middleton's
mother, was a most abnormal young man.'

'Oh!'

'Yes. Very interesting. I wish you had been there
with me. We could have compared notes. She did
not realise the significance of what she told me. That
was obvious. She gave me a remarkably complete
sketch of a melancholiac with marked homicidal—
perhaps suicidal—tendencies, and described a most
extraordinary *ménage à trois* with which she and
her husband had to cope up to the time when
Middleton cast off Mrs Passion, who was then

Martha Fluke, and brought Mrs Middleton back here to Neot House.'

'One thing,' said Jones. 'How was it that no one identified the dead body as that of Pike and not Middleton?'

'No relatives appear to have come to the funeral, and, according to Mrs Middleton's mother—who's had a terrible time, poor woman—the coffin was screwed down by the time she arrived, and she was not allowed to see the body at all.'

'I see. Smart work, but a bit suspicious-looking if anybody had had the gumption to see it.'

'True, child. Of course, Mrs Pike had to be kept away from the body.'

'Because it was her husband.'

'Yes.'

'But we don't *know* it was her husband, do we? It's only what we suspect. We haven't *proved* anything, you know.'

'No. But we shall, I daresay, when the police have exhumed the body.'

'You are giving these theories to the police, then?'

'Yes, child.' There was a short pause, and then she added: 'By the way, at about twenty minutes after the murder was committed, Mrs Passion, you think, was in this cottage.'

'Think? *I know!* Good heavens, I've seen the woman daily for weeks. I couldn't mistake her if I tried,' said Jones. 'You referred to this before.'

'You've seen her suitably clad, and you recognise her step. Remember that on the occasion we are referring to she was wearing a raincoat, that rather conspicuous and quite shady hat, and a pair of men's boots.'

'Oh, but, look here, I *know* it was Mrs Passion! I'd swear to her in a court of law if necessary.'

'That's what Mrs Passion is depending on, dear child.'

'You don't mean that *someone else* visited me on the night of the murder?'

'I believe so, but that again we cannot prove at present. I think it possible, in spite of what you say about recognising her, because otherwise it would be so extremely odd in her to visit you like that.'

'Oh, I don't know. She's a funny customer,' said Jones. 'But what about Mrs Pike as a suspect?'

'Possible, if the dead man had been Middleton, but he wasn't. Besides, I expect she has an alibi. Passion was ill, and I am prepared to assert that Mrs Passion asked her to go in and keep an eye on him. Oh, something else that will interest you. I really believe that we are in a position to be able to prove whether little Richard or Henry Pike is the Middleton heir.'

'Really?' said Jones. 'How so?'

'When I was at the house of the late Mrs Middleton's mother,' said Mrs Bradley, 'I discovered, by accident, that the father was colour-blind.'

'Good old Mendel,' said Jones. 'Colour blindness *is* a Mendelian dominant, isn't it?'

'An important one, from our present point of view.'

'Colour-blind grandfather should mean colour-blind grandson,' went on Jones. 'That's the way it works, isn't it?'

'Yes, roughly speaking. Colour blindness is sex-linked, of course, and usually passes from a colour-blind father to grandsons through an unaffected daughter.'

'But, surely,' said Jones, 'a colour-blind father and normal mother should have normal children? Although I realise, of course, that two colour-blind parents would be bound by the Mendelian law to have colour-blind children.'

'True,' said Mrs Bradley. She poked him in the ribs and added: 'Likewise, if the daughter of a colour-blind father, herself normal, marries a colour-blind man, the colour-blindness will appear in all their children both male and female. Then, if one such colour-blind woman marry a normal man, all the sons of that union will be colour-blind and all the daughters normal.'

'Therefore,' said Jones, grinning, 'if we find that Richard is colour-blind he is the rightful heir, and I have to abandon my desire to adopt him, but if he proves to be normal, as I am jolly certain he will, he *can't* be the late Mrs Middleton's son, and if that happens to be so, he may be an illegitimate son of the late unlamented Middleton, or the legitimate offspring of Passion and Mrs Passion.'

'If Richard should be colour-blind, we shall have to test the Passions and old Mrs Fluke and make inquiries about Mrs Passion's father and both of Passion's parents with respect to colour-blindness,' said Mrs Bradley, with a sudden scream of laughter. Jones groaned, and then smiled at her. She beamed upon him, and added in pleased tones: 'Nervous system toned up again, I see, dear child. You didn't even start at that raucous noise I made. Come along. Let's find something red and something green.

'Cheer up,' said Jones. 'He may not be one of the cases that mixes up red and green, you know. There *are* other types of defective colour sense!'

There was no doubt about the result. Henry Pike was unable to distinguish between red and green. Richard's colour sense was normal.

'Q.E.D.,' said Jones triumphantly, 'Now to get the truth, the whole truth and nothing but the truth out of Mrs Passion and Mrs Fluke, and then we shall see.'

'Very well, dear child,' said Mrs Bradley. 'But it is only a negative proof, you know. It proves that Richard is *not* the Middleton heir, but it does not prove conclusively that Henry is.'

'As long as Richard isn't, I don't care who is,' said Jones positively.

'Yes,' said Mrs Bradley. 'Another point, child. Has it ever occurred to you that there might be some connection between the murder at Neot House and the nervous breakdown of the vicar?'

Jones whistled.

'So that's what you're after!' he said. He paused. But you said yourself he left the house too early to commit the murder. But where's his motive for killing anybody? In any case, I don't believe him capable of murder. Besides, the murderer was Middleton.'

Mrs Bradley cackled.

'Bless you, bless you,' she said, giving him a prod in the ribs that made him catch his breath. Jones removed his long thin body out of reach, and then said earnest

'Seriously, now, give me your reasons for supposing that the corpse was not Middleton. Apart from the blackmail business.'

'These,' said Mrs Bradley. 'Middleton is a very clever man; so clever that his brains run away with him. I repeat, emphatically, that if he had put a bold face on matters after his wife's death, ignored the rumours in the village, and lived on at Neot House, no one would ever have suspected him of anything, and even if he had been suspected, nothing could have been proved. But he couldn't leave things alone. He had to think out and carry through that daring and appallingly stupid disappearance. That's the proof we have, it seems to me, that he murdered his wife.'

'I see,' said Jones.

'And that isn't proof positive,' Mrs Bradley hastened to add.

'Well?' said Jones.

'I don't believe it would be easy to murder a man of Middleton's mentality. He was quite abnormal and is certain to have been insanely suspicious. I am certain he would never have allowed himself to be decoyed downstairs and hit on the head with a poker.'

'I see,' said Jones again.

'Another thing,' said Mrs Bradley. 'At the inquest the body was identified by Mrs Tebbutt and by no one else. That may be a suspicious circumstance and it may not.'

'And, as we know already, the Tebbutts are not to be trusted,' said Jones. 'Oh, I see. You mean, if the corpse wasn't Middleton and she swore it was——'

'More than that,' said Mrs Bradley. 'I interviewed Mrs Tebbutt, as you know. Her information was interesting. For instance, she told me a number of obvious lies, as well as suppressing the truth.'

'Oh?' said Jones. 'That *is* interesting.'

'Yes, child.' She produced her notebook and turned over the leaves until she came to the entry she sought. 'Oh, and she was far too communicative.'

'How do you mean?'

'Well, she didn't know me; had never heard of me; would have been justified in refusing to answer a single question I asked her. Instead, she flung information at my head by not only answering my questions but in supplying gratuitously the notion that her stepson might have committed the crime in a moment of panic.'

'Really?'

'Oh, yes. And produced chapter and verse in support of her statement.'

'Well, I'm blessed!'

'Further, she recited for my benefit a fairly

complete and comprehensive history of Mr Carswell Middleton.'

'*Did* she?'

'Of whom no one else—not even the late Mrs Middleton's mother and the solicitors who have had charge of Richard, and whom I questioned closely on the matter—had so much as heard.'

'Oh-ho!'

'Yes, child. Then she let out the fact that she and Mrs Passion are sisters, and yet she denied ever having lived in Saxon Wall.'

'That was foolish, because Mrs Gant at the post office would be sure to recognise her.'

'Other people, too. Then, when I asked her whether she saw Middleton go upstairs at half-past ten, she hedged at first, and then declared that she had.'

'She may have forgotten at the moment,' suggested Jones, 'whether she saw him.'

'Quite,' Mrs Bradley agreed. 'There was one important point she kept from me, however.'

'What was that?'

'That although she did not commit the murder, she knew all about it,' Mrs Bradley answered. 'That was why she locked the dining-room door so that Tom could not get in.'

'Oh yes. Afraid the boy would raise the alarm, I suppose, if he thought his employer was dead?'

'So long as he could be induced to think it was his *employer*, there was no great harm done,' said Mrs Bradley gently. 'If it had been his employer, there might have been no reason for locking the door. The only point in locking the dining-room door was to keep Tom out, so that when the corpse was identified as that of Middleton, he was not in a position to contradict what was said.'

Chapter Eighteen

'I rather tell you what is to be feared
Than what I fear. . . .'

WILLIAM SHAKESPEARE
Julius Caesar. Act I, Scene 2.

AFTER having been kept under observation for a
week in Mrs Bradley's London clinic, the vicar had
demanded that he should be permitted to return
to Saxon Wall.

'So what about it, child?' asked Mrs Bradley.
Her sharp black eyes studied the vicar's haggard
face, as she sat opposite him in the study at the
vicarage after his return.

'I can't possibly tell you. The wretched
woman told me in confidence. I couldn't have
stopped her, and, from all that I can gather,
Middleton was a desperately wicked man, unfit
to live, and certainly unfit to take charge of a
child.'

'I see. So, knowing when and where and by
what means the murder was to be committed,

you thought you would be well advised to give yourself an alibi.'

'Good gracious me! I never thought of such a thing!'

'Oh, didn't you?' said Mrs Bradley, innocently. 'Then who supplied Mrs Passion with the notion that you had gashed your forehead with broken glass from a rose-window?'

'It was such a valuable rose-window! It was simply hellish of the boys to damage it like that!'

'I know it was. I know something else, too,' said Mrs Bradley.

'What are you talking about?' The vicar had a hunted expression. Mrs Bradley laughed. She was more than ever like a serpent, the vicar decided, watching her, fascinated and yet repelled.

'This,' she said, nodding her head slowly and rhythmically. 'Village people don't understand the religious symbolism of a rose-window, do they?'

The vicar passed his tongue over his lower lip, and did not answer. Mrs Bradley waited, to give him time to make some remark, but, finding that he had nothing to say, she continued: 'Neither do they understand the law of tabu.'

'Oh, don't they?' said he. There was fear in his eyes.

'I beg your pardon. Yes, of course they do. Just as much as *you* do,' said Mrs Bradley, grinning.

She paused again, while the vicar shifted his body as though he found his armchair uncomfortable.

'But not, once again, the symbolism connected with it,' she went on, as the vicar again offered no comment. 'That's African, that business of the string of feathers, isn't it?'

'I suppose it is,' said the vicar. He put two fingers inside the front of his clerical collar, as though it were too tight for him.

'If you wanted the woman, you should have taken her,' Mrs Bradley continued, in a carelessly conversational tone; but, in spite of it, the vicar leapt up and shouted:

'For God's sake, how do you know?'

'The string of feathers told Hannibal Jones the truth. He was a psychologist before he became a novelist, you know. Then he was both!' She chuckled. 'Psychologist enough to know how to make more than twenty-five thousand people buy every book he wrote, poor, lost soul that he was!'

'Lost soul! Lost soul!' muttered the vicar wildly. He began to gabble, as though he had learned the next sentences by heart, and was afraid he would forget them. 'There were twelve of us at home, and my mother and father both came of large families. That sort of thing conditions a man's reactions.' He grimaced. Mrs Bradley nodded. 'I resisted the temptation and chucked her out,' he continued. He gazed, unseeing, at the far corner of the room, shadowed and soft now that the afternoon sun had left it, and added, with a ghoulish pleasure that interested Mrs Bradley more than he could have realised: 'A pity she has to wear those ugly, clumsy garments. She was Middleton's mistress at one time, so I'm told.' He giggled. 'I don't know what the feathers had to do with it.' He giggled again, more wildly. Mrs Bradley watched him, interested.

'And Nao is a Japanese, and clever. Besides, you see, it was the choosing of the summer house,' she said, as though in explanation. The vicar looked at her, bewildered.

'I didn't put them there,' he said. 'I found them, and they frightened me.'

'Oh, yes, you *did* put them there,' said Mrs Bradley gently. 'You put them there after you had repulsed Mrs Passion and driven her away. That's how Mr Jones knew anything about it. That's how I knew, too. It was'—she cackled and became briskly professional—'an almost perfect symbolisation of your emotions. Read it up.'

'Cocks' feathers! Cocks' feathers!' said the vicar. His spasmodic grimaces were horrible. 'Cocks' combs and cocks' feet nailed to the scullery window! Nailed there to keep her out! To keep her out! To keep her out!'

'You're mad,' said Mrs Bradley.

'Mad!' The vicar leapt from his chair, his hands clenched, his teeth gritted together. He looked like a ferocious beast as he stood over the little old woman. She put up a yellow claw and pushed him backwards.

'Sit down; control yourself,' she said. Snarling, and not altogether human, he obeyed the note of command in her voice as a savage animal might obey the menacing crack of a whip. As he sat down again, Mrs Bradley noticed that his left sleeve was saturated with water almost up to the shoulder seam.

'You're wet!' she said, pointing to it. The vicar glanced at it indifferently.

'Oh, that!' he said. He touched the wet sleeve and mumbled unintelligibly. Then he shrugged and lapsed into moodiness. The bandage was no longer round his head; neither could she discern any trace of a scar. His neuralgic pains seemed better, or, at any rate, less severe, for the scarf was gone also, although his thin face bore an unyielding expression of grief and pain.

They sat there a long time. Then the vicar said boastfully: 'I can get them, you know, if only the drought holds. They'll *have* to come here for water. They can't hold out against me if I corner the water supply, can they? I've got a shot-gun and Nao has a revolver. We can hold the well against the lot of them. Birdseye will help! I can depend on Birdseye! Perhaps Jones will come! And there's always Tebbutt from Neot House, and Corbett from the Long Thin Man. They'll all come! They must come!' He ended on a shout of triumph.

'Tebbutt may be arrested for the murder of Hanley Middleton,' said Mrs Bradley calmly. 'I shouldn't depend on him.'

'Oh? But he didn't commit the murder. That was Mrs Passion, I tell you. She said she would—and she did,' he shouted again.

'Then how was it that she visited Mr Jones at a time when it would have been impossible for ber to have been at his house if she had committed the murder?' asked Mrs Bradley.

'It must have been someone else who visited Jones.' The vicar nodded his head as though pleased at his own suggestion. Then he looked cunningly at her, but there was fear in his expression. Mrs Bradley watched him carefully, then she said:

'When I was talking to Mrs Tebbutt she began talking about "our" Martha. She corrected herself hastily, but the truth was out. She supplied Mrs Passion with an alibi—or so I imagine—by going to poor Mr Jones dressed in a raincoat and a large black hat which helped to shade her face—he was to view her by candlelight, you see—and a pair of men's boots, which would effectually alter the sound of her footsteps, so that Jones, accustomed to Mrs Passion's tread, should suspect nothing. Both realised that the fact of the woman's appearance would be the uppermost thought in Mr Jones' mind. Neat, I call it, and really rather clever.'

'Whose idea do you think it was?' demanded the vicar hoarsely.

'Mrs Passion's. Richard is a most intelligent little boy.'

'It was because of the child that she intended to kill Middleton,' said the vicar decidedly. 'You hear me? It was because of the child.'

'Undoubtedly.' She grinned again, and the vicar, recoiling, said:

'You'll have to tell the police about her, won't you?'

'I have no choice at all,' said Mrs Bradley definitely. The vicar looked relieved, but blinked very fast.

'You will have to tell the police! You will have to tell the police! You will have to tell the police!' he reiterated wildly. Mrs Bradley nodded and grimaced. He nodded blandly, too. She could almost see him hugging himself with pleasure and relief.

'You don't think old Mrs Fluke had anything to do with it?' he said, and leered at her.

'Why should you ask that?' Mrs Bradley inquired.

'Just that she also took care to provide herself with an alibi, didn't she?'

'With the dead frogs?' Mrs Bradley chuckled. 'It may have been accidental that she chose that particular night.'

'And that particular time?' said the vicar. Mrs Bradley shrugged and changed the topic.

'Passion was ill, was he not?'

'I didn't hear that.'

'Oh, yes. So ill that Mrs Pike, in Mrs Passion's absence, was compelled to go in and look after him.'

'While Mrs Passion committed the murder?'

'While Mrs Passion was in Mr Jones' cottage,' said Mrs Bradley, grinning mirthlessly. The vicar shivered, as though the air was cold; or, more, perhaps, as though a sudden draught from the open window had blown chill upon him.

'But she *wasn't* in Jones' cottage,' he said feebly.

'No,' said Mrs Bradley. She rose. 'Good-bye, Mr Hallam.' The vicar started at the name, and then looked slightly confused. 'By the way, if you really intend to bring the village to heel, you'll need to find some method of cutting off supplies at Neot House. There's plenty of water there. It only needs pumping, you know,' she added, not particularly kindly.

'I realise that,' said the vicar, 'but I don't think it would occur to the villagers to go up there for it. They're an odd lot. Very conservative, you know. No, I don't think I need fear the water supply at Neot House.' He spoke with almost ludicrous conviction.

'Take my advice,' said Mrs Bradley, as she made for the door, 'and get away for a rest and change. You need it badly. If you don't go, I'm afraid you will regret it.'

'And what's your fee for that advice?' asked the vicar, sneering.

'To be allowed to reach the gate in safety, unmolested,' said Mrs Bradley, giving him an odd look in which amusement and warning were nicely blended. Stupefied, he gazed at her. Then he almost ran to the door and opened it. Nao, who had been about to enter the room, staggered, but recovered himself.

'Mrs Passion, white-heated, to see Mr Hallam,' he said.

'I don't want to—I *can't* see her! Send her away at once!' said the vicar wildly.

'I'll take her back with me,' said Mrs Bradley. She held out her hand to him.

'Come to the gate and see me off your land,' she said. Then she raised her voice and called: 'Mrs Passion! Come! Where are you?'

'Has gone,' said Nao politely, re-appearing with a shopping basket. 'Household requirements,' he said to the vicar, tapping the basket with a slim hand, yellower than Mrs Bradley's own. 'Not want me?'

'Not at present,' said the vicar, gazing contemptuously after him as, basket on arm, he trotted away.

'I'll just let him get along,' said Mrs Bradley, once more settling herself comfortably into a chair. The vicar walked to the window and gazed out. After a lapse of about four minutes Mrs Bradley rose again.

The vicar, who had been standing with his back to a little table, came forward a step or two, and held out his left hand as though to bid her good-bye.

'Wrong hand,' said Mrs Bradley, but as she spoke she stepped adroitly to his right and seized the hand he held behind him. His face went white. He cried out suddenly in agony, and wrenched his hand away. Mrs Bradley smiled evilly, more like a serpent than ever. He stamped on the ground and clasped a badly dislocated wrist. Mrs Bradley kicked a hunting knife out of the doorway before her before she bent and picked it up.

'You'd better let the doctor see that wrist. And mind you behave yourself back here in Saxon

Wall. You don't want to go back to London to my clinic, do you, now?'

He was crouched like a beast in the doorway. He snarled, but did not spring.

Chapter Nineteen

'I do remember once in secret talk
You told me how you could compound by art
A crucifix impoisoned,
That whoso look upon it should wax
blind. . . .'

ANONYMOUS
Arden of Faversham. Act I.

'So that's how it stands,' said Jones. 'Proof positive,
I should call it. Nobody could possibly be as
fond as that of the woman who visited me that
night. Still, "beauty is in the eye of the beholder"
of course.'

'Yes,' said Mrs Bradley dubiously. 'I have
interviewed the man Passion. Of course, a
brachycephalic head is not always a symptom of
feeble-mindedness,' she added in parenthesis.

'And Mrs Pike was called in by Mrs Passion to look
after him whilst the murder was being committed,'
said Jones. Mrs Bradley shook her head.

'No, she wasn't. Odd, isn't it? Mrs Passion did

not leave the cottage until eleven, when he was feeling a little better, and she returned to it——'

'But, look here,' Jones broke in, 'it doesn't matter at what time she returned, does it? If she didn't leave the cottage until eleven she could not have committed the murder. The fellow was dead as a door-nail by a quarter-past eleven. She couldn't have done it in the time. Or do you think Passion is lying?'

'I don't think so. His story is remarkably circumstantial. I tested it in every way that occurred to me. Besides, don't you notice something else that's rather odd?'

'How do you mean?' asked Jones.

'Everybody was just a little bit on the late side with the alibi, dear child. Just think of all those nice alibis. Mrs Passion's is for ten minutes to eleven until twenty past. Mrs Fluke's is for just roughly eleven o'clock. The vicar and Nao saw her, and, presumably, she them, at approximately that hour, you remember. Mrs Tebbutt, who provided Mrs Passion's alibi, did not leave the house until, at the earliest, twenty minutes to eleven, and probably not until a quarter to.'

'Then how did she get to me by ten to? Oh, in Middleton's car, I suppose?'

'Yes. And she did not behave as though she had cut it rather fine, did she? On the contrary, her idea seemed to be to stroll in and then to remain on your premises as long as possible.'

'Yes,' said Jones helplessly. 'But what about that locked door? If Mrs Passion went to Neot House with

the intention of murdering Middleton, how was
it that someone else was murdered by Middleton
instead?'

'We don't know, child. I think there *must* have
been a plot to murder Middleton, because all the
alibis were a trifle late, and had been invented, not
to cover the murder that did take place, but the
one that missed fire. Somehow, Middleton managed
to turn the tables.'

'Whoever committed the murder certainly knew
in which attitude Middleton was accustomed to lie
on the settee. I suppose it's quite certain that the
body was placed on the settee in that position so
that anybody glancing into the room should not
suspect that anything was wrong.'

'Or that it was really Middleton who had been
murdered, child. By the way, you remember the
body of the cat? Now, who was it put down cock-
fighting and adder-hunting in this village, did you
say?'

'Hallam. But he wouldn't kill a cat, would
he?'

'He would if it were badly hurt.'

'Yes, but why should a cat be badly hurt?'

'I don't know, child. I think it would take Hanley
Middleton to tell us that. A man who would
cause his wife to die of blood-poisoning following
child-birth, and who would murder a man on the
operating table, would not shrink from inflicting
injury on a cat, I imagine. One never knows, of
course. People are odd about a good many matters,
but I think they are most odd over the things they

consider cruel. I could multiply instances, but you know as many as I do, I expect.'

'But what was Hallam doing at Neot House?' asked Jones. 'Oh, of course! I remember why he went. He wanted to discuss the question of providing the villagers with water. He wanted to ask Mr Middleton to grant supplies to the villagers if the more obstinate of them refused to go to the vicarage.' He paused, and then said: 'So the murder was unpremeditated?'

'Well, it ought to be urged, in the vicar's defence, that Mrs Passion had already announced her conviction that Mr Middleton would be better dead, and had expressed the firm intention of killing him. The idea of murder was in Hallam's mind, although perhaps not the idea that he should commit murder. The sight of the cat may have clinched matters.'

'Good Lord! What are you going to do about it?'

'Well,' said Mrs Bradley, 'one of the Tebbutts may be convicted and sentenced.'

'And if that occurs ?'

'I shall suggest to the vicar that he plead guilty. If the defence have any sense they will see that a plea of self-defence is put forward. You remember how badly the vicar gashed his head?'

Jones gazed at her in admiration. Mrs Bradley poked him in the ribs. Jones writhed, and moved out of reach. Then he asked:

'But, look here, I've found a snag, I think. Hope so, anyway.'

'Say on, child.'

'When Mrs Fluke saw Hallam and Nao at about eleven o'clock, they were busily engaged in removing the quatrefoil glass, weren't they?'

'Were they?'

'Well, what about the time of the murder, then? *Hallam* hasn't a car! And the vicarage is nearly a mile and three-quarters from Neot House, isn't it?'

'He cycled, dear child.'

'Oh, Lord, yes, of course. Well, what are we going to do now?'

'Get out of Saxon Wall as soon as possible. We've made it too hot to hold us.' She cackled harshly.

'Taking Richard?'

'That depends. Henry ought to have his rights, I think.'

'And I want Richard.'

'So does Mrs Passion.'

'Well, she can't have him. She sacrificed him to Mammon once, and she can do it again. I'm for clearing out tomorrow without a word to a soul. We can always pretend that Richard's guardians want him up in London and we can deal with the Pike end of the thing—the inheritance and all the proofs and so forth—up there.'

'I am not at all sure,' said Mrs Bradley, eyeing him with sympathy, 'that it won't be a great deal better to let sleeping dogs lie. Richard is a dear little boy, and he is very attractive. But he has a bad heredity. You ought not to adopt him. Let him go his own way. You don't want to bring trouble on your wife. It isn't fair.'

'And it isn't fair on Richard to condemn him

because of his father and his mother. What kind of Christianity is that?' cried Jones, amazing himself by his words. 'And if he's a bad hat and gets into trouble later on, I'll get him out of it, or go to gaol instead of him. Damn heredity! He shall forsake his father and mother and all their works and ways! I'll face the risk, and, as for Frances, I don't care very much what happens. It's the boy I want.'

'And you can't have him until you've dispossessed him of the Middleton money and estates, and given them over to Henry.'

'Who, in my opinion, is the rightful heir. Let's have Mrs Passion in, and prove it.'

'Very well.' Mrs Bradley rang the little handbell, and Mrs Passion entered.

'Sir?'

'Sit down, Mrs Passion,' said Jones. 'We now know all about the murder of Mr Middleton, and——'

'I didn't do it, Mr Jones. No, neither with the bow of Jonathan nor the sling of David, nor with Saul's sword on which he killed himself, nor with the help of any mighty men of valour.'

'We know all that. Do you know who did kill him?'

'I do. He were struck dead by the hand of heaven. "Vengeance is Mine: I will repay, saith the Lord!" And sure enough so it was. I beant rightly certain whether I would have lifted my hand or no, when it came to it, but it did not come to it. He was even laid back again on the sofy, nicely disposed.

"In the midst of life we are in death," and alive he looked, but when I spoke to him, he, having ears, heard me not, and, having eyes, saw me not, and, having lips, neither kissed me nor spoke to me.

'And whose son is Richard?' asked Jones, not attempting to challenge her identification of the murdered man.

Mrs Passion answered:

'He is my natural son, by Hanley Middleton, who be dead.'

'And who, then, is Henry Pike?'

'He also is Hanley Middleton's son, but by his lawful wedded wife, who be also dead, too and all.'

Jones said: 'I want to adopt Richard, Mrs Passion.'

She nodded, and suddenly giggled.

'Why not?' she said. 'He's a nice little fellow, although I say it.'

'You have no objection?'

She shook her head. Her eyes became glazed and heavy; her face was expressionless and pale. She had rolled her hands in her apron.

'Only, take him away from here. The devil's in the village,' she said. 'I want Richard took away from here.'

'Is she mad?' asked Jones, when the woman had gone. Mrs Bradley shrugged. 'At any rate, I'm going to take her advice,' he added. 'Tomorrow we go. You'll come, of course?'

'Yes, I shall come,' said Mrs Bradley. 'The devil's in the village! How extraordinarily true. Is she giving us a hint, I wonder, or did the words slip out by accident?'

She cackled mirthlessly.

'I *would* like to know about that alibi,' said Jones. 'Do you think she'd tell me if I asked her point-blank?'

'She might.'

Jones went to the door and called out: 'I say, Mrs Passion, could I trouble you again?'

She came at once, and stood waiting to hear what he had to say.

'That night—the night when Middleton was murdered,' Jones began.

'Sir?'

'Was it you who came here, or was it Mrs Tebbutt?'

'It was neither, Mr Jones.'

'Who was it, then?'

'It was someone sent.'

'Sent?'

'Yes, sir. By that wicked old Fluke, to get me into trouble.'

'What on earth do you mean?'

'It was Mrs Tebbutt, my sister that is. But she never knew. It was wicked old Fluke, putting it on her.'

'Hypnotising her?'

Mrs Passion shook her head. The word meant nothing to her.

'Her told I to tell ee not to go helping parson at that there old treat.'

'Oh, did she? Why shouldn't I?'

'Her cast it up and see it were an unlucky day for ee, that's all.'

'Is this a warning, Mrs Passion?' asked Jones, curious to hear what she would reply to the question.

'Parson's hurt his hand,' said Mrs Passion unconcernedly. Jones exchanged glances with Mrs Bradley.

'It's certainly uncanny,' she said, suddenly leaning forward and gazing intently and unwinkingly at Mrs Passion.

'Yes, mam,' said Mrs Passion, in her dull flat voice, as though she were agreeing to something that Mrs Bradley had said. Mrs Bradley said quietly and distinctly:

'Who killed Hanley Middleton?'

'Parson killed him.'

'Why?'

'I don't remember for why.'

'Why did *you* intend to kill him?'

'My mother told me to. Her told me as Mr Middleton had wronged me.'

'When was that?'

'Long enough ago. I don't remember when. I don't want to remember. I won't remember. I can't bear to remember.'

'Oh, yes,' said Mrs Bradley. 'Yes, you can. Tell me when it was.'

'Nay, I don't want to.'

'Yes, you do. You know you do. Tell me, and then that will be the end of it, and you won't be troubled with it again.'

'Nay, I won't tell ee. I won't tell anybody. You'll tell Mr Jones, and I can't abide for him to know. Don't ee tell Mr Jones, now, will ee?'

'Tell him yourself, then. He won't mind.'

'All right, I'll tell him. It was when I were eighteen, Mr Jones. I be only just on thirty now. Ay, I know you'd think I were more, but I amna.'

She paused, her mouth working, her breath coming with a slightly snoring sound, and her eyes open but obviously sightless. She was completely hypnotised, and, having once been brought to the point of confession, made no more ado, but told them the pitiful story. At the end of it she came out of the hypnotic trance a trifle sleepy, but otherwise normal, and appeared to have no recollection of it. Mrs Bradley talked to her awhile of household affairs and then dismissed her.

'So old Mrs Fluke was at the bottom of the affair. She knew Middleton's reputation before ever she sent the girl to service at Neot House, it seems,' said Jones. 'The question is, what are we to do now if one of the Tebbutts is arrested for the murder?'

'It depends which one is arrested,' said Mrs Bradley.

'Which one?' said Jones.

'Certainly. Mrs Tebbutt has no alibi, dear child.'

'Why, of course she has! Didn't she come to me to cover Mrs Passion?'

'Yes, indeed she did,' said Mrs Bradley definitely.

'Well, that was her alibi, then.'

'But was it?' Her black eyes, sharp as a bird's, met his. '*Was it?* What was she doing between half-past ten and ten to eleven, then, child?'

'But I can't understand! You said that the vicar committed the murder!'

'Well, he had the opportunity, you know, and, in a sense, the motive.'

'And now you say that Mrs Tebbutt did it.'

'Do I, child?'

'And before that you said definitely that it must be Middleton. You mean you don't know which one of them it was?'

Mrs Bradley cackled.

'The vicar is suffering from a severe nervous breakdown,' she informed him. 'Frankly, at the moment, child, he's mad. It's impossible to credit what he says. I'm having him moved tomorrow.'

'You don't think he did it, then?'

Mrs Bradley cackled again.

'Do you know,' she said, 'I believe if you saw the vicar at this moment, you would find him very greatly changed. The bandages did make a difference.'

Jones sighed.

'Poor Hallam. He's such a fine chap, really.' He paused. 'That brings us back to Mrs Tebbutt, then.'

Mrs Bradley nodded, but, as Jones knew from past experience, her nodding was not necessarily a sign of acquiescence.

'And if the police arrest her, you won't interfere?' he asked. 'And on the other hand, if they don't arrest her, you won't put them on her track?' he continued without giving Mrs Bradley a chance to answer his first question. She answered the second, however.

'I shall not put them on her track,' she said.

'But if they arrest some totally innocent person——' said Jones.

'They won't,' said Mrs Bradley confidently.

'What makes you certain that Mrs Tebbutt did it?' asked Jones, curiously.

'I am *not* certain that Mrs Tebbutt did it,' replied Mrs Bradley. 'It is still quite possible that Mrs Passion did it.'

'But, under the influence of hypnotism, she has just said the vicar did it.'

'I know,' said Mrs Bradley, 'and she may be right. But remember, please, that I did not succeed in hypnotising Mrs Passion until *after* she had made that statement, therefore it is possible that the statement is a lie.'

'Well, but why didn't you wait until she was completely under your influence before asking her?' demanded Jones.

'Moral scruples,' said Mrs Bradley blandly.

Chapter Twenty

'My gende friend, beware, in taking air,
Your walks grow not offensive to your
wounds.'

ROBERT GREENE
James the Fourth. Act V, Scene I.

'So, officially, Hallam is gone again, and the vicarage is empty?' said Jones, a day later.

'Officially, yes,' Mrs Bradley replied. 'Actually, he is in hiding in a back bedroom of the Long Thin Man, and will join us here this evening as soon as I give him the signal that the coast is clear.'

She concluded on a hoot of laughter that caused Jones to eye her apprehensively.

'But the Chief Constable's coming to dinner,' he said.

'He's come,' said Mrs Bradley, pointing out of the window, 'and, as Mrs Passion is busy making the cakes for the Sunday School outing, Tom Tebbutt (whom you so kindly brought back from Southampton) and I have been trying our hands at

cooking. The dinner'—she waved a yellow claw—
'will be a cold collation. There is a bird, a tart,
some cream and a delicious cheese.'

'After weeks of Mrs Passion's stew,' said Jones,
'my stomach yearns to the repast. Let's let the
gentleman in and get down to it. Is Tom going to
wait at table? And is he behaving himself?'

'Lily Soudall is going to wait at table. Yes, Tom
is puzzled but obliging.'

'Oh, you borrowed Lily for the occasion, I
suppose?'

'No. She gave notice at the doctor's yesterday.'

'What for?'

'She didn't say.'

When the meal was over, they sat in the open
doorway looking out on the banks of phlox and
lavender and the first shaggy dahlias, while Mrs
Bradley talked, and the sounds of dish-washing
came, together with snatches of conversation, from
the scullery.

'I want the case looked at from another angle,'
Mrs Bradley said. 'Suppose the dead man isn't
Middleton—'

'But are you *sure* he isn't?' the Chief Constable
inquired. He was a man between thirty-five and
forty, looked lazy, was imaginative, and had for
Mrs Bradley the half-humorous deference of a son
for his mother.

'Of course I'm sure he isn't, child,' Mrs Bradley
retorted. 'But I thought it would be nice to have
the bodies dug up, and prove it.'

'But I can't have bodies dug up just as I fancy,

you know. Can't you give your adopted nephew any idea of what you're getting at?'

'Yes,' said Mrs Bradley. 'I don't believe Hanley Middleton is dead.'

'Hanley Middleton? But he died under an operation donkeys' years ago.'

'Hanley Middleton is not dead. He is Doctor Mortmain, Tebbutt, or the vicar,' said Mrs Bradley calmly. 'Unless, of course, he is our innocent-looking Mr Jones here.'

'But what gives you that idea?' inquired the astounded Jones. 'Hallam and Mortmain I met before the murder was committed. They *must* be what they seem. Tebbutt—well, I don't know.'

Mrs Bradley shook her head.

'Consider the supposed arrival of Middleton in the village,' she said.

'Fishy in a way,' said Jones, 'particularly now we've made up our minds that there never was a Carswell Middleton.'

'But the dead man was formally identified as Carswell Middleton by his servant, Mrs Tebbutt,' said the Chief Constable, puzzled.

'Didn't both the Tebbutts identify the body?' Mrs Bradley inquired, although she knew they had not.

'Well, as a matter of fact, I believe not. Tebbutt himself seems to have been a bit knocked over by the shock, and he was under the doctor and couldn't turn up at the inquest. But it made no difference, because his wife turned up and identified the dead man without hesitation as Carswell Middieton.'

'The son, young Tom Tebbutt, wasn't called upon, then, to identify the body?' Jones inquired.

Hearing his name, Tom stepped out of the back door and came round to them.

'You call, sir?'

'No, Tom. You didn't go on to the inquest and testify that the murdered man was Mr Middleton, did you?'

'Not me, Mr Jones. Weren't asked. Dad, he was going, so mother said, but he were still too bad, so Mrs Passion went along with mother, and mother, she had to look at the corpse and swear.'

'Mrs Passion is your aunt, isn't she, Tom?' asked Mrs Bradley.

'Not as I knows of, mam.' He looked surprised.

'Oh, of course!' said Mrs Bradley, as though she had just remembered the fact. 'Mrs Tebbutt is only your stepmother, isn't she?'

'That's right, mam.'

'Tom, when you peeped in at the dining-room window that night, did the dead man *really* look like Mr Middleton?'

'Well, he had Mr Middleton's way of lying down, mam, and that's all I know. Soon as I see somebody there I went to bed.'

'Tom, at what time of night was it that you and your father and stepmother and Mrs Passion chased the vicar out of the grounds of Neot House?'

Tom looked confused and began to stammer an angry denial that the incident had ever happened.

'I had it from an eye-witness, Tom,' said Mrs Bradley, grinning. 'Come, now. Don't waste our time. I can't think why you haven't told me about it before.'

'I don't know what time it was,' said Tom, truculently.

'It was before eleven, wasn't it?'

'I can't say when it was.'

'What had the vicar been doing, Tom?'

'Putting rubbish in our well.'

'Oh, dear me! Whatever for?'

'So's everybody got to go to him for water and say their prayers in church and send their little 'uns to Sunday School before he'll give any. That's why.'

'Yes, I see. And you caught him at it and chased him off the premises?'

'What if I did? They wasn't your premises, I suppose?'

'There's no need for impudence, Tom, especially to ladies,' said Jones, beginning to lose his temper with the boy.

'I ain't impudent. And if you wants to go poking your nose into something else that don't concern you, I wish you'd find out why they don't let me go and see dad when he's lying there all by himself.'

'Hasn't your stepmother told you that he is suffering from an infectious illness?' inquired Mrs Bradley.

'Yes, more than once. But if mother allows of that there Mrs Passion to go in and out, why for can't I? That's what I be wanting to know. I beant a little 'un that's got to be took care of, but so's I shan't go in, do you know what they've been and done?'

'Put a billy goat on guard at the door,' said Mrs Bradley, laughing, 'and not the one that belongs to the Misses Harper, either.'

'Well, for the Lord's sake!—' said Tom aghast. He crossed his fingers and avoided her bright black eye.

'Come, come!' said Mrs Bradley, laughing. 'It doesn't take a witch to see goat-prints on an otherwise innocuous lawn, child. They exercise the goat after dark, you see.'

'Do they so?'

'Yes. After dark. At about half-past eleven, I should imagine.'

'So if I bided me time,' said Tom slowly, 'I could slope in when the old goat wasn't there, and have a look at dad.'

'Yes. And leave the weapon in your bedroom, Tom. It won't be needed,' Mrs Bradley advised him.

'Weapon?' He turned green. 'I anna got no weapon. I wouldn't—you don't think I'd go for to be revenged on my dad?'

'I hope not, for your sake, young man,' said the Chief Constable, addressing him for the first time. Tom caught his eye, gulped, and, at a word from Mrs Bradley, made haste to leave them.

'So that's Tom Tebbutt,' said the Chief Constable, slowly. 'In other words, the young fellow who's going to make it unnecessary for me to get permission to exhume those bodies.'

Mrs Bradley patted him delicately on the shoulder.

'First prize for general intelligence, child,' she said.

'But I don't understand,' said Jones. Mrs Bradley called loudly for Henry Pike, whose face appeared immediately above the fence which separated the cottage gardens.

'Go to the Long Thin Man now, Henry, please,' she said. Henry smiled and nodded. In the quiet of the evening they could hear him running down the road.

'Wheels within wheels,' said Mrs Bradley cryptically. She glanced sideways at the Chief Constable. He was lying back in his deck chair, his feet up on the canvas rest with which all Jones' deck chairs were provided; his mouth was half open and he appeared to be asleep. Mrs Bradley lowered her voice a little. 'The chief difficulty in discovering the identity of any murderer is that there are often so many suspects to choose from,' she said.

'How many people, then, do you imagine might have had some reason for murder?' Jones inquired. Mrs Bradley produced from a capacious pocket in her skirt a notebook and pencil, but before she could answer, he continued:

'But, for the life of me, I can't think why you want to look further than Mrs Passion. She had the motive, she had the opportunity, she provided herself with an alibi and, if you ask *me*, she has the temperament.'

'The temperament,' repeated Mrs Bradley. 'Yes, child. As good psychologists, we ought not to lose sight of that important item. The temperament for murder—an inexhaustibly interesting subject. I have it, you have it, the vicar has it. Mrs Tebbutt has it, Doctor Mortmain has it. To how many other people in Saxon Wall would you say it has been vouchsafed?'

Jones laughed, and protested that he did not know.

'Besides, why drag in ourselves and the doctor?' he inquired. 'We are not among your numerous suspects, are we?'

'No,' said Mrs Bradley, with a peculiarly unnerving grimace.

'Well, who are the others? I really can't think of any more.'

'I believe we once discussed the possibility of the two Miss Harpers,' suggested Mrs Bradley. She leaned forward so that she could tap him on the knee with the end of her silver pencil. 'We might question those women further, child, you know.'

'But they have been questioned.'

'By the police. Not by me. I just allowed Miss Phoebe to ramble on, you know.'

'Well, police questioning is not to be despised. They understand how to get hold of information, do the Roberts. You'd know they did if ever you'd been nabbed for anything.'

'I *have* been nabbed,' said Mrs Bradley mincingly.

'What for?' asked Jones, amazed. 'Contempt of court?'

Mrs Bradley stroked the sleeve of a jumper she had knitted for herself in five shades of purple, two of which did not blend happily with the rest, and smiled reminiscently.

'For murder,' she replied, with modest conciseness.

'Good Lord, yes! I remember. But you didn't do it, did you?'

'Of course I did it,' the little old woman replied. Jones groaned.

'But you didn't kill this unknown man, did you?'

'No I didn't kill him, child. You haven't forgotten the Tebbutts, mother and son?'

'Not father?'

'Father, possibly. Not very likely. He is not on my list. What say you to old Mrs Fluke?'

'Wicked enough for anything, but she has an alibi.'

'Well, you think she has, so let her pass for the moment. What do you think about a motive for Passion? Passion's alibi is curiously suspect, child, when one comes to think about it.'

'Why? The poor devil was sick as a dog. Shouldn't think he felt much like committing murder. Suicide would be more likely, I should think.'

'You have a coarse mind, child. Did it strike you that he was at considerable pains to tell everybody how very sick he was?'

'Oh, well, persons of his mentality are always

proud of their illnesses. Now what about the vicar, whose case we have also discussed. Aren't you going to bring him back on to the list?' asked Jones with levity. Mrs Bradley shook her head at him.

'The vicar has never been removed from *my* list,' she said.

'But Crevister?' said Jones, becoming serious. 'You are joking,'

'Not exactly. You see, Doctor Crevister may have had a motive for the murder which at present we don't know. He is one of the few people connected with the case who was actually living in Saxon Wall when Middleton committed the other murders.'

'Besides,' Jones added, 'I suppose to a certain extent it's bred in the bone, this "birds of a feather" business.'

'This—?' inquired Mrs Bradley. Jones grinned.

'You know quite well what I mean. For instance, if I am with a man for a quarter of an hour, I know, long before that quarter of an hour is up, whether he's any sort of a writer. I can spot one a mile off. Doctors and lawyers, I take it, are equally gifted.'

'I see.' Mrs Bradley pursed her lips into the semblance of a little beak. Jones looked at her. Then he said:

'Look here, what are you getting at? I'm willing to bet anything you like to suggest that you've got something up your sleeve. So out with it. Am I to prepare for a shock?'

Mrs Bradley shrugged.

'I am puzzled by a good many things,' she said. 'And there are a good many questions for which I want answers.'

'For example?'

'For example, child, who *was* it that first trailed the red herring of a Mr Carswell Middleton? It's interesting, that. You see, so many people had it pat.'

'Including Passion, who's more or less mentally deficient,' said Jones, thoughtfully. 'You mean, he'd been pretty carefully coached before I had that conversation with him the day he was mowing the cricket pitch?'

'Exactly. He had been very carefully coached. *Very* carefully. And he really *was* sick when he said he was. And there's another interesting point. We deduced that there was no such person as Carswell Middleton, and it turns out that there *is* no such person as Carswell Middleton.'

'Well?' said Jones. Mrs Bradley, chin on hand, considered him.

'Well, child?'

Jones laughed and shook his head.

'No clue, either across or down, leaps to assist my faltering intelligence,' he said. 'Therefore, say on.'

'How many people still living in the village today knew Hanley Middleton by sight, do you imagine?' asked Mrs Bradley. Jones, knitting his brows, replied that he supposed that there must be quite a number.

'Quite a number,' agreed Mrs Bradley. 'Did it ever strike you, I wonder,' she continued, going off at a tangent suddenly, 'that although Mrs Passion may have needed an alibi that night, she may have needed it for reasons totally unconnected with the murder?'

'Spare me!' said Jones, placing his hand on his heart.

'You think it over,' Mrs Bradley advised him.

'It *was* Mrs Tebbutt who came to my cottage that night?'

'It was Mrs Tebbutt. Of that one fact I am absolutely certain.'

'And she came in order to provide Mrs Passion with an alibi?'

'Undoubtedly, child.'

'But not an alibi for the murder at Neot House?'

Mrs Bradley cackled. Jones frowned in thought, and then he shook his head.

'No. I can't solve it,' he said. 'Give it up, please.'

'I think she had an appointment at Neot House with Hanley Middleton.'

'But she didn't murder him? Ah, another thing! Who hit me on the head that night, do you suppose? The murderer?'

'I think it was one of the Tebbutts, but I'm not at all sure,' said Mrs Bradley.

'You mean Tom's a nervous boy, and saw me crawling, and took a pot shot for luck?'

'Possibly. But I think it far more likely that you

were within an ace of seeing something which the Tebbutts did not care to have disclosed.'

'I say! What rotten luck! I wish I'd seen it. I suppose you know what it was?'

'Well, no, I don't, child. But I can guess.'

'And what would I have gained by seeing it, whatever it was?'

'Exactly nothing, child. As far as I can tell, it would not have made the slightest impression on you. It would not even have caused you a moment of surprise.'

'What was it, then?'

'Oh, just an empty room in Neot House, child, just an empty room. And now stop talking about the murder, because here comes Mr Hallam, and I don't want to upset his nerves. Aha! And Mrs Passion!'

Mrs Passion approached the group very slowly, and, addressing herself to Jones, said, in her expressionless voice:

'Anything I can do, Mr Jones, before I go to bed?'

'No, thank you, Mrs Passion. There'll be plenty of washing up in the morning, but it can wait.'

'Oh, so Lily Soudall don't spoil her nice hands with dirty dish clouts and soda water,' said Mrs Passion.

'Oh, Lord, I'd forgotten Lily! Just go round to the back and tell her she can go, will you! And young Tebbutt, too.'

'Tom Tebbutt?' For an instant her lack-lustre

eyes took on the expression of those of a hunted hare. Then she recovered. 'If I diddun think Tom Tebbutt was after a job at Southampton.'

'He was. He got the sack, and is afraid to let his parents know,' said Jones, with easy mendacity.

'By the way, Mrs Passion,' said Mrs Bradley, 'you might sit in that small basket chair, and tell us, once and for all, who killed Hanley Middleton.'

'Hanley Middleton!' said Mrs Passion stupidly. Her pallid face was a blank which expressed more surprise than any contortion of the features or display of histrionics could have done. 'Was it Hanley Middleton was killed? Oh, of course! What am I saying? No, no! Carswell! It were Carswell, Mr Jones!'

The silence was broken by Jones.

'I shouldn't say any more, Mrs Passion. It's silly to incriminate yourself before you need.'

Mrs Passion giggled.

'If I killed Hanley Middleton I'd be willing to hang, for I'd have killed the devil himself,' she said. 'I thought it was his brother, as would take away from my Richard everything as was his. I changed the little babies over, and give Mrs Pike the lawful one, and put my little Richard, that was Hanley Middleton's son, in place of him. Then came this Carswell Middleton, that was young enough to marry and have sons of his own, maybe. So he got killed dead as an old cow, and my sister, she locked the door on the poor dead body, so no one should see it till day.'

She folded her hands in her lap, and added, with another giggle:

'I do lay my ruin at the door of Hanley Middleton, and after that I done his wife wrong, so sweet and gentle a young woman as she was. I really did ought to tell somebody about it, and it did all ought to be told—crying out to be told, so it be—before I die.'

'No, no!' said Jones with sudden violence. He turned to Mrs Bradley, as though to suggest that she should prevent the telling of an obviously lying and therefore possibly an incriminating tale, but Mrs Bradley, her sharp eyes fixed on Mrs Passion, and her mouth pursed into a bird-like beak, appeared to be avid with interest and in no mood to assist in an interruption of the story.

Jones sank back in his seat and crossed his long thin legs. Hallam's head was in shadow. The light fell aslant Mrs Passion's dead-white face. About her neck was a single rope of pearls. She fingered them with her coarse-skinned hands and suddenly giggled again.

'Funny about they beads,' she said. 'He give them to me when first she went away. She came back, though. I knew she wasn't dead, although he swore she were. He swore as how he'd killed her, like he killed my first little baby I bore to him.

'That was the time he killed the cockerels. I reckon he was possessed. I thought so at the time, and since then, why, I be pretty sure of it.'

'Possessed?' said Hallam, suddenly. Then he

relapsed into his former attitude, and said no more while she told her story.

'He was left the place by his uncle,' Mrs Passion continued, 'and none of us hadn't heard tell on him till he came to live in these parts after he married his poor young wife.

'Mother, she helped bewitch him, belike, for he wasn't nothing only miserable and quiet and staring when he first came hereabouts, but as time went on, and mother cast her spells about him, he got worse and worse, and turned cruel, and hunted for women and ruined two or three good girls and then we what wasn't good, and took we up along of the big house, he did, time she, poor creature, went back to her father and mother in London.

'Thing is, he wanted her to die, but was too frit to set about and kill her, so he came along to mother and ask what was best to be done.

'Mother have Irish blood, and she showed him the way to rot her away like a sheaf of corn that's buried underground. He took and done it wrong somewhere, for nothing come of it, and when they went to see how the sheaf was doing its work, they found it gone. Mother, she was terrible upset and anxious. It worried her for weeks to try and think how sheaf had been spirited away.'

Mrs Bradley nodded, and suddenly cackled. Mrs Passion shook a head as heavy as that of the eldest oyster.

'No laughing matter, living with mother after that,' she said, 'so when my robust lord thought to take himself along up to London, I seemed best advised to go. But with carrying his second child for him he put me off and naught to it but to wed with Passion as had cast sheep's eyes for a twelvemonth or more, tell him never so often I were a bad lot he was better without.' She paused, and ogled Jones, who avoided her eye.

'Meanwhile, herself got with child, Hanley Middleton must have been took demented when she died just about three weeks afterwards.'

Mrs Bradley leaned forward.

'Come, come, Mrs Passion,' she said, in her most soothing and honeyed accents. Then she gave a screech of laughter that almost jerked Hallam and Jones to their feet, and added gleefully: ' "Now, don't tell me a lie for you know I hate a liar"—how did he kill his wife, and why?'

Mrs Passion's pallid face went livid. She put up a roughened hand as though to ward off a blow, but, in doing so, performed a gesture which would have been recognised from China westward to Peru. Mrs Bradley laughed again.

'I am not the devil,' she said, 'and I do not possess the evil eye.'

Nevertheless she fixed her bright black orbs on Mrs Passion, nodded her head slowly, solemnly and rhythmically and stated calmly:

'We know he killed Mrs Middleton in such a way that no one could swear it was deliberate and intentional,' she said, 'but murder it was, and you knew it. *And what happened to Pike?*'

Mrs Passion threw her apron over her head.

'It was nothing to do with me! I didn't have

any hand in any of it. He were the devil himself, that's what he were, so be it, and he told me I must look in the coffin and swear it was himself that lay there, when it was Pike all the time.'

Jones leaned forward.

'What was the purpose of killing Pike?' he asked. 'We thought it was to provide Middleton with a means of escape in case anybody investigating the circumstances of his wife's death, thought that he had killed her. Is that so?'

Mrs Passion took down her apron and faced him.

'I ought to tell you that Pike anyway would have died,' she said, with dignified finality. 'There wasn't no doubt. So Hanley nipped up to the cottage with me as soon as we heared what he seemed like—all the pain and sickness and that—and mother and me fetched him out of the back door and laid him in a cart of turnips we'd come with, so no one would think aught of us being there at the back, and so with him up to the big house and a wodge of cotton wool across his mouth to stop him screaming. Mother was ever a one for the devil's work, and me, I was angry with Pike that had called me a foul name.'

'Yes, but it *was* murder,' said Jones, 'because the operation was performed by an unqualified man. Besides, Middleton had poisoned Pike after you had experimented on that poor wretch, your husband.'

'It was done by Doctor Crevister, poor old man, and a young fellow from Stowhall hospital,' said

Mrs Passion dully, ignoring Jones' remark about
Passion's illnesses.

'Nonsense,' said Mrs Bradley. 'You know quite
well it wasn't! Don't you remember that Hanley
Middleton sent a telegram to the hospital in Doctor
Crevister's name, declaring that the patient had
died, and so the surgeon would not be needed?'

Mrs Passion shook her head.

'Nothing of that,' she stated again with finality.
'Hanley Middleton and me was in the little drawing-
room together and he kept dancing up and down
and saying:

'"So perish all mine enemies!" I thought he was
crazy. I'm dead sure he was.'

'I say, Mrs Passion, who's Richard's father?' said
Jones with dramatic suddenness. 'Will you tell me,
please? I'd very much like to know.'

She fingered her apron and smiled.

'I'll tell ee who it wasn't, for I know what you
be after.'

('The devil you do!' thought Jones.)

'He anna son of Hanley Middleton. There anna
any devil's blood in Richard.'

'This is important to me,' said Jones, excitedly.
'Tell me the truth! You will tell me the truth about
this, won't you?'

'I be. Time I was whoring along of Hanley
Middleton, I took up with a young theayter
gentleman in London. Gentleman never knew, and
Hanley, he purtended to think as how it wasn't his'n,
and so cast me off. And it *wasn't* his'n neither! But
he never knew that! He only purtended! But 'twas

true! And I have the laugh of him yet. Ay, and *you'll* have the laugh of him before you finished, won't you, too and all!'

Jones had never seen her look so animated. Then her face clouded over.

'You won't go telling of him, will you, Mr Jones?'

'I don't see how I can, now he is dead,' said Jones.

'Dead!' said Mrs Passion. A gleam of amusement and scorn showed in her sombre eyes. 'You don't believe that, I know. More don't that devil's hag that hunts beside you.' She pointed at Mrs Bradley, who was making rapid notes. ' 'Tis her I fears, not you. She sees first and she sees fur. Ay, further nor most she sees, and deeper, and now that old pond be dry on Godrun Down, we'll see what'll happen, us will.'

'And what do you think will happen?' asked Mrs Bradley, not a bit put out. Mrs Passion put her hand in her apron pocket and withdrew five lumps of sugar.

'Seven children by the long thin man,' she muttered. 'Ay, you can take Richard, and welcome, and let Henry Pike come into his own again.'

Chapter Twenty-One

'There resteth all. But if they fail thereof,
And if the end bring forth an ill success,
On them and theirs the mischief shall befall,
And so I pray the gods requite it them.'
THOMAS NORTON and THOMAS SACKVILLE
Gorboduc.

'Go home, child,' said Mrs Bradley to the Chief Constable when Lily, Tom and Mrs Passion had taken their separate ways to their own beds. The Chief Constable eyed her, and said, as he rose to his feet and knocked out his pipe:

'No devilment, please.'

Mrs Bradley was about to prod him in the ribs, but knowing her, he side-stepped, and, chuckling, walked into the cottage for his hat. Mrs Bradley followed.

'You believe, then, that you can identify the murderer?' he said, when they were out of earshot of Jones. 'My people are only waiting for the doctor's permission to arrest Tebbutt. That I suppose you know.'

'What motive had Tebbutt for the murder?' Mrs Bradley inquired.

'Middleton slept with the wife. Didn't you hear that? Some old woman spread it all over the village and when we put it to Mrs Tebbutt she admitted that it was true.'

'The devil she did!' said Jones, just behind them.

'I wish they could bring it in as manslaughter,' the Chief Constable continued. 'You can see exactly what happened. Tebbutt lost his temper and smashed Middleton over the head. Any man might have done the same thing.'

'Yes,' said Mrs Bradley, patiently, 'that's if the murdered man was Middleton, child, but I tell you he wasn't!'

'Well, he was identified as Middleton. You can't get away from that.'

Mrs Bradley sighed. Then she grinned. The Chief Constable went out to the front gate and started up his car. Out of the shadows in the parlour rose the Reverend Merlin Hallam. He crept to the window and watched the Chief Constable's departure.

'And now,' said Mrs Bradley, returning briskly to the cottage, '"boot, saddle, to horse and away."'

'"Some to kill cankers in the musk-rose buds,"' said Jones, lighting the oil lamp and fiddling scientifically with its wicks. '"Meaning to say,"' he added, blowing out the match and drawing the blinds, '"he did not choose to leave the oyster bed." Also, "Watchman, what of the night?" Not to mention: "Sister Anne, do you see anyone coming?" and also: "We are seven"—I mean three. Both are lucky numbers, fortunately.'

'Tonight,' said Mrs Bradley, with extreme relish, 'we crawl over bog, bush and moorland to defend the vicarage against all comers. Have you given Nao all my instructions?'

'Every single one,' said Hallam. 'Moreover, he left the vicarage (officially) at just after eight-thirty, and should have been in the castle ruins about a quarter of an hour ago.'

'Good. And you can trust him?'

'Utterly. He hates the villagers. What about the well at Neot House?'

'Our first task is to put it out of action. That has been arranged. We are going to push about two tons of solid stone into it. They will never get it out again without a derrick,' said Mrs Bradley briskly.

'Two tons of stone?' said Jones, completely fogged. 'What *are* you talking about?'

'And can we depend on the Corbetts?' asked Mrs Bradley, utterly ignoring Jones, and continuing to address Hallam.

'To the last ditch,' replied Hallam, his voice confident and excited.

'Well,' said Mrs Bradley, 'good night, then. I am going to bed. "When my cue comes, call me."'

The two men sprawled in armchairs. Jones, in the midst of wondering how soon the vicar proposed to return to the vicarage and allow him to go to bed, dropped into an uneasy sleep. In the middle of a muddled dream he was awakened by a light tapping on the parlour window. He started up, drew up the blind and quietly opened the casement.

'What is it?' he said. 'Who's there?'

'All the village. They are bringing wood. They will burn down the vicarage. Come at once.' It was Hallam's servant Nao. 'There must be twenty or thirty people. All are angry, and the morning comes.'

Jones went to the door and opened it, and, as the Japanese entered, Mrs Bradley, fearful and wonderful in a bright blue silk dressing-gown on which great dragons, gold, and red-gold and bronze, sprawled in the insolent splendour of Chinese hideousness, came downstairs and observed in her mellifluous voice:

'There's only one thing for it, Jones, my friend. The long thin man will have to come to life on Guthrum Down. That leopard skin from the hearth. The shortest prop—no, the longest copper-stick. The blue-bag on your cheeks and arms and thighs. Quick, get your clothes off while I find the properties!'

She darted into the kitchen. It took her three minutes to get Jones into his impromptu fancy dress. When he was dressed, he looked taller and thinner than ever. Mrs Bradley applied the damp blue-bag freely to his face to act as a disguise.

'Now, up the lane with you, as though you were coming upon the vicarage from Guthrum Down,' she said, 'whilst we drive your car to the multitude, and cry the tidings of terror. Hurry! You've got your boots on for comfort, but take them off if you can before the crowd sees you.'

Nao ran out to start up the car. Dawn was near. A greyness, in which their faces looked pale, unearthly and elfin, gave faery significance to the adventure. The car sped on its way, and Jones suddenly shouted in Mrs Bradley's ear:

'"Cry havoc! And let slip the dogs of war!"'

Mrs Bradley gave a yelp of glee and shouted in reply:

'"If music be the food of love, play on!"'

Nao trod on the accelerator, and the car leapt onward down the westward-running road. About a hundred yards from the vicarage he turned it sharply to the right up a lane that ended in a sheep-walk that led on to Guthrum Down. He stopped the engine, climbed down, and motioned Jones to get out. Mystified, a prey to a kind of nightmare excitement, but absolutely obedient, Jones sat on the dewy grass and pulled off his boots while the others drove away.

As soon as the car had disappeared round the bend and the sound of its engine had faded, Jones became aware of the tumult of the besiegers. The English blood in his lean and ludicrously-decorated body turned dogged, however, at the thought of danger, and the Welsh blood which he inherited from his father thrilled to the thought of a fight against odds. He was amused at the idea of descending upon the village in the guise of an avenging elemental spirit and frightening it out of its life; the notion filled him with great gusts of invincible laughter. Putting his boots on again, and beginning to run because the early morning air, with its misty promise of another scorching, cloudless day, was at the moment chilly against his naked body, he made good time down the lane, and, swinging his copper-stick and singing a Welsh revivalist hymn, he came upon the assembled villagers like the Assyrian—a particularly masterful and imposing wolf upon a rather disorderly fold.

The first person to become critically aware of his presence was a certain Elias Pibb. He was a loutish boy of two-and-twenty, and he had a flaming, crackling branch of apple wood in his left hand, and in his right a heavy stone.

Jones had taken the impromptu torch from him and kicked him with a (by this time) bootless foot before the rustic was aware of his presence. The yell he gave when he turned and saw Jones clove through the general hubbub like the noise of a shell above the distant sound of rifle shooting, and caused a dozen heads to turn.

'The long thin man! The long thin man!' he yelled. Jones, who had stubbed his toe on the youth and was feeling proportionately savage, jabbed him in the ribs with the copper-stick and bellowed into his hair from the rear, 'Lasst uns erfreuen,' and then, at the top of his voice, as the lad, with a scream of terror, began to run from him, 'Shule, shule agra! Shan von vocht!'

Panic spread. The people had believed in the

long thin man for so long that his manifestation and sudden incarnation were terrifying but not surprising. None questioned the reality of the apparition. All, after one horrified glance, turned and fled at the sight of it.

'It's the devil again!' screamed one.

'It be Judgment Day!' yelled another. The women's shrill, terrified voices had their usual effect of turning a sudden scare into an unreasoning, stampeding flight from the horror. They fled, not knowing why. Jones, thoroughly roused by the pain in his toe, leapt after them, brandishing the blazing branch in one hand, the club in the other, and yelling at the top of a voice which had always been masterful, and which now, under the mingled influences of mental stimulation and physical agony was sufficiently stentorian to do justice to a town crier:

'Lero lero, lillibulero, Lillibulero bullen a la!' he yelled. And, to complete the rout, he bellowed joyously (for he had come at last to a patch of yellowish sun-scorched grass by the side of the road and his feet were easier) 'Quot estis in convivio! Na horo eile! Na horo eile! Rah! Rah! Rah!'

The mob stayed not upon the order of its going, and when the last sobbing runner was out of sight round the bend, Jones, panting and sweating, entered the vicarage, helped Hallam, Nao, and, to his illogical amazement, Mrs, Passion, to put out the tongues of flame which were beginning to crackle on the woodshed roof.

Hallam's face was marred with gashes made by stones. His hands were blackened, and his clothing was wet and torn. But he pushed his hair from his eyes with his forearm and smiled at them.

'He's recovered,' thought Jones. 'Now they've shown their hand he's relieved.' He glanced down at his own bare shins protruding from the ends of a pair of the vicar's trousers, caught Hallam's eye, and grinned.

The fire had not taken serious hold. When it was out they spent the next hour clearing away the piles of brushwood and kindlings which the villagers had piled against the house. The well was choked with rubbish of every description, but fortunately the first object thrown in had been an ancient sieve which had become wedged about five feet down, and the refuse which had been dropped on top of it had been caught and held.

'Bit of luck,' grunted Jones.

Mrs Bradley chuckled.

'Not luck, but foresight,' she said.

'You didn't know they'd throw rubbish into the vicar's well?'

'Oh, yes, of course I did. They were depending upon the water supply at Neot House. Nao's orders were to commence the stopping up of the vicarage well himself so that nothing should foul the water. Then any rubbish anyone else shot in would rest on top of *our* carefully disposed rubbish, with the result that you see.'

'And tomorrow——' began Hallam.

'And Doctor Mortmain will be in Southampton,

and won't know that in spite of our serious consultations about your mental health you are still at large,' said Mrs Bradley, grinning.

Jones, who had at last removed all traces of the blue-bag from his countenance, demanded suddenly:

'I say, Hallam, what *did* happen here on the night of the murder?'

'I went to Neot House to arrange, I hoped, that the new owner would supply the villagers with water should things become too desperate.'

'Yes?' said Jones.

'I went on my bicycle and I arrived at the house at about a quarter to ten. I had been advised by Mrs Tebbutt that Middleton was not in the habit of going to bed before midnight, and that he disliked being interviewed during the day.

'I left my bicycle against the side of the house and rang the bell. The door was opened by Tebbutt, and I was shown into a room which was furnished sparely but comfortably, and in about a quarter of an hour Mrs Tebbutt came in to tell me that her employer was not, after all, disposed to see me, but would do as I pleased about the water.

'Scarcely had she left me when young Tom Tebbutt put his head in at the door, and told me, in a whisper, to go as quickly as ever I could, because I was in grave danger.'

'Good gracious me!' said Mrs Bradley.

'I thought Tom Tebbutt was mad,' continued the vicar, 'but, as there was nothing to stay for, I left the house and was just wheeling my bicycle on to the drive preparatory to riding home when the most dreadful hue and cry broke out behind me.

'I admit that I was seriously alarmed, and that I acted under the influence of panic. My nervous system—but I won't make all these wretched excuses. It's enough for me to confess that instead of investigating matters and facing the consequences, I mounted my bicycle and made across the lawn to the gate and so down the road faster than I have ever ridden in my life. What the hue and cry was, and how it affected me, I have no idea whatever; nobody except Mrs Tebbutt knew that I was going to Neot House that night, and I believe my pursuers numbered, at the most, four or five persons, of whom some, I am convinced, were women. No one will ever know what I felt, when I realised that, but for my cowardly flight from a noise and a few stones——'

'So *that's* how you cut your head!' said Jones, relieved.

'I might have saved a fellow creature from being murdered in that house. Poor wretched man!'

Mrs Bradley turned to Jones. 'Has it never struck you that in this affair there is one obvious and unexplained phenomenon, dear child?'

'How do you mean?' asked Jones.

'Well, where's Tebbutt?'

'Tebbutt? Still at Neot House. Isn't he ill in bed there?'

'Is he?' said Mrs Bradley. She grimaced in a terrifying manner and added grimly:

'I am not addicted to the making of wagers, but I am prepared to stake any sum short of fifty thousand pounds that Tebbutt is not at Neot House.'

'But the doctor attends there daily.'

'He does not attend Tebbutt.'

'You can't prove that.'

'Have you noticed how badly the vicarage paths need weeding?' inquired Mrs Bradley with apparent flippancy. 'Or you could consult Birdseye. Anyhow, as soon as Tom Tebbutt bursts into the guarded room where his father is supposed to be lying dangerously ill of an infectious disease, and reports to me that his father is not in the room, I am going to have the police search the house. If Tebbutt still does not materialise, I am going to have Middleton's body exhumed and re-identified.'

'But you don't think——' Jones exclaimed in horror.

'Oh, yes, I do,' said Mrs Bradley.

'I'm lost,' said Hallam. 'But I would like to ask one question. You mean to imply that the dead man was Tebbutt, and not Middleton, don't you? Well, how did he come to be murdered?'

'The blackmail, of course,' said Jones. 'But, look here, Hallam! You can't have looked at the time. I came to you here at half-past nine that night to tell you about my talk with old Doctor Crevister. Don't you remember the fearful neuralgia you had?'

Suddenly he broke off, and they stiffened, listening. From the ruins came extraordinary sounds of tumult.

'We ought to see what's happening,' said Jones.

'They're certainly up to mischief,' Hallam observed. As though by previous arrangement, both men started forward.

'Stop!' said Mrs Bradley. 'You can do nothing that will help matters, and you may do harm.'

'But they're hunting something, and they're cruel people,' said Hallam.

'Be still,' said Mrs Bradley. 'You would only break your necks if you went over there now. It's a very dangerous place at any time, and especially so this morning.'

'But what can it be?' asked Hallam, very pale. Jones himself was sweating with nervous fear.

'I must go,' said Hallam. 'There's something being done to death out there. And where on earth is Nao?'

Chapter Twenty-Two

'Enter a Devil.'—(Stage direction.)
ROBERT GREENE
*The Honourable History of Friar Bacon
and Friar Bungay.*

'WE shall know very soon whether the man they buried was Tebbutt,' said Mrs Bradley. 'The Chief Constable was sufficiently impressed to have applied for an exhumation order.'

Jones was pleased; Hallam horrified.

'They're not going to disturb my churchyard?'

'I wonder what the deuce that noise in the castle ruins was?' said Jones, to change the subject. They argued about it, on and off, until the middle of the morning. Then Jones, who was at the window, called for silence.

'Here's a deputation come to ask for water I expect,' said he.

The water shortage in the village had become acute. Even the dewpond on Guthrum Down was nothing but a disheartening patch of thick wet mud, and the village pumps had long since given up work. Most people had been going to the Long Thin Man or up to Neot House for water, and once a week a lorry came in from Stowhall and the people bought from it. But the water was soon used up, and a week was a long time to wait for more.

Besides, not only the people, but the animals, needed water. The parched grass, heavy-headed crops, and the brownish leaves (already falling from the trees although it was still high summer) were dying under the unfailing, dry, fierce, unaccustomed heat of the sun.

Jones put his head out of the window as the procession of villagers reached the vicarage gate. In his right hand he held a small automatic pistol, and in his left a white handkerchief. He surveyed them as they came to a halt before his quizzical and critical gaze. They were too numerous to be called a deputation and they did not like the look of Jones' automatic. There was a certain amount of embarrassment and scuffling, and an apparent universal desire to let someone else get within range of it.

They did not look a very fearsome lot. Nearly all were women, for the men had not dared to absent themselves from work. Foremost among the crowd there was certainly old Mrs Fluke, kept in the place of honour, Jones suspected, by repeated proddings from the rear, and near her were Mrs Pike and the water diviner, Thomas Part. Of Mrs Passion there was nothing to be seen, and Mrs Tebbutt did not appear to have joined the muster.

Jones raised his voice and spoke cheerfully but with decision.

'I have a loaded gun here and I will fire it if anyone advances beyond that gateway without my permission. If you have anything to say to the vicar you are to send forward a small deputation when I wave my handkerchief.'

'We wants some water, and parson knows it,' shouted a voice.

'Why don't he let us help ourselves?' queried another.

'Water be free to all, beant it?'

'What call have he not to pray for rain, then?'

'We ain't sending no deppitation. Us reckons you got the police up there along of ee.'

The last came from the water diviner, who carried his hazel wand. Jones made no reply. The others were out of sight of the crowd. Suddenly a stone smashed against the wall of the house near the window, so he fired the pistol, but high above their heads. Some of the women screamed; some retreated. The boldest shook their fists at him, and one of them shouted:

'You dursn't do that if our chaps was here, you dirty Londoner!'

'Who brought Old Satan walking from Godrun Down?' another screamed.

'Stealing other folks' little 'uns!'

'Who killed Middleton?'

'Who slep' along of witches and harlots?'

'Who ruined doctor's serving wench?'

'They'll rush the house in a minute,' Jones said,

over his shoulder. He was wrong. After a short colloquy and a shower of stones and opprobrious remarks and epithets, the little mob moved off.

'We may expect them back this evening when the men come home from work,' said Hallam. But he did not seem perturbed. Instead, it was as though, his blood mounting to battle fever, his mind and spirit were gaining in temper and resolution. Although not essentially a man of action, he had the power of dramatising himself and of willing himself into a frame of mind at once victorious and serene.

The time was now almost mid-day. During the early part of the morning Lily Soudall had joined the party at the vicarage, but of Tom Tebbutt there was no sign at all. Jones found himself wondering whether the lad had broken into his father's sick-room, and, if so, what he had discovered there. Suddenly he found Lily at his elbow.

'Oh, sir,' she said, 'that Japanee!'

'Nao? What about him?' asked Jones.

'He's burying Mrs Fluke, and if she rot away, I'll never be quit of dreaming about her, sir.'

'Stay here a minute and keep your eyes skinned. If you see anybody coming, even if it's only the postman, yell blue murder. Understand?'

'Supposing it's my mother, sir, come to see what I be at?'

'Yell just the same. Don't fail us. Where is Nao?'

'In the garden.'

'What in hell are you up to?' asked Jones, when he had found him.

'Rotten tree, big magic, and that old Fluke, denizen of above, shall be seized by a demon and translated,' replied the Japanese.

'Oh, rot. I thought you had shed all those ideas. Didn't Mr Hallam convert you?'

'Mr Hallam, yes. But that old Fluke, I have concocted her from the wood of the guelder rose, and may she rot away with this tree which fortune has bestowed upon this garden.'

'Look here,' said Jones, exasperated, 'is it something in the air that makes witchcraft flourish here? You'd better not let Mr Hallam catch you at this, you know, so near the churchyard.'

Instead of replying, Nao began to walk towards the wall which separated the vicarage garden from the churchyard. He looked round once to make certain that Jones was following him.

'You make Middleton body not to be Middleton, I think?' he said quietly, when they reached the gate in the wall which was the vicar's short cut to the church.

'Who told you that?' asked Jones, for he had supposed that Mrs Bradley would keep that one of her theories a dead secret until the exhumation order had been put through. Nao inclined his head in the direction of the house.

'The small wise woman said it to me. Has thought of body-snatchers tonight or some time very soon.'

'Body-snatchers?'

'Should said body not be Middleton,' the Japanese patiently explained, 'certain persons unknown would have interest in keeping same dark.'

'Good Lord! Of course they would!' said Jones. 'I wonder what we ought to do?'

'Said honourable woman refuses to telephone police. Desperate and highly illegal act can only be performed under cover of all-enveloping night, I think.'

'That's right,' Jones agreed. A thought struck him. 'I say, Nao, what really happened here on the night of the murder?'

'I cannot tell. Clerical individual came on bicycle. Head cut. Hot and bothered. Must take out priceless stained glass.'

'Oh, so that bit of the story is true?'

'Quite true. Much concerned for priceless glass to save it from beastly people.'

'And he had a ladder?'

'No ladder,' said the Japanese unhappily.

'Come, come,' said Jones. 'Of course he had a ladder. And he said he was thankful it was a quatrefoil and not a trefoil, didn't he? And with you a little knowledge is a dangerous thing, isn't it?'

He walked off whistling. The Japanese gazed after him unresentfully, then shut the gate in the wall, and walked round the back of the house to the kitchen. An old-fashioned dresser, about eight feet long, stood against one of the walls, and underneath it was a space usually given up to several pairs of boots and shoes, which were placed there ready to be cleaned. These had been cleared away, and in their place was a long box covered neatly with the remains of an ancient plush curtain. Small cactus plants, spiny, goblin and distorted, decorated each end and the middle of the box, and the Japanese removed these and the curtain, and then lightly polished the exposed surface of the receptacle. A small brass plate in the centre informed him that Carswell Middleton was aged forty-three years.

Having finished his polishing, Nao replaced curtain and cactus plants, and set about preparing lunch.

'A little knowledge,' he said gravely to Lily Soudall, when she inquired why he did not put his cactus plants in the window as Christian people did, 'is a dangerous thing. Therefore, youthful miss, I say to you that in my country—' he delved into the box where the potatoes were kept, and settled down to peel them.

'Oh, Japan!' said Lily. 'That's different. Is it true they worship a mountain? Though, for the matter of that, Mister Nao, I wouldn't say but what some of these people here aren't no better than a lot of heathens, the way they talk about that there hump on the top of Godrun Down.'

'That hump is a grave,' said Nao. 'Very, very old. Unquiet spirit lives there. Walks. Is restless.'

'Lor!' said Lily. 'Give over that sort of talk! I shan't dare go to bed! You know as well as I do it was Mr Jones and that Mrs Bradley having their little joke.'

Nao smiled.

'You and I, Miss Lilian, we also.'

'Also what?'

'Also have our little joke.'

'Not if I know it,' said Lily, primly. 'Not with a Japanee.'

'You mistake.'

'I'd better, unless you want Jasper Corbett's fist in your face, he's that hasty-tempered and jealous.'

The Japanese continued to smile.

'He does not practise ju-jitsu, I think.' He smiled. 'I like him. But you mistake. The cactus plants. Our little joke.'

'Oh, them!'

'They will grow through the eye-sockets of dead men.'

'Oh, do dry up. Give anybody the horrors!'

She backed away from the cactus plants, Nao, still smiling, continued to peel the potatoes.

After lunch, Jones decided to go to his cottage to bring back the books that he wanted, and the two beds. He walked to the Long Thin Man to borrow a conveyance, but before he got there he encountered old Mrs Fluke, who immediately offered him the loan of the two perambulators which had transported her furniture from her own cottage to that given up to her by Birdseye.

'But how do you know I'm going to move any furniture?' asked Jones, surprised. Old Mrs Fluke fingered the edge of the sackcloth apron she was wearing and then scratched the side of her nose with a forefinger the colour of the soil. She grinned. Her whole demeanour was that of one who finds

herself mistress of the situation through her own wit
and foresight and Jones felt, if not actually alarmed,
rather uncomfortable. She gave the impression of
one who held all the trumps when her opponents
did not even know what the trumps were. He
said:

'Somebody left you a windfall, Mrs Fluke?'

She wagged her head. Suddenly she removed the
old check cap she was wearing, and Jones observed
that every hair on her head had been shaved off.
She was as bald as the bust of Julius Cæsar, and
her dirty white scalp was in unpleasing contrast
to her earth-brown wrinkled face. She looked to
Jones a cross between a picture of Gagool which
had fascinated him in his youth, and the great
condor at the Zoological Gardens in Regent's Park.
He looked at her in amazement. Mrs Fluke broke
into a wheezy and unregenerate cackle.

'I am not a-running any risks,' she said, 'of
being mistaken for a witch, Mr Jones. Folks is so
ignorant hereabouts.'

'You're running every risk of catching your death
of cold,' said Jones, who found the sight of her
scalp peculiarly nauseating. 'You don't want to get
pneumonia, do you?'

' "They have sharpened their tongues like a
serpent: adder's poison is under their lips," ' said
old Mrs Fluke, disregarding Jones' contribution to
the conversation and carrying on a monologue of
her own. 'Be you having my old prams, or beant
you?'

'Will you push one?' asked Jones.

'Ay. Surely I will. Sixpence in money, and my right o' way through parson's garden.'

'No monkey tricks, then.'

'I dunno what you mean. Oomen of my years knows how to respect themselves, I should have thought.'

'Very good,' said Jones, 'but I shall keep my eye on you, so don't you dare start any funny business when you get near the vicar.'

Mrs Fluke chuckled and put on her cap again.

'Where are those perambulators?' said Jones.

As they walked back to the vicarage with the rolled-up mattresses and the books, the sun was overcast with clouds. Old Mrs Fluke let go her perambulator, and, with a squawk of rapture, pointed to the sky.

'Rain! Rain!' she said. Jones glanced up indifferently.

'Not on your life,' he said. 'It's only heat haze.'

The perambulators were hastily unloaded, and, having been rewarded with a florin by Jones, Mrs Fluke took her departure, loosing a last fusillade of Hibernian blessings on him.

'She's a perfect old Tartar,' said Jones to Mrs Bradley, 'but, really, one can't help liking her. When will the bobbies be here?'

'Not this evening. No attempt will be made until after dark, I am sure. I don't want the police here yet.'

'There's something worrying you,' said Jones. Mrs Bradley would not admit to being worried, but confessed that she was puzzled over the non-appearance of Tom Tebbutt.

'The boy should have been here by now to tell me that the sick room at Neot House is empty,' she said.

'But perhaps it isn't empty. You may be mistaken. Tebbutt may be ill in bed after all.'

'Impossible,' said Mrs Bradley finally.

'But you think that somebody may make an attempt to remove the coffin containing the body of the murdered man?' said Jones, who wanted to know why she supposed that this would be so.

'Yes. But not necessarily tonight,' repeated Mrs Bradley. 'I am not certain that Hanley Middleton is in the village at present. I wish we could send a man up to Neot House to discover what has become of Tom Tebbutt,' she added.

'You're uneasy about that boy. Let me go,' said Jones; and at nine o'clock he set off for Neot House, alive, this time, to the risk he ran of sustaining another knock on the head. He imagined, however, that Mrs Bradley had not anticipated any such occurrence, or she would have insisted upon his being accompanied.

He walked up to the front door, knocked and rang; but before the bell had done pealing he was aware that he was trying to gain admission to an empty house.

Although it was not yet dark, bats were beginning to essay their jerking, feckless flight, swooping and darting round the eaves of the house, and a young owl was crying to the approaching night.

Jones' Welsh blood began to go chilly, and his imagination began to cause him to hear creeping footsteps about the empty house. The words "no living thing" suddenly came to his mind, and, for no reason, refused to leave it.

'No living thing . . . no living thing . . .' said Jones under his breath. He could feel the hair rising on his scalp and the gooseflesh crawling about his shoulders as he pronounced the words. Suddenly there was a rushing noise inside the house, the sounds of overturned furniture, and, with a crash that sent Jones' heart up into his throat and the sweat starting all over his body, something came hurtling against the inside of the door.

'Poltergeist!' said Jones, gulping down his terror and trying to take a scientific view of the phenomenon. But he found himself retreating. The crash came a second time. How many more times it came he did not know, for he soon found himself at the end of the drive and in sight of the road.

He fell in at the door of the Long Thin Man and ordered a brandy and soda.

'Why, what's the matter, Mr Jones?' inquired young Jasper, serving him.

'The devil's loose in Neot House. I've been up there to find Tom Tebbutt.'

'Tom Tebbutt? Why, haven't ee heard the news?'

'Of course not. Tell me.'

'Why, Tom were picked up on top of Godrun Down. Took him to the doctor's straight away, they had to. Poor chap was fair dazed and couldn't say nothing of what he'd done to himself, Mr Jones.'

'And he's at the doctor's now?'

'Likely to be. They say he can't be moved for some days yet. Doctor thinks to get him to Stowhall hospital and put the X-Rays on him to see what's broke and all.'

Jones stayed only to finish his drink. Then he made for the doctor's house to see Tom. The doctor himself opened the door.

'Ah, here you are. I'm glad you've come. I'm called away. Will you sit by the boy? The police may want to know anything he says when he regains consciousness—if ever he does!'

'He's very bad, then?' said Jones. The doctor did not answer. He led the way upstairs, and there in a white bed in the smallest room lay Tom with a bandaged head.

'You can't do anything. There's nothing to do,' said the doctor. Without waiting for any kind of response from Jones, he hurried away. A moment later Jones heard the engine of the car which was garaged at the back of the house.

Jones rang the bell for the maid. No one answered it. He rang again, but there was no response. He was alone in the house with the injured boy. He picked up a silver-backed hair brush from the dressing-table and stepped to the side of the bed. A slight dimming on the bright surface of the silver informed him, to his relief, that the boy was breathing. Jones left the bedroom door wide open and went into the front bedroom of the house. It gave indisputable evidence of accommodating two people. Jones scratched his jaw.

But he had not come there to investigate Mortmain's private affairs—he recollected that Lily Soudall had left the doctor's service rather suddenly—but to look out for some passer-by who could take a message to the vicarage.

The village street was deserted. Jones began the wearisome business of gazing up and down the street, returning to make certain that Tom Tebbutt needed no attention, and then tip-toeing back to the front of the house again. He was experiencing that helpless and anxious feeling common to sensitive persons who are left with the sole responsibility of dealing with a situation which they do not understand. Jones found himself hoping that the boy would remain unconscious until Mortmain returned.

Suddenly the street was filled with tumult. Jones left the injured boy's bedside and leapt to the front bedroom window. A procession was passing. It appeared to be composed of the whole village. Men, women and children, all were there. The only notable absences were those of the two Passions and Mrs Gant from the post office. Even Mrs Pike, wild-eyed and wild-haired, was there. The people at the sides and rear of the procession appeared to be spectators rather than participators, but the bulk of the village was *en fête*, if such an expression can be used to describe an assembly in which seven-eighths of the parties were completely, and the remaining eighth, partly, intoxicated.

They were singing a hymn tune, but the words which floated up to Jones' amazed and horrified ears were blasphemous and filthy beyond anything that he had ever heard. At once, and completely, he believed every one of the vicar's oft-stressed jeremiads about the viciousness and vice of the community where he had come to stay. Saxon Wall, uninhibited, was a fearful and terrible thing.

The lustiest singer, and the chief master of gesture as well as of words and music, was the water diviner, Thomas Part. Twirling a hazel wand like the bâton of a drum major, he headed the procession, capering like a satyr and bellowing the scurrilous words of the ditty with a gusto which Jones had only once seen equalled, and that by a drunken undergraduate on Boat-race night.

Most of the men were armed with cudgels and some carried scrips full of sharp flints. Even the women had broomsticks, hayforks and pebbles, and, in the rear of the procession, came a grim-looking group drawing the wheelwright's largest barrow, laden with coils of rope.

'What in hell?' thought Jones. He crept back and looked at Tom. There seemed nothing to be done for him. On the other hand, the people at the vicarage might be in grave danger from the drunken mob. There were not less than forty people in the procession, and Jones knew enough of the herd instinct in men to realise that as soon as the fun began the onlookers would readily become participants.

He wondered where the liquor had come from, but reflected that with people as angry as the villagers were, a little beer would go a long way towards making them utterly unmanageable and irresponsible.

He slipped out by the back door of the house, scaled the fence, broke through a hedge, leapt a bone-dry ditch, and began to run. He was soon level with the procession. He crouched down under cover of the hedge, which separated him from the road, and, once past the leaders, he began to sprint. Blown, sticky with perspiration, heaving and gasping, he projected himself at the front door of the vicarage and crashed on the knocker.

'They're here!' he said, tumbling in on top of Nao. 'Barricade everything! Is the well guarded?'

Less than five minutes afterwards they could hear the approaching procession, but instead of coming as far as the vicarage, it turned off into the churchyard. Before his intention was realised, Hallam had dashed out of the house and across the garden to the gate in the wall which gave on to the churchyard.

'Come on! They'll kill him!' cried Jones. Followed by Nao, Lily Soudall and Mrs Bradley, he raced after the vicar.

But the mob were not prepared to enter the church. The building was dedicated to Saint Thomas the Apostle, and over the Perpendicular porch, standing in a small, rounded niche, was a statue of the saint. Willing backs made the ascent of the porch a safe and simple matter, willing hands dragged the statue down. It was caught in sheets brought by the women, and placed in the wagon.

Jones and Nao held the struggling Hallam.

'It's all right,' said Mrs Bradley, soothing him. 'The figure is only an early nineteenth century restoration, child, and, in any case, they'll bring it back when they have done with it.'

Hallam ceased to struggle.

'What unholiness are they up to, anyhow?' he said.

'See "The Golden Bough," dear child.'

'Not magic?'

'Well—yes and no, child. Yes and no!'

'How long will they be?' asked Jones.

'Where is the nearest water?'

'At the top of Godrun Down,' said Lily Soudall, 'though it beant no more than a patch of mud by now.'

'Well, the point is, I've left Tom Tebbutt all alone in the doctor's house. He's got concussion or something. He's not recovered consciousness.'

'Where is Mortmain?' asked Hallam.

'Goodness only knows!' said Jones. 'There's something sinister about that man, I shouldn't wonder.'

'Doctor Mortmain is not in mischief. He is helping me hide the body,' said Mrs Bradley. She hooted with mirth at the sight of their startled faces.

Chapter Twenty-Three

'I have been sometimes thinking, if a man
had the art of second sight for seeing
lies, as they have in Scotland for seeing
spirits, how admirably he might entertain
himself. . . .'

SWIFT
The Art of Political Lying.

TOM TEBBUTT had regained consciousness. His first
remark to Mrs Bradley, who had entered the
doctor's house by way of the kitchen window,
and who was soon in the act of removing a blood-
stained bandage from his head with celerity and,
apparently, professional callousness, took the form
of a question.

'Was it that there Mrs Passion as poisoned I?'

'Goodness knows,' said Mrs Bradley.

'Dad wasn't in the bed,' continued Tom.

'I thought he wouldn't be,' said Mrs Bradley. She
examined the blood on the bandage, pursed her
lips, grinned tigerishly and, rolling the bandage,

tossed it into the fireplace and gave her attention
to a superficial cut on Tom's left eyebrow.

'"What done that? Mice," ' said the boy, eyeing
her amusedly.

'What did happen to you, Tom?' asked Mrs
Bradley.

'Well, I busted in, and dad, he weren't there,
nor the bed any different to what it ever were,
so far as I could see—embroidered bedspread and
all—nothing took off nor folded away, and all the
winders shut and the same stuffy smell—not the
smell of people, just the smell of dust and front
room furniture—you know how—and I tackles her
and says: "Where be dad?"

'Her takes her time about answering, and then
her says: "Dad be passed away, and us didn't like
to let on to ee for fear ee'd start in roarin'!" *Me*
roar for *'im*!'

There was silence. Then Mrs Bradley said:

'Could you get as far as the vicarage, Tom?'

'Ay, if I beant sick on the way.'

'Be off with you, then. Tell them I'm gone up
Guthrum Down to learn a little folk-lore.'

Tom grinned.

'Village be gone up-along to give that there idol
a bath.'

'St. Thomas' statue, Tom.'

'Ay. That's right. Parson pray to she.'

'It isn't she, you ignorant booby.'

Tom grinned again. His face was pale, but he
appeared entirely good-tempered. Mrs Bradley
nodded slowly and rhythmically. She had guessed

accurately the temperament of Tebbutt senior.

'Anyhow, I'm off,' said Mrs Bradley, 'as soon as you've told me what took you to the top of Guthrum Down.'

'When?'

'When the men found you and brought you to Doctor Mortmain.'

'I weren't up Godrun Down.'

'Amusing,' observed Mrs Bradley, appearing to lose all interest in the subject.

'Mother brought me here-along, when I said I reckoned I were poisoned with they mushrooms Mrs Passion cooked for me.'

'Did Passion eat any of them?'

'Ah. He were sick as a dog.'

'Dear, dear!' said Mrs Bradley absently. 'Passion's being as sick as a dog is such an unlucky sign or portent in this village, isn't it?'

'He's sick before a death, no doubt of that. Or so *she* says.'

'She being——?'

'Mother.'

'And she brought you here?'

'She did. And I done a faint along the road, and I never woke up till I see you in the room.'

'Hm!' said Mrs Bradley, sniffing delicately.

'I reckon I were poisoned right enough.'

'Undoubtedly, child.'

'And for the purpose, like.'

'Yes.'

'Because I found out dad weren't in the bedroom.'

'Oh?'

'I reckon they done in dad.'

'What makes you imagine that?'

'Or else he done himself in because he done in Mr Middleton.'

'Describe Mr Middleton, Tom.'

'Big, black-haired, red-faced fellow. Flashing eyes and white teeth when he laughed. Joke and a shilling for everyone, and not half a one for the ladies, he wasn't, but only to rescue 'em like, out of clutches.'

'Out of——?'

'Clutches. You know—unwelcome attentions and that.'

'I see,' said Mrs Bradley. She bestowed on the smiling youth a smile of her own which wiped the pleased expression from his face and replaced it with a stare of fascinated apprehension. Hers was a pleased smile, too; the pleased smile of a tiger which licks its lips when it beholds its prey. Tom got out of bed and put his boots on. Then, with a look which mingled apprehension and defiance, he removed the blood-stained bandage from the fireplace and twisted it round his head.

'Well, I'll be off,' he said, moving towards the door.

Mrs Bradley let him go. She went to the front of the house and watched him as he went along the road. Then she let herself out at the front door and walked back to the vicarage. Her thirst for folk-lore appeared to have been assuaged. Arrived at the vicarage she poked a bony yellow forefinger into the ribs of the unsuspecting Jones, and demanded, cackling with joy, which person in the village possessed a copy of his collected works.

Jones had the grace to blush—a feat of which his acquaintance believed him incapable.

'I believe the Misses Harper have one of my earlier books, and loan it out occasionally,' he said.

'Tom Tebbutt's borrowed it,' said Mrs Bradley. She eyed him with the kindly smile of a boa-constrictor which has engulfed a donkey and is preparing for a week or two of slumber.

'I hear the village returning,' she added suddenly, holding up her finger. The village was making considerably less noise in its descent of Guthrum Down than it had made going up.

'I hope they've brought St. Thomas back,' said Jones. 'What, exactly, did they want him for, Mrs Bradley? You gave us the reference, but I must have forgotten the text and I'm immensely curious about it.'

'They are taking him up to the pond on Guthrum Down to cast him into the water, child, that's all. It is a way of pointing out to him that the village wants rain to fall. I thought the custom was French, but they seem to have heard of it here.'

'Good heavens!' said Hallam, aghast.

It was very nearly dark. From the upper windows of the south side of the vicarage Guthrum Down loomed like a heavy cloud. Two stars appeared to the right of it, and a long wash of greenish sky behind it marked the end of the summer day. The villagers, unwilling to face the long thin man after

sunset, were already in the village street. Their
singing and shouting was carried a long distance
on the still air of the evening, and there was
something threatening and something pathetic in
it. It was as though they were defying the gods,
and knew that their defiance was useless because
it was unregarded. It was as though they knew
they were shouting at something which had no
ears; which had never been able to hear.

They brought back St. Thomas' statue to the
churchyard. The rain-clouds which had given their
false promise earlier in the day, had passed over the
village hours since, on the shoulder of the south-
west wind. The people entered the churchyard,
looked at the sky, and left St. Thomas standing
beside the west door.

'Too fed up even to knock spots off him,' said
Jones, peering through the dusk to where the knot
of black-clad people were standing around the hand-
cart on which the statue had been transported at
immense labour up the hill. 'Tired, too. Most of
'em seem to have cleared off home.'

There were not more than fifteen people at the
church door. Jones went out to them. Amid silence,
he walked up to the statue and touched it. It was
wet and slimy with mud.

'Good Lord! Is that what the dewpond is like?'
he asked in friendly tones. A growl from the men,
and, from some of the tired women, a sob, were
the replies that he received. He turned and went
in to Hallam and Mrs Bradley.

'They'll have to have water, Hallam. However

godless they are, they've got to have water,' he said.

'I am going to them now,' said Hallam. His face was very pale. He looked straight in front of him as he walked. He put Jones aside when the other offered to accompany him.

'They are my people. I shall go alone,' he said.

'They're in a funny mood,' Jones warned him. Hallam smiled.

'So am I, my friend.'

Mrs Bradley placed herself between him and the door. She waved a skinny claw.

'Not yet, dear child, not yet,' she said. She lowered her voice, and added, with a sense of ultimate conviction in her tone which caused Hallam to bow his head and Jones to stare in surprise:

' "The people that walked in darkness have seen a great light: they that dwell in the land of the shadow of death, upon them hath the light shined." '

The villagers began to disperse. A stone struck one of the windows and shattered it. A few more rattled against the side door. But the demonstrators seemed utterly tired and dispirited, and after some lurid threats in respect of what would happen on the morrow, they departed.

'Now for the body-snatchers,' said Jones with relish. Mrs Bradley shook her head. Hallam, with a murmured excuse, had gone into his study.

'They may not come tonight,' she said. 'By the way, I must have a message taken to Doctor Mortmain. I wonder who could go?'

'There's Lily,' said Jones. 'Or what about Nao?'

'Nao? Splendid,' said Mrs Bradley briskly. She summoned him.

'Doctor Mortmain? Can go,' said the Japanese with suspicious readiness.

'Wants an excuse to get into the village,' said Jones, when he had gone. 'I say, what about Hallam? Does it strike you that—oh, you wouldn't realise the difference, though. You didn't know him before the time of the murder. But it's dashed odd, all the same.'

'Where is Lily?' demanded Mrs Bradley, whose thoughts seemed to have strayed.

'In the kitchen, I suppose,' Jones answered. 'Do you want her?'

'I think she has gone home to her mother,' said Mrs Bradley, not answering the question.

'Why on earth? Oh, scared of the villagers and their little demonstration, I suppose? Poor girl! I should think she finds the village a change after Surrey.'

'She's found Jasper Corbett, child. She'll be married soon. By the way, has it struck you that for such an unusually awful village, Saxon Wall has a high percentage of most respectable inhabitants?'

'From which you deduce——?' said Jones courteously. Mrs Bradley cackled, and her reply, when at last it came, took the form of a doggerel verse by Gilbert, which she sang, to a tune she fondly imagined to be Sullivan's, in a voice which was unarguably contralto:

'Nothing venture, nothing win:
Blood is thick, but water's thin:
In for a penny, in for a pound,
It's love that makes the world go round.'

Then she led him by the arm to the kitchen.

'Look,' she said. Jones looked. All that he could see was a large dresser with a space underneath it which had the appearance of a place where shoes were habitually kept. He wondered why he thought this, and then recollected that he had visited the kitchen once to talk to Nao about his employer, and he supposed that his visual memory retained what his reasoning mind did not—the spectacle of shoes under the dresser.

The space was now empty. Jones turned to Mrs Bradley and raised his eyebrows.

'The coffin was there this afternoon,' Mrs Bradley explained.

'The coffin?'

'Tebbutt's coffin, child.'

'With Tebbutt in it?'

'Certainly. But labelled Middleton.'

'How do you know?'

'By taking thought, child.'

'Oh?'

'And now,' said Mrs Bradley, turning towards the door, 'for a little walk up Guthrum Down to find where they have laid him.' Her remark set Jones laughing.

' "Good morrow to the Day so fair;
Good morning Sir to you:
Good morrow to mine own torn hair
Bedabbled with the dew," '

he observed, as he followed her to the study.

'And make certain that the revolver I gave you is loaded and in working order, child. Can you fire a revolver?'

'I can.'

'Good. Then you shall protect us both, and as we go——' she leered horribly—'I will a tale unfold.'

'A tale?'

'Even so. There were once four suspects——'

'Four?'

'Yes, child. You, Tebbutt, Doctor Mortmain and the vicar.'

'But Tebbutt's dead, I thought?'

'That fact may prove that he is not the murderer.'

' "Nay," ' said Jones, grinning, ' "you must name his name, and half his face must be seen through the lion's neck; and he himself must speak through, saying thus, or to the same defect——" '

'There were once four suspects,' repeated Mrs Bradley firmly, 'and their names were Jones, Tebbutt, Mortmain and—well, let us say, the vicar.'

'Only one of them was called Middleton,' Jones interpolated.

'Quite right, child. Which is the shortest way up Guthrum Down?'

'I don't suppose I can find my way in the dark.'

'Tut, tut,' said Mrs Bradley, pronouncing the words phonetically. She stepped delicately on to the vicarage lawn. 'And walk quietly, child.'

'Don't advise me to be careful,' Jones said, gripping the revolver. 'My blood is up. I've had a cosh on the head and I'm thirsting for revenge.'

Mrs Bradley poked him in the ribs, and, by mutual consent, they abandoned conversation until they were clear of the sleeping village. The doctor's red lamp was burning, but his house was otherwise in darkness.

'He's back again,' thought Jones. A moment later they were crossing the village green.

Chapter Twenty-Four

'That the question of insanity in a case
of murder should be left for decision
to the wisdom of a jury, seems to be
outrageous.'

DR BERNARD HOLLANDER
The Psychology of Misconduct.

'IT's this way, child,' said Mrs Bradley. 'We were
looking for a murderer. If I mistake not, we were
looking for a madman, too. It is arguable that all
murderers are mad, but this particular murderer,
Middleton, was the kind of madman for whom
mental homes were designed and intended. He was
of the genus Bedlamite. Observe: he had killed a
woman and two men. Why?'

'Are you asking me why, or is it a rhetorical
question designed to create attention and a
due regard for your own intelligence?' asked
Jones.

'Child,' said Mrs Bradley severely, 'answer me
directly.'

'Well, if you are seriously bent upon obtaining a reply, I confess that I don't know. Oh, wait a moment! It was to provide himself with his own dead body, wasn't it?'

'Well, we supposed so. All along, that has appeared a feasible idea, and the only one that seemed to fit the facts. But——'

'Yes, that's so,' said Jones, as he stumbled over a mole-hill. They were leaving the rough grass of the village green, and soon were walking over the heather which grew on the lower slopes of Guthrum Down. A great moon, climbing the shoulder of the hill, began to light their path and to discover tracks through the bracken to which the heather gave place, and, at last, the remnant of a flinty sheep-walk which mounted to the dewpond on the crest. 'We shall be spotted a mile off in this moonlight,' he added, glancing about him.

'It doesn't matter now,' said Mrs Bradley. 'I concluded,' she went on, as calmly as though she were not making a breath-taking statement which left Jones standing with astonishment and dismay, 'that the murderer was the vicar.'

'You don't mean that Middleton is Hallam?' he said, amazed beyond measure by this startling theory.

'Middleton was mad. I deduced that from what I learnt of his habits from the late Mrs Middleton's mother. Now, if our conclusions are correct, it follows that, if Middleton has been living in this village, a madman has been living here.'

'So far, so comprehensible,' said Jones, placing a

hand in the small of her back to help her up the gradually steepening incline.

'The vicar was the only lunatic in the village,' said Mrs Bradley, 'therefore, logically, Middleton and the vicar were the same person.'

'Yes, but——'

'One moment, child. Apart from the fact that the vicar was mentally unstable, there are suspicious circumstances surrounding his conduct on the night of the murder which need considerably more explanation than they have received.'

'Look you,' said Jones, breaking in. 'The man is a good man, therefore he is not a murderer.'

'So was Saint Paul a good man,' said Mrs Bradley tartly. 'Do you remember the stoning of Saint Stephen? Besides, even judged by your incomplete and sentimental standards of conduct, he is not nearly as good a man as you are, and you——'

'Are singularly imperfect,' said Jones, finishing her sentence for her and then laughing. 'Very well. Let that go. But I like the man. He is my friend. I know he is not a murderer. I shouldn't like a murderer. Nobody could.'

'The warders liked Belle.'

'Oh, Belle. That's different. Belle was a beastly woman, anyway.'

'Don't be ingenuous, child. There is nothing I dislike more in a man of the world than nauseating naïveté of that sort. No wonder you can write those disgusting novels!'

'Never again,' said Jones humbly. 'My next——'

'After the detective story?'

'—after the detective story—is to be entitled Beatrix What-is-it, after the famous thingummy of Dante, with special reference to Beatrice Adela Lestrange Bradley, who dashed from my lips the poison-cup of chloroformed best-selling, copper-bottomed, gilt-edged fiction, and led me forth to indulge in the pure, wholesome and exhilarating sport of murderer-hunting. Say on. After all:

> "in such a night
> Stood Dido with a willow in her hand
> Upon the wild sea banks. . . ." '

'Now, about Hallam,' said Mrs Bradley. 'On the night of the murder Hallam certainly went to the vicarage.'

'Yes, he was seen by Miss Phoebe Harper, wasn't he?' said Jones.

'He was chased out of the grounds of Neot House, and later he was reported to have spent some time in removing the thirteenth-century glass from a small quatrefoil window in the church. As a matter of fact, I don't think he did do this on the night in question.'

'But——' said Jones.

'I think,' said Mrs Bradley, 'that he removed the stained glass at least two days beforehand.'

'But why on earth should you suppose that?' asked Jones. 'We know that he cut his head on a piece of the glass, don't we?'

'Of course, we ought to decide which vicar we are talking about,' said Mrs Bradley.

'Well, I'm talking about Hallam,' said Jones, slightly mystified by what appeared to be a pointless remark. He was certain, however, that Mrs Bradley had deduced several facts which were still unknown to him.

'So am I,' said Mrs Bradley urbanely, 'and I suggest that Mr Hallam would never have made the elementary mistake of confusing a small quatrefoil with a rose-window. What do you say to that?'

'Well, now you mention it, of course, the church doesn't possess a rose-window.'

'And has it ever struck you,' Mrs Bradley continued, 'that no village boys in the world would have bothered about smashing that small quatrefoil when a large, handsome, Early Perpendicular east window was there to excite the unmannerly to the work of destruction?'

'Golly,' said Jones, deeply impressed by this line of reasoning. 'Then—no, hang it! I can't see it now! I thought I could for a minute, but it's no use.'

'You remarked a little while ago that I had never met Mr Hallam before the date of the murder, didn't you?' said Mrs Bradley.

'I did. You hadn't, had you?'

'No, child. But you had.'

'What are you getting at?'

'The man who lived at the vicarage from the night of the murder until the night the villagers set fire to the house was not Mr Hallam, child.'

'Not Hallam?'

'No.'

'But—good Lord! You're right! You *must* be right! But how on earth did I never spot it?'

'First, Mr Hallam was not so very well known to you that someone who had studied him could not deceive you by impersonating him.'

'Oh, but I say! I must be blind!'

'Not at all. You remember the heavily bandaged head and eye? You remember the huge scarf that comforted the terrible bout of neuralgia? You remember the long time spent in bed, and the trick of ducking the head under the bedclothes and the fancy to have the curtains closely drawn? You remember that the doctor was not allowed to approach the bed, and, on a later occasion, was refused admission? You remember the husky tones of whispering agony? You remember the changed outlook?'

'Yes,' said Jones. 'I remember all that. Of course, he did seem extraordinarily changed, but then, I thought he was going crazy, you know.'

'Not going—gone. Didn't you find the change rather sudden?'

'I've had no experiences to compare with your work in mental institutions, you know. But, now I come to think of it, he *did* take the most acute pleasure in detailing all those nauseating stories about the morals of the village. And didn't he tell the doctor he was Moses? Still, I suppose that really it's not surprising I was deceived. Everybody else was, too.'

'Indeed?' said Mrs Bradley. 'I can tell you some who weren't.'

'Mrs Fluke, for one, I suppose?'

'Why should you pick her out?'

'Well, those sacks of frogs. I'm sure she smelt a rat.'

'Who else, child?'

'I don't know. Mrs Passion?'

'Why Mrs Passion?'

'The summer house incident. I can see everything now. She knew what Middleton wanted, but he dared not give himself away.'

'Yes. Oh, and that reminds me. Mr Hallam had been a missionary in Japan, I think.'

'Of course he had. Brought Nao home with him.'

'Yes. Well, why start in on Polynesian and West Indian magic? That struck me at once as being odd, and out of character. He made many slips. That was a bad one.'

'Oh, heavens! I *am* a fool!'

Mrs Bradley's voice was kindly, as she continued:

'And his sudden change of front about the water. The real Hallam was more than willing, I understand, to give the village people water from his well. The impostor Hallam was not.'

'But how on earth did he persuade Hallam to get out of the vicarage?'

'He didn't. Mr Hallam was attacked near the lodge of Neot House at just after ten on the night of the murder, and was conveyed to the castle ruins in Middleton's car. Nao and I released him and took him to the Long Thin Man without the knowledge of Mrs Corbett, who has rather a long tongue, but with the connivance and assistance of Corbett and young Jasper.' She chuckled. 'This was done whilst you were nursing your headache after the blow you received at Neot House.'

'Yes. Who struck that blow?'

'Mrs Tebbutt, I think. She's been in deadly terror, that woman, ever since her husband was murdered.'

'Why? She didn't kill him, did she?'

'No. But she expected to be the next victim unless Middleton's orders were carried out to the very letter.'

'What were his orders?'

'On no account to let anyone suspect that Tebbutt was dead. Tebbutt was ill in bed and could see nobody; those were her instructions.'

'And she thought I'd come snooping——'

'Which you had!'

'And laid me out with a half brick or something. Not so bad! And Tebbutt was killed——'

'Because he had blackmailed Middleton.'

'But how do you know that?'

'I don't. But it must be true. You see, child, I think there is no possible doubt that Middleton must have spent at least part of the time since his wife's death in a mental home. His madness is recurrent, and on a fairly long cycle, I should imagine.'

'Have you discovered this asylum? Do you know where it is?' inquired Jones. Mrs Bradley shook her head. Her face looked thinner and more peaked than ever in the brilliant moonlight.

'I don't intend to look for it,' she said.

'But it would be invaluable proof——' began Jones.

'I don't want proof.'

'Why not?'

'I will tell you when we return to the vicarage. I hope Mr Hallam is enjoying himself at Doctor Mortmain's house.'

'What do you mean?'

'Just exactly what I say, child. Nothing more.'

'Then that's a change!' said Jones, laughing. By this time they had arrived at the top of the hill. Before they halted Jones asked one more question.

'I suppose you're certain about the Hallam business? I mean, could *Nao* be taken in? After all, he'd lived a good many years with Hallam, hadn't he? And yet he never batted an eyelash, so far as I could see.'

'Nao helped me find Mr Hallam.'

'Oh, yes. But still——'

'Thank goodness for Japanese impassivity,' said Mrs Bradley, cackling. 'A European servant would have given himself away to Middleton half a dozen times, however careful he was resolved to be. Nao, I am certain, never did. I told him what I wanted him to do, and he obeyed me.'

They had reached the top of the hill. The barrow of the long thin man looked unfamiliarly significant under the moon. Mrs Bradley sat down on an outcropping of limestone rock to rest. After a moment Jones sat down beside her.

'The coffin is not up here, it seems,' he said. He had not expected that it would be.

'No,' said Mrs Bradley. She peered at her watch. At the end of about ten minutes she rose and intimated that they would descend to the village.

'Mortmain was *my* choice,' said Jones, breaking a pause which had lasted, he thought, too long.

'Mortmain? Oh, because he's a doctor, you mean? Yes, but, child, he's sane. We had to look for a madman; for someone obviously and entirely insane.'

'Well,' said Jones, grinning, 'if that's all you wanted, you wouldn't need to look much farther than the Misses Harper, would you?'

Mrs Bradley cackled.

'Let's go and see Doctor Mortmain, and ask him where the body is,' she said.

'Of course, he hid it for you. But I thought you thought the body would be in the barrow of the long thin man.'

'It will be, later on,' said Mrs Bradley. 'Come along. I never intended shouldering the responsibility of finding it up here.'

But when they arrived at Doctor Mortmain's house she led Jones past it and on to old Mrs Fluke's cottage, the one she inhabited by courtesy of the (so far as Jones was concerned) still unmaterialised Birdseye.

A candle was burning in the kitchen and old Mrs Fluke, a nightcap drawn decently over her hairless scalp, was seated at the table with a pack of cards. As she shuffled them she mumbled, and as she mumbled it seemed to Jones that the candle flame burnt lower and higher rhythmically, uncannily and aptly, according to the changes in her tone.

They had lifted the latch and walked in, uninvited and apparently unnoticed, for the old woman did not look up nor give any other indication that she realised their presence. At last she pushed the cards together in an untidy heap and addressed Jones, chuckling.

'I smell rain upon the wind, so I do.'

'Good for you,' said Jones cordially. Old Mrs Fluke looked at Mrs Bradley, and touched the dirty nightcap.

'Not to have no more talk about witches and their hair, I shaved mine off,' she said confidentially, as one of a sisterhood to another. Mrs Bradley nodded.

'Eh?' said Jones.

'It is supposed in some districts,' Mrs Bradley observed, 'that a witch's familiar spirit clings in her hair.'

'And for why did Hanley Middleton go for to keep parson shut up in they old ruins like that?' old Mrs Fluke continued. ''Twas cruel hard on poor young fellow. Us always liked parson, though us quarrelled with un. I done my best wi' they frogs to show Hanley Middleton what a cruel old Pharaoh us did think him, and how he did ought to have let parson go, but it wasn't no good, I reckon.'

She looked at Mrs Bradley, and chuckled hoarsely.

'Come across, Mrs Fluke,' said Jones. 'When did you know that Mr Hallam had left the vicarage, and that Middleton had taken his place?'

'When it happened. Just after when he killed that there Tebbutt our Eliza married. Sure, wasn't that the brave one, then, to be trying to get the better of his old mother-in-law the way he did!'

'Look here, who killed the cat?' asked Jones.

'Tom, he killed it. It was hurt, I reckon, and I know Hanley Middleton had been a-praying to it, and Tommy killed it.'

'A debased fertility cult, founded partly on Isis worship, was introduced hereabouts by Roman legionaries in the second century, I believe,' interpolated Mrs Bradley. 'Middleton was experimenting with it, I expect. I have always supposed that the cat was one of the first signs that Hanley Middleton had come to the end of one of his lucid intervals. Tell us about the night of Tebbutt's death, Mrs Fluke.'

'Nowt to tell ee. I reckon you knows more now than I do, though how it come about you do is more than I can make out,' replied the old woman. 'Shan't trouble denying there's witches after this, I shan't, say parson what he like. Tebbutt and our Eliza brought Hanley Middleton back to Saxon Wall, and they kept him close, too, but not so close we didn't soon know all there was to know about their goings-on. And our Martha and me, we guessed there was something behind it all. But a main sight too smart was that Tebbutt—such a life he led that poor boy of hisn, too and all.'

'Hanley Middleton was being blackmailed by the Tebbutts, then, because they knew he had murdered his wife?' said Jones.

'Who can tell?' replied old Mrs Fluke, giving a coquettish push to the night-cap. 'That there Tebbutt thought he knew how to manage mad people, you see, him having minded 'em in a lunatic asylum once upon a time before he married, and thinking you only had to be cruel to 'em to make 'em do just what you wanted. Of course, our Martha laid her head to theirs, her knowing all about Pike and having that to lay against Hanley, and I don't know but what I wouldn't have told 'em what I knowed about him trying to kill poor Miss Constance by black magic earlier on, soon after they was married, but none of 'em wanted me to have my share, not even our Martha, curse her for a greedy guts and a bad lot and a fair trial to her poor old mother from her birth onwards! Anyway, one day, soon after Mr Jones got here, Hanley turns round on Tebbutt and tells him he's Moses, and he's going to live at the parsonage. Told him he would lead the village forty years in the wilderness, he did, and off he went. Well, that Passion our Martha married, he went and helped Hanley and Tebbutt put parson in the underground of them old ruins. He done that, Passion did, because he once heard parson talk of him as a Natural—which he is, if ever there was one—and that heathen man that does parson's housework, he was fair outrageous to find him when it happened. Well, that Japanee, he found out where they put him, because he took a nasty hold of Passion, that hurt him like the devil's pincers, so Passion told us afterwards, and Passion helped get him out.'

'Out of the cellar in the ruins?' asked Jones.

'Ay. The parson, he went up along to Neot House to ask about the water and to tell Tebbutt, private like, that he better persuade his master.

'Hanley had gone up there hisself—beguiled, we thought he was, by Tebbutt—and Tebbutt, he was going to kill him, because they couldn't hold on to him any longer, and was afraid he'd tell the police on 'em.'

'For blackmailing him?' asked Jones.

'Ay. And being cruel to him, and such.'

'So *that's* why everybody had an alibi!' said Jones.

'Yes, child,' said Mrs Bradley. 'You remember that, for the murder of Tebbutt, all the alibis were a little late. For the murder of Middleton they would have been better timed.'

'I see.'

'Ay,' broke in old Mrs Fluke, unwilling to be robbed of the position of raconteuse, 'our Eliza made out to be our Martha'—she chuckled, apparently at a vision conjured up of Mrs Tebbutt in hat and boots—'she were always a bolder piece than Martha, only she knew better how to do the best for herself, Eliza did! And Martha, she were late up there for the fun, I think, because she was dosing that there Natural of hern——'

'Oh, yes,' said Mrs Bradley. 'That reminds me. The sick man in bed whom the police could not arrest——'

'Passion,' said Mrs Fluke. 'We kept him down with foxglove.'

'Didn't Doctor Mortmain attend him?'

'No. He used to come, but there! We never let him in except to look at our Eliza's veins.'

'I told you the vicarage garden needed weeding,' said Mrs Bradley to Jones.

'Passion's got a wonderful constitution,' Mrs Fluke continued. 'He got over it. Us let him go later on. He's got his uses, Passion has, though you wouldn't think it to look at him.'

'But Hallam's—no Middleton's—alibi. The taking out of the glass,' said Jones.

Mrs Fluke shook her head.

'Hanley didn't take no glass. That was parson, because he feared, if the drought ended up in thunder rain, that little window like the four-leaved clover might get broke, I think. Hanley, he only climbed!'

'Climbed?'

'Ay.'

'On the church?'

'Ay.'

'Come, come,' said Mrs Bradley to Jones. 'He had just murdered Tebbutt. What else should he do but climb?'

'Oh, Sigmund Freud?' He breathed a sigh of relief and comprehension.

'They only chased parson out of it and took a

hold of him and shut him up again,' continued Mrs Fluke, to ensure once again she was not being elbowed out of the conversation. 'The Tebbutts see that parson would spoil their game if he knowed what was on. They might have killed him but they didn't dare, once *you* had made a friend of him, you see!'

'Why ever not?' said Jones. Old Mrs Fluke wagged her head. On the whitewashed wall of the cottage the shadow of her night-cap made a terrifying devil-dance.

'We all knowed you soon as we seed you, Mr Jones. We'd all been waiting a thousand year or more. And when you came walking in—so pleasant and friendly you was—we waited and we watched. And then we knowed. And then we told Tebbutt what didn't know.'

'Knew what? I don't see how you mean.'

She wagged her head again.

'Me and our Martha, ay, and others, too, we all took all the looks at you we could, and we see what we did see.'

'And what was that?' asked Jones.

'The long thin man and his shadow. The long thin man and his shadow, Mr Jones.'

'But I'm not the long thin man! The long thin man is a myth. He's a—he's a village tale. He isn't anyone!'

Old Mrs Fluke looked upwards at the rafters.

'I smell the rain on the wind. You don't know who you be, and you don't know what you be. The village'll go to church tomorrow. Ay! And the rain'll wash 'em clean! Sure, it'll wash 'em clean.'

It was after midnight when Jones and Mrs Bradley reached the vicarage.

'I suppose Nao has gone to bed,' remarked Mrs Bradley.

'Not yet,' said the Japanese, apparently from under their feet. Jones gave an exclamation at his sudden appearance, but Mrs Bradley appeared unmoved by it.

'Everything ready for the Chief Constable?' she inquired.

'All is in order, honourable madam,' replied the Japanese politely. His face was impassive and his eyes secret, and Jones, staring curiously at him, was aware that behind that smooth mask there was laughter.

'What's the joke, Nao?' he inquired.

'That that which was said to be, is; and that which once was, is not; and who knows what an exhumation order from the Home Office may bring to light?' said Mrs Bradley, in what was, Jones sorrowfully informed her, an unnecessarily airy and flippant tone.

'And whatever has happened to the village?' he inquired. 'Have they sunk their differences with Mr Hallam?'

Nao smiled.

'After death of lamented Middleton——' he said.

'What?' said Jones.

'Hanley Middleton has been dead some little time,' said Mrs Bradley in a reassuring tone.

'After death of aforesaid beastly person,' Nao continued urbanely, 'I removed corpse of one Tebbutt from coffin disinterred for the purpose, and substituted—adroitly, I trust—one corpse as per label. Coffin is in *status quo,* and tomorrow Mister the Chief Constable will be shown suicided body. Dog eat dog,' explained Nao, benignly.

'It was the best way,' said Mrs Bradley, when the Japanese had gone. 'The police will exhume Middleton's body, and the late Mrs Middleton's mother will be called upon to identify it. She won't realise that it has not been dead as long as it ought to have been.'

'But what about Tebbutt?'

'The Chief Constable knows some of the truth. Nobody will be arrested and charged with the murder of Tebbutt, because it will be established beyond a doubt that Middleton murdered him and then committed suicide.'

'You know,' said Jones, 'I still don't know what happened to Middleton.'

'He fled when they set the vicarage on fire that night.'

'Where did he go?'

'To the castle ruins, child. And the villagers followed him there.'

'Oh?' There was a very long pause; then Jones said anxiously: 'But you didn't know that at the time?'

'Oh, yes, I did,' said Mrs Bradley.

'But—then we could have stopped them! You remember you wondered what all the noise was about?'

'I knew then what all the noise was about,' said Mrs Bradley quietly. 'They hunted Middleton through the ruins, fell upon him, and beat him with loaded sticks.'

'Adder-hunting!' exclaimed Jones.

'Old Satan,' added Mrs Bradley in parenthesis.

'But surely you didn't allow a man to be beaten to death! It's indefensible!' said Jones. He gazed at her in horror. Mrs Bradley nodded.

'Indefensible,' she said. 'You see, when the first man found him, he was already dead.'

'How do you know?'

'Nao flung him from the battlements of the ruin, and he fell on his head and was killed. When the others came upon him he was already dead. Middleton could not help being cruel, you remember. He did not treat Nao very well, I fancy, during the time he was impersonating Hallam. Nao asked my permission to kill him, and it seemed much the simplest way out of a difficulty. The villagers, you see, were certain to fall upon him once the well at Neot House as well as the water at the vicarage was put beyond their use.'

'But if he was dead they couldn't chase him through the ruins.'

'No. It was Nao they chased. I explained the situation to him, and he saw at once that the people must have their sport. His brother is valet to a fox-hunting marquis, he informs me. He understands the English love of the chase.'

'So he led them a dance as far as Middleton's body?'

'Yes, child, which looked as though it had fallen from the battlements, the body of a suicide.'

'Hm!' said Jones. 'Your sex's morals are peculiar to your sex, thank goodness.'

All day the rain held off. Black clouds raced across the heavens, torn, chaotic and ragged, and in the still rainless evening a very big congregation filled the tiny church. Late that night Mrs Bradley invited Jones to accompany her into the village. She led him to the cottage he had occupied, and told him to knock on the door. He thought at first that the cottage was untenanted. However, he knocked again, but again there was no response.

'Now what?' he asked, turning to Mrs Bradley.

'Knock once again,' she said. The cottage was in darkness. Once again Jones thundered on the door. The door opened this time.

'Come along in,' said Mrs Passion's dull and heavy voice. 'I been expecting of ee this good hour an' 'alf.'

Prodded from behind, Jones entered. Mrs Bradley followed. Mrs Passion, carrying a lighted candle, preceded them into the parlour. Jones looked apprehensively about him for lumps of sugar, but there were none to be seen.

'There's storm in the wind,' said Mrs Passion, suddenly. The brilliant moon was swallowed up by clouds. The air was sulphurous with thunder.

Lightning from over the top of Guthrum Down cut the room suddenly and vividly in twain, discovering Jones staring wildly into Mrs Passion's face.

'Where's Middleton?' he cried. Mrs Passion giggled.

'Happen Hanley Middleton's in hell. Your Japanese have broke his neck,' she said. 'How be my little Richard? Tell me, how be he?'

'He's well,' said Jones. 'You can come and see him on his birthday.'

'Not I,' said Mrs Passion shaking her head. 'It shan't be me to stand in his way no more.'

The longest and loudest peal of thunder Jones had ever heard drowned the last two words. A flash of lightning that made of their tense pale faces staring masks, heralded another and a louder thunder clap.

'The skies are falling!' said Jones.

'Ay, so they are!' said Mrs Passion wildly. ''Tis the devil abroad! He's falling adown the wind! He's cast out of heaven, and Michael's master there. Michael's the master of the fort of heaven! Praise be to God! Praise be to God, I say!'

Rain that hissed and pelted, rain that came straight and heavy, rain that dashed down upon the hard-baked earth and leapt away again, rain that saturated trees and the unreaped crops and tore down fruit from the overloaded branches and beat out flat the heavy summer flowers, fell as though the bowl of the sea were inverted, and floods greater than Noah's were spilt upon the earth.

None of them had seen such rain. It fell like an

avenging cataract of fury, relentless, unceasing, terrifyingly noisy and triumphant; they stood there listening to it, awe-stricken in the face of the terrible mercy of God.

END PAPERS

1. CONSTANCE MIDDLETON. Constance Middleton's mentality would have pleased a student of Gestalt psychology. A Freudian would have perceived in her a powerful Inferiority Complex, and might have suspected inhibitions due to an Œdipus *perversion* (as Mrs Bradley prefers nowadays to call it) but the fill-the-gap type of mentality which she exemplified, and about which the other modern schools become so tiresomely circumlocutary and so wildly inventive, is sufficient justification for the whole Gestalt theory.

2. HANLEY MIDDLETON. Hanley Middleton was in Pompeii *(see* Part I, Chapter I) from sadistic and morbid inclination, and had spent most of his time in the small museum there gazing upon the bodies of the slain. The carcass of the dog had given him particular pleasure.

Elms *(see* Part I, Chapter I) are the trees peculiarly devoted to witch-craft and the practice of magic.

The burying of a sheaf which has been fashioned

in the likeness of a human being is Irish magic. Atavistic instinct may have caused Constance to destroy the sheaf. It is not at all likely that she realised that Hanley was working magic with intent to kill her by causing her to rot away with the rotting grain.

Hanley's madness was of the circular type as exemplified in Clouston's Cycle. That is to say, Hanley suffered from periodical melancholia followed by actual mania, from which he emerged into sanity before relapsing again into melancholia. The rhythm of the three periods is always irregular, and in Hanley Middleton approximated (as near as Mrs Bradley could calculate from the meagre material at her disposal) to Clouston's third cycle:

Melancholia two years.

Mania three years.

Sanity one year, and so on in rotation.

There is distinct evidence that Hanley was launched into a 'sane' period immediately after the murder of his wife. The arrangements for the substitution of Seaman Pike for himself, and the fact that Doctor Crevister accepted him as the surgeon from Stowhall hospital are not proof positive of Hanley's sanity at the time, but do give some indication of the state of his mind.

3. BEER. Not only the inhabitants of Saxon Wall, but Jones himself, (an author, and therefore no mean judge) found that the beer at the Long Thin Man in the time of the Corbetts was of excellent quality.

4. GOATS. The *other* goat (*see* Part II, Chapters II, XV, XXII) which was never satisfactorily accounted for, was, as a matter of fact, the property of Birdseye, and had been borrowed by the Misses Harper (he thought) for breeding purposes.

5. HALLAM. The real vicar of Saxon Wall, although interested in cricket, was a keen golfer. A propos of this, Jones informed Mrs Jones, later, when they were in London, that Hallam was 'a putter of sitting balls; devotee of a game invented and perfected in a land where, for historical and topographical reasons, it was almost impossible to conceive of sports and pastimes being conducted in the team spirit or played on the level.'

6. SPEECH IN SAXON WALL. The adage that speech is intended to conceal rather than to reveal thought certainly held good in Saxon Wall. Nevertheless, Mrs Passion (*see* Part II, Chapter VI) apparently intended to warn Jones that it was proposed to hide the captive Hallam in part of the ruined castle. Unfortunately she expressed herself so obliquely as to render her warning useless.

Mrs Bradley later expressed the opinion that the inhabitants of Saxon Wall were incapable of making straightforward statements. In her unprejudiced opinion, even their lies were elliptical.

She hazarded a guess that this peculiarity dated from the days of the Norman Conquest, when the Saxons of those parts, too cunning to tell direct lies to their overlords, resorted to these maddening half-statements and oracular pronouncements.

Jones, however, thought that they were hag-ridden people, who were afraid that the powers of evil could weave words into nets and thus catch the unwary away to the devil. Jones, of course, was half-Welsh, and all his scientific training had not persuaded him to prefer a rational explanation to a romantic one. That is why, until weaned from the pernicious practice, he wrote bestsellers.

7. Time Table.	Middle of June, Hannibal Jones discovered Saxon Wall.
July 27th.	Jones takes tea with the Misses Harper.
	Quarrel betwen Mrs Fluke and Mrs Passion.
	Jones listens to Mrs Corbett.
July 28th.	Jones talks to Passion.
August 2nd.	Jones interviews Doctor Crevister.
	The vicar has neuralgia.
	Jones has an unwelcome visitor.
August 3rd.	Jones hears about the murder.
	Arrival of Richard.
	Jones knocked out.
August 4th.	Arrival of Mrs Bradley.
	Mrs Bradley interviews the Tebbutts.
August 7th.	Mrs Bradley interviews the Misses Harper.

	Jones and Mrs Bradley interview Mrs Pike.
August 8th.	Mrs Bradley takes the vicar to London and interviews Constance Middleton's mother.
August 15th.	Mrs Bradley brings the vicar back.
August 16th.	Jones becomes an elemental spirit.
August 17th.	Uproar in the castle ruins. Rain.

8. Horns and a Tail. One of the most curious and interesting features of the general mentality, if such a term is permissible, of the inhabitants of Saxon Wall, was a noticeable inability to distinguish between essential good and essential evil. For instance, they thought that the long thin man who was buried on the hill-top was a sleeping devil and yet they called the hill itself Godrun Down. They conceived Jones to be the manifestation of this devil, and yet they took it for granted that Jones was on Hallam's side. Incidentally, the village accepted unconditionally the Scriptural interpretation of madness, i.e., demoniacal possession. It had also some of the traditional Oriental respect for mentally deranged persons. (It is not proposed to enter the old-fashioned arena of the great Aryan Controversy in support of this last statement.)

9. Drugs and Insanity. Valerian (see Part II, Chapter

XVI) and hyoscin hydrobromide are sometimes used as soothing, quietening and sleep-inducing agencies in cases of extreme violence and excitement. A drug used in cases of melancholia is paraldehyde. No doubt Tebbutt understood how to treat Middleton's outbursts and usually had him pretty well under control. Middleton, like most lunatics, however, was cunning as well as crazy, and, having waited his chance, killed Tebbutt with the (heavier) poker. He seems to have shocked himself into sanity, as was also the case after the murder of his wife.

This, at any rate, was Jones' opinion, but Mrs Bradley's possibly more scientific theory was that in each case the murder was actually the culminating point—the peak, as it were—of the period of insanity, and that the subsequent descent into sanity (or near-sanity) was in the natural sequence of events.

10. MRS TEBBUTT'S FEARS. *(See* Chapter XV).

(*a*) She was physically afraid of Hanley Middleton.

(*b*) She could not trust Mrs Passion and/or Mrs Fluke, and, most unwisely had put herself into the power of them both. She had given Mrs Passion an alibi for the night of the murder, and therefore had none for herself, and she knew that Mrs Fluke was privy to the plot to kidnap Hallam and disapproved of it because she had been refused a share of the spoils of blackmail. (Incidentally, it never transpired to what extent the Tebbutts had blackmailed Middleton.)

(c) She was afraid of Doctor Mortmain, who guessed what was going on, and whose sense of humour was beyond her understanding.

(d) She was afraid of Tom, a violent and undutiful boy, and only administered an emetic after poisoning him when she realised that he so hated and feared his father that he would be the last person to cause trouble when he learned that his father had been murdered.

(e) She mistrusted Mrs Bradley, and suspected her of knowing almost as much about the murder as Mrs Bradley really did know.

(f) She was alarmed because she could not keep Passion permanently in bed at Neot House to impersonate Tebbutt. It may be remembered (see Chapter XIV) that Passion broke away in order to accompany little Richard to gather water-cress. Passion was the most unreliable of allies, and, like many mentally defective persons, was curiously and obstinately wilful in spite of his apparent meekness.

11. Extraordinarily Accommodating Behaviour of the Chief Constable. This, and the curiously anomalous position occupied by the farmer Birdseye, are the most interesting and sinister features of the whole affair, and are equally inexplicable. It is true that Sir Odysseus was afraid of Mrs Bradley, and that she had known his mother, but this hardly accounts for the almost inspired manner in which he kept out of her way and left her to her own devices.

As for Birdseye, only a student of early Liturgical drama and of Miracle and Mystery plays would be able to account for the part he played. 'Noises Off' may cover 'more things in heaven and earth, Horatio, than are dreamt of in your philosophy!'

GLADYS MITCHELL
February, 1935.

VINTAGE

MORE VINTAGE MURDER MYSTERIES

EDMUND CRISPIN

Buried for Pleasure
The Case of the Gilded Fly
Holy Disorders
Love Lies Bleeding
The Moving Toyshop
Swan Song

A. A. MILNE

The Red House Mystery

GLADYS MITCHELL

Speedy Death
The Mystery of a Butcher's Shop
The Longer Bodies
The Saltmarsh Murders
Death and the Opera
The Devil at Saxon Wall
Dead Men's Morris
Come Away, Death
St Peter's Finger
Brazen Tongue
Hangman's Curfew
When Last I Died
Laurels Are Poison
Here Comes a Chopper
Death and the Maiden
Tom Brown's Body
Groaning Spinney
The Devil's Elbow
The Echoing Strangers
Watson's Choice
The Twenty-Third Man
Spotted Hemlock
My Bones Will Keep
Three Quick and Five Dead
Dance to Your Daddy
A Hearse on May-Day
Late, Late in the Evening
Fault in the Structure
Nest of Vipers

MARGERY ALLINGHAM

Mystery Mile
Police at the Funeral
Sweet Danger
Flowers for the Judge
The Case of the Late Pig
The Fashion in Shrouds
Traitor's Purse
Coroner's Pidgin
More Work for the Undertaker
The Tiger in the Smoke
The Beckoning Lady
Hide My Eyes
The China Governess
The Mind Readers
Cargo of Eagles

E. F. BENSON

The Blotting Book
The Luck of the Vails

NICHOLAS BLAKE

A Question of Proof
Thou Shell of Death
There's Trouble Brewing
The Beast Must Die
The Smiler With the Knife
Malice in Wonderland
The Case of the Abominable Snowman
Minute for Murder
Head of a Traveller
The Dreadful Hollow
The Whisper in the Gloom
End of Chapter
The Widow's Cruise
The Worm of Death
The Sad Variety
The Morning After Death